Lost and Found

Children's Books by Jackie Smith

My Sister's Cat

Hairy-Scary Things

There's a Bump in my Bed

No Time for Play

Grandma's Gift

Lazy-Daisy

A Small Texas Miracle

Going to the Principal's Office

Charlie's Harley

The Indian Who Wasn't

The Cat Who Wanted to Fly

Kennedy's Curiosity

The Cat, the Rat, and Me

The Sock Thief

The Mommy Monster

Non-Fiction Trilogy

Starting Point

Moving Forward

Finish Line

Novels

The Hourglass

Destiny

The Lost One

Once More with Feeling

The Bargain

The Chameleon

Lost and Found

The Orange

Long Journey Home

Death of an Angel

Not My Child

The Throw-a-Ways

Old Fashioned Girl

Lost and Found

Jackie Smith Ph.D.

To order additional copies of this book, contact:
Bookwhip
1-855-339-3589
www.bookwhip.com

This story is dedicated to

Kathy Plevich,

Who defines the very title of peacemaker,

not taking sides or judging others but

bringing out the best in *everyone*.

She helps guide the rest of us into a calming,

peaceful and productive place where all

can be heard without censorship but instead,

with understanding and acceptance.

God blessed me with your

presence in my life, Kathy.

TABLE OF CONTENTS

PART ONE

CHAPTER ONE

Who am I?

I t wasn't as if she impulsively leapt into it. A lot of thinking, planning, and decisions all went into her final move before the actual physical action. She theorized that the immediate reaction would not come either quickly or be expected. No, they would only gradually take notice or mark down the interesting, but unimportant fact she wasn't there; in any of the usual places she could generally be found. That was one of the results when you are the kind of individual who is easily ignored or forgotten. She was used to thinking of herself as indivisible.

If necessity is, indeed, the father of invention, then expectations are bred by habits and repetition. She planned carefully for the time when most of them would be involved with their own concerns and their usual selfish but consistent activities. She knew that most of the time her presence (or lack thereof) would make her almost invisible to them, as always (as she normally felt she was). The main difference between the others and herself was that she was genuinely unselfish. She was more interested in the behavior and beliefs of others than given to examination of her own. Observant and given to retrospection, she was honest in her assessment and evaluation of the motives and knew each of her family better than they knew her. Realistically, she was on target and not given to misjudging or projecting her own values on others. There was a fearlessness about herself that others took for recklessness, which would be wrong. She was thoughtful and knew her capabilities well enough to judge whether the action would be worth the risk or not.

She had never been a writer of written lists, choosing instead, to keep these tightly recorded effectively, but totally mentally. The most difficult part of the planning had been the accumulation of any financial means she estimated she would need for her success. She had never received any allowance or allotment for a share of the family's' monetary wealth; in fact, just the opposite. Once in a while when a well-meaning distant aunt or grandparent sent her a crisp monetary gift in a birthday or Christmas card, it was immediately confiscated "for safe-keeping" by the adults in the family, never to be seen again. Their common excuse for this was they needed to be saving for college someday. Even when she was brave enough to venture forth with a request for some spending money for any reason, she would be given, instead, a multitude of reasons as to why it was impossible. She listened, gave every indication of acceptance, then proceeded to find another way to accomplish her goals.

This led to a reinforcement of her own resourcefulness. She offered her services to neighbors for errands, chores, and opportunities. She discovered these tasks would bring a small, but appreciated monetary reward. The money she received for these efforts was kept silent and secret to herself alone, allowing her family to think she was a generous, caring, but foolish child who helped these neighbors because she was either too stupid to realize she could request payment for walking the dog, ironing simple linens, painting the fence or garage walls; "ah-la-Tom Sawyer", raking the leaves or sweeping the porch and shoveling the snow from the walk. Several times one of the others would remark that these things were "good for her" and also added to the reputation of the family as being "good neighbors". Her mother and father also voiced the opinion that keeping herself busy with these chores certainly kept her out of trouble or too busy to run with the wrong neighborhood children.

This added to her isolation from any peers; even at school she kept to herself and was as close as to be invisible as to fit with her slight, gamin, soft-spoken and withdrawn physical appearance. Occasionally when someone would seek her out for some reason or another, most could not remember with any certainty as to where or when they had last seen her. Was it yesterday? No? Perhaps the evening before?

She was relieved when she realized this would make her plans easier. It would make it almost as though she really didn't exist; in fact, had *never* existed and was just a product (somewhat cloudedly) of their collective imaginations.

As she began to run her plans over again and again in her mind, she worried about the mounting enthusiasm she had for her project, and that some of her own excitement would leak through to others; it was certainly not in her usual personality traits that she demonstrated any excitement or any new behavior which called any notice to herself. She was what she was; simply, for the most part, *there*.

She often felt this sense of being invisible must have always been a part of her. Yes, there was a side of her that most people were unaware of…And while it played a part in *who* she was, it was not the definitive part. She loved her family; and did not want people to immediately assume the wrong answer for her actions. She knew she should be careful of how she presented her behavior so as not give away her plans.

She was not unhappy with her parents, her brother, her family. She knew she had been adopted as an infant. This had never been an issue with her. She knew her mother loved her as deeply as any biological mother would be.

Her entire family was aware of the story of how her parents (for several years) had hoped for a baby and had finally decided to apply for adopting a child. To the west of their small town was a Catholic Orphanage. The story her mother and father shared with her was what she liked to call "a fairytale, once upon a time, romantic" description. It wasn't just that they filed for an adoption, passed all the comprehensive "red tape" with flying colors.

No, her story was very different. Her parents had received a call informing they had an infant. A girl. The most amazing part of all the story was the fact that the infant didn't come from any of the unwed mothers who lived at the home. Instead, the administrators told of waking up to an infant's cries seeming to come from outside. When they investigated; almost like a "Moses" story, was a wicker basket with a swaddled infant who was making her presence known with her lusty cries.

When asked where her name had come from, she was told that her adopted mother was addicted to historical novels and was reading a book on Queen Victoria. Thus, she became Victoria. However, right from the beginning, always called Vicki.

As often seems to happen in such circumstances, two years later her mother got pregnant and her brother was born.

No one questioned her as to what she dreamed of becoming as an adult; no one shared their thoughts as to her possible talents or gifts. She was never the top in her school classes, nor the bottom, she was never a leader or the last one chosen for the team and her opinion was never asked. When there was a need for a volunteer or someone forced to share, almost automatically it fell to her and she accepted it without complaint or any whining.

Often, she would wonder who am I? What is my purpose? When will I know? How will I find out? She was embarrassed (even to herself), with these questions and knew she could never voice such inquires to anyone.

Once in Sunday school class she embarrassed herself and other class members when they were discussing how God created everything in seven days and she raised her hand and asked, "Yes, but who created God?"

She immediately felt stupid and ostracized and barely made it through class when trying to muddle through the teacher's less than satisfactory answer. The only lesson she learned from this was to be quiet, blend into the background, and never ask questions. Once, when watching a movie about lawyer and trial proceedings she heard one of the lawyers give the advice that when cross-examining a witness to never ask a question you didn't already know the answer. She thought this the most ridiculous advice ever. Why ask it at all if you already knew the answer?

There were some questions children were not allowed to ask. She became good at finding; if not perfect, then at least answers which alleviated the questions. Early on she became adept with researching her own questions.

She admitted she had never felt physically, mentally, or even emotionally abused in any way; and yet she could not erase the feeling she was not where she belonged. Part of this feeling undoubtedly arose because she was so out of step with the rest of the family and because of her adoption past. She felt most adopted children held the same questions occasions.

She felt her father, while patient and efficient in his job; lacked any real imagination. Vicki said to him once, "Dad, you must be secretly from Missouri. You're the original "show me" guy.

Her mother was an accountant and lived totally in a world of numbers; and of black and whites; no grays, but more importantly, no bright splashes of neon colors, either.

She grinned to herself, lying in bed one evening as she thought, *I must have missed my stop somewhere and someone else got plunked down in my place and me in someone else's. Often, she thought they spoke different languages and she spent most of her time trying to explain herself or her feelings to them. Often, it was easier just to keep them to herself. She was in touch with her own personality well enough to realize it was easier to let them jump to the wrong conclusion than to try to explain things to them.*

She remembered when some other children at school tried to convince her there was no such thing as Santa-Claus, or the Easter Bunny she had argued long and hard against their claims. Her disappointment; not with their views, but with her mother's refusal to refute their claims and back up her belief caused a breech with her mother (hidden from her, of course) which never really ever went away.

Her mother's accounting position with a local lawyer seemed the ultimate boring and useless career possible, in Vicki's eyes. This was reinforced after she went to one "Take your daughter to work day" with her mother.

She told her mother afterwards, "Mom, know what would be really great about your job?"

"What?"

"If you actually got to go to court with Mr. Henderson (her mother's boss). Listen to the jury and the judge and all the witnesses."

Her mother laughed and replied, "Well, that's not going to happen. Remember I told you Mr. Henderson works in a civil court. He deals with deeds, and wills, and lawsuits. Nothing exciting there. As you grow older, sweetheart, I'm afraid you are going to find the real world is pretty routine."

Not mine, Vicki told herself.

When Vicki saw a movie about two old men who decided they had missed out on many things they wanted to do with their lives, she immediately pulled out paper and pen and, labeling it at the top, began a list of things she wanted to do with her life before she was too old.

1.   Get the lead in the school annual drama production.
2.   Write a novel.
3.   Go up in a balloon ride in New Mexico.
4.   Adopt a child from Africa or at least an orphanage.
5.   Make the Dean's List in college.

6. Have her own place to live; with ceiling to floor bookshelves on three walls, and a rolling ladder like in Mr. Henderson's office with all his law books.
7. Visit other countries.

As time passed, she would add to the list or change some of the entries; for instance, under visit other countries, she put "Africa, Egypt, Australia."

On the evening before her journey began, she lay out her clothes for morning; jeans, t-shirt, thick socks, hiking boots and hoodie.

The night before she left, she waited, in the stillness of a house in which everyone except herself was sleeping soundly and sitting at her small desk, wrote several notes.

The first was to her parents:

Dear parents,

Don't worry about me...I have not been kidnapped nor taken prisoners by aliens, and in reality, I am not running away from home. It is rather that I am running towards my future. I don't know when you will find this note...You have always been good about respecting others' privacy and belongings; but when you do, please accept this as something good and of my own free will. It has nothing at all to do with my being adopted. I could never doubt how much you love me. It has always been what gave me my identity and my security. No one else is involved; nor even privileged to be in my confidence. If all goes to plan, you will be totally blind-sighted about this and have no guesses as to where I am. I apologize for any worry or guilt you may try to accept for my actions, but know, instead, that this is something I have been planning for a very long time.

I know there will be a strong desire for you two to think this has something to do with my adoptions, my motivation is <u>not</u> to *seek any information on my birth mother and father. You are, in my mind and heart, my parents.*

I love you both very much.

Vicki

The next was written and put into an envelope which she addressed simply: Mrs. Marshall.

Dear Mrs. Marshall,

Just to let you know I am giving notice I can no longer mow and edge your grass on Thursday afternoons. You may be able to talk my brother Tony into taking on this chore; although if you do so, remember to keep on his ass (pardon the language) because he can be very lazy at times in fact, most times. He doesn't know of our financial arrangements, so don't let him talk you into more than the five dollars you pay me currently. It is plenty. I will miss you and your cheerful little companion, Brownie.

Affectionately,

Vicki

P. S. I will miss the lemonade and chocolate chip cookies as well.

The final note was addressed to Tony and read:

Dear Tony,

I don't have any sage advice to give you, but I do leave you all my books. Treat them with care, they were my most treasured possessions. In exchange I am confiscating one of your multi-task scout knives. You have two so you shouldn't be too mad with me for this. Take care of the family, do something spectacular with your life. You are smarter than you realize, just lazy.

Much love,

Vicki

She sealed each enveloped and put them in the center of her neatly made bed, except for the one addressed to Mrs. Marshall and this she put in the front pocket of her heavily laden backpack.

As she checked and rechecked her supplies she thought, it wasn't as if she was just going to leave with no destination in mind, willy-nilly like some kind of crazy person. That would have been totally out of character for her.

Many times, she had seen the mountain people come down the slopes to trade or get things they did not grow or make themselves. Once in a while they would set up little portable stands with the crates they brought in their homemade crafts and barter and sell homemade artifacts. Sometimes her parents would allow her to purchase an inexpensive necklace or pin beat out from tin or made of carefully polished wood on leather strings.

She had questioned her parents (especially her father) and he had told her some of them had never even see a television or even (in some cases), a radio. They did not have electricity in their homes nor running water and when she said she felt sorry for them he had laughed at her.

"Don't be. They are some of the most contented people I've ever met. All they ask for is to be left alone."

Vicki had tried to imagine what their homes were like and how much she loved her own modern technology such as her cell phone and her favorite television shows.

When she asked him about their schooling, he said their parents taught them. He even described going one time to one of their "Save Jesus" church revivals with his great-grandmother and the passionate songs and messages which had so impressed him.

He had told her how years ago people had come in, trying to buy up great acres of land to strip the timber off and how some of the town's lawyers; like her mother's boss, had helped them hold on to their farms, and not charged them a penny to do it.

She had long had a great desire to meet some of these people, and she felt like they would not take advantage of her; nor would they be too nosy about her and her own business.

She could sense her father's respect for them and thinking of how much she respected him, she felt she could trust his instincts about these people.

CHAPTER TWO

The Journey Begins

The most difficult part of the plan seemed at times to be making the right choices in what to take and what she could do without. Vicki was aware that in the past few days as she prepared for her journey, she often increased the contents of her backpack depending on whether she had just eaten or was due to eat soon. Almost like going to purchase groceries with her mother. If they went when they had recently eaten, they bought less. If they were hungry, they bought more. She knew she had to travel light, she weighed probably seventy-five pounds and though this was spread in a healthy distribution over her small bones, and she considered herself strong, she knew she was not a genuine athlete, and not exceptionally strong. She laughed and told herself, *if you are not careful, girl, there will be more food in your backpack than clothes or other necessities.* The last night she relentlessly went over her inventory and once again checked the backpack hidden in the back of her closet, counted out the sparce amount of money in the little brown coin purse and swapped several items for others. She had considered choosing a book from her shelves of favorites; but realized she would grow tired of repetitively reading the same one over and over. Instead, she took several pens and a brand-new composition book. She loved the fresh, empty pages brimming with possibilities, and for the first time in her life vowed to journal regularly.

Then she carefully and silently left her room, closing the door gently behind her. Pausing briefly, she listened to the quiet house and then went downstairs and out the back door. There was a full moon, and the backyard was a familiar view, easy to cross and the grass soft on the bottom of her hiking boots.

She reached the back gate and went through it, closed the gate, and walked the short way to the mailbox in front of Mrs. Marshall's house, opening it and sliding the last note inside.

She went into the woods across from her home which led to and surrounded the small park and children's playground, remembering her plan to try to keep hidden for as long as she could. People (especially adults) would immediately wonder where she was going in the middle of the night and be suspicious of what mischief she would surely be up to. Everyone knows children, especially in today's world, had no business being outdoors after dark, alone and unchaperoned by grown-ups.

She often wondered at the excuses the adults in her life used to persuade her to "act your age", then, conversely to "give it time, you're too young for that". She knew this clearly was dictated by what the adults wanted and had nothing to do with her own goals or abilities.

Her pace at first was fractured and uneven, sometimes stumbling in her haste to get as far as she could before daylight. Then it leveled out and she reached some good kind of rhythm which was comfortable and easy on her breathing. She felt like she could go on and on, perhaps forever, at this pace. This must be somewhat akin to the rhythm joggers spoke of. She had always loved walking, especially in the fall when the woods were such a burst of joyful colors, but now it was summer and would turn hot very quickly after mid-morning. Her plan was to get as far as she could during the night, then hole up somewhere safe and sleep the heated day away.

It was strange she didn't feel worried about finding a place to rest, but she felt as though it would work out. She had lived in this area all her life and knew the hills behind these woods like the back of her hand; having hunted rabbits, squirrels, deer, and other game with her father and her brother. Her brother wanted her banned from these hunting trips and even her mother thought it unladylike and unsuitable for a girl to want to tag along but she persevered until they gave in and allowed her (though begrudgingly) to come. Now she grinned when she remembered Tony's hot argument, "Why don't you go take ballet classes or something? Girls don't belong on hunting trips."

"You go take ballet," she had replied, adding, "You're just worried because I'm a better shot than you."

She had two watches with her. On her wrist, her new wristwatch and in her backpack, her grandfather's pocket watch he had given her before he passed away. She resisted the urge to look at either one to gauge her progress, but did stop a little later as the sun began to rise. She paused to look at the orange, reds, and yellows of the beautiful sunrise coming up and to drink sparingly of the water in her canteen. Birds were beginning to come out and signal each other. Once she got close enough to the small creek, she stopped and wet her face and hands in the cool water. She congratulated herself on being smart enough to put her hair in braids; it kept the hair off her neck and her bangs out of her face.

In the distance she could hear the beginnings of the world coming to life, but when she reached the "Y" where the small wooden bridge forced a decision she had to choose. She must go left towards the small farming community of Wainscot, or right, deeper into the woods and heading towards the low and deceivingly close mountains. She almost started skipping. When they came looking for her, the followers must make a decision as well. Once she got to the edge of the mountains, she would feel must safer from discovery. If she had judged her progress correctly so far, she would be in a good place before the heat of the day descended on her and she had to stop for her daytime rest.

Since it was a Saturday, she knew her family would not waken her for breakfast. It was every man for himself on Saturdays. Usually by the time she went downstairs, everyone would be occupied with their own plans for the day. She felt sure she would have most of the day without any alarm.

Her mother's days off were only Saturday and Sunday so most of her day would be spent catching up on the week's laundry and doing household chores she had no time for during the week. Vicki correctly estimated it would be late in the afternoon before an alarm was sounded. Even when they noticed her made-up bed, the notes and her absence, they would think she had risen, eaten and gone off to do something herself. This thought gave her an unexpected but comforting feeling of freedom. It was like being on Mars or something. No one else but herself.

She heard the muted sounds of an owl and remembered her class reading the poem by Alfred Tennyson, "The Owl". It had become one of her favorites and she especially could relate it to the beginning of a new day (or even adventure) like this morning. The dew, the stirring of others as each began another day in their lives. The white owl giving out his call for others to wake and begin the day.

Nature did not frighten her; as her brother had discovered when he attempted to frighten her with the grass snake he had caught, or the rubber spider he threw at her once. She felt God had a plan when he created all creatures and therefore, they were all deserving of their own place and purpose. If they left her to her own devices, she would leave them to theirs. Sort of *live and let live*, she thought.

Feeling the warmth of the morning beginning to elevate, she stopped long enough to remove her hoodie, and carefully fold and roll it tightly as her brother had taught her once; to save space and minimize wrinkles when packing. She placed it in her backpack, took a small drink of water from her canteen, and resumed her walk.

There was not a lot of shrubbery or ground-cover to hinder her walking; they lived in a forest primarily filled with pine trees. Outside of the preponderance of pine cones, the ground was primarily covered with pine needles. She remembered the bird feeders her class had made from pinecones; coating them completely with peanut butter, then rolling them in birdseed, and hanging them from trees. She had been thrilled to see birds light on them and enjoy the treats. Having made these, she was never again satisfied with purchasing a store-bought bird feeder. She had once helped her grandfather assemble and put up a Martin-house. It was interesting that such a bird as a martin could help cut down on the mosquitoes in the backyard on a summer evening. She thought the birdhouse looked like an apartment house with all its' openings.

She was not a big breakfast eater but began to feel the first stirrings of mild hunger and thought of the energy bars in her backpack. Still, conscious of her limited supply of food (and money) she resisted the urge to get one out yet.

Briefly she thought of her family and wondered if they had awakened yet. She reasoned it was still too early, especially for her brother on a Saturday. Her parents might have let the dog out when he scratched on their door or the kitchen door to the back porch; but poor old Gus was old and slow with his arthritis and would go only out in the yard far enough to relieve himself and then return to the porch to find some of the early morning sun to lie and dream.

She wasn't worried about the possibility of Gus being useful in tracking her, or even if the sheriff were eventually called in with a dog; she was doubtful their small town even had access to a tracking dog; but she also planned to go wading in the summer warm creek for a distance as the sun rose. She would tie her shoe laces around her neck like she had seen in a movie, cuff and roll her jeans up and take a good long portion of her walk in the water. She firmly believed they could not trail her if she did this successfully. And, she thought, when she got out of the creek, she would get out on the opposite side to further complicate their efforts. She grinned when she thought of her brother. He would, of course, try to take charge, using his scouting experience as his expertise. He always wanted to be in charge. *Little did he realize,* she thought, *that she had absorbed more of his training second-handed than he himself, had initially been taught. And…she told herself, he was always over-confident in his abilities and his personality of always believing he was right would keep him from listening to others in their hunt for her. Surely, they would hunt for her…? Of course, they would,* she quickly amended to herself.

Finally, the growling in her stomach increased enough to make her feel justified in finding a noticeably flat rock, large enough for a comfortable seat, and getting an energy bar out. She debated on adding one of the small tangerines, but self-righteously talked herself out of it; cautiously telling herself she didn't need it and to conserve it for later. She had important things going for her; but all her decisions and choices now could play an important part in the success or failure of her adventure.

She was determined that later she did not want to have any thoughts of "If only I had…" For instance, even such a choice on how much or how little to eat now could play a part. Normally she could eat with a healthy appetite, and yet rarely gained a pound. She had small bones which was why others always characterized her physical description as "dainty" and feminine. She looked several years younger than her age due to this small stature as well.

At first, after enjoying dangling her feet in the water of the creek and munching contentedly on her energy bar, she just relaxed and mentally thought about her family back home. Had they discovered her absence as yet? Did it raise a big enough stir to call the sheriff's office or had they dismissed it as a normal Saturday morning? Had they even gone inside her bedroom far enough to find the notes as yet?

She debated about taking her rest stop early, she felt like with the small sleep she had the evening before, (what with her excitement) she could probably easily nap. Almost immediately she dismissed this idea as foolish. She needed to put as much distance between home and herself as she could before any good-sized alarm could be raised. She carefully wrapped the wrapper from the energy bar around a rock and taking a rubber band from her backpack pocket, thoroughly wrapped it and then watched as it sank to the bottom of the creek when she threw it as far towards center as she could. It was difficult not to feel confident about her keeping on task and eliminating any and all clues which might result in her early capture. Now seemed a good time for step two. She pulled a bar of soap from her backpack and suds up her hands, and then the rock where she had sat and touched things. Then, she splashed double handfuls of water over and over on the rock-seat, hoping it would take away her scent. She didn't know it would any difference at all, but thought it worth a try. Then she took her boots, tied the shoestrings together and having tucked the socks firmly and safely in the toes, she hung them around her neck, rolled her jeans up as high as possible and gently walked into the middle of the creek. The deepest part was only knee-high, and the water was warm and relaxing in its early summer temperature. Since she usually went the entire summer bare-foot, her feet were toughened and showed the wear and tear of many hikes and different surfaces. At first, she picked her way rather tentatively over the creek bottom, but rather than sharpness in the rocks, it was a pleasant surprise to find a lot of moss cushioning her feet. She noticed herself humming a bit in satisfaction, and would have preferred to whistle; however, she was afraid she would be overheard.

She hooked her thumbs around the laces of her boots and had a brief thought: *I can't believe I am really doing this.*

CHAPTER THREE

The Family

Tony would normally sleep in on Saturday mornings, but he and his best friend, J.R. had planned an early morning fishing excursion and Tony's father had promised a lift to Decker lake on his way out of town for his monthly regional business meeting in Knoxville. He liked to drive in the early morning before any of the weekend traffic headed out, so left before sunrise. This suited the two boys who shared a firm belief that during hot weather you had to get to the fish very early or they would stay on the bottom and not even pay attention to the dangling bait. This worked fine for Tony's father because he could drop them off at the lake, get to San Antonio for his meeting and then get home in time to swing by and pick the boys up at the lake and still have most of his Saturday left.

He would have liked to go with the boys but his experience did not agree with theirs' on the behavior of fish during hot summer weather. He wagered to himself they would come home empty handed, but nevertheless, having enjoyed the outing.

Vicki had completely forgotten her father's business trip to Knoxville which meant he would not even be at home for a minimum of four hours, maybe more if he stopped to eat somewhere along the way. And since Tony rarely shared any of his plans with her, he would not be home until much later, either. It would be hours before anyone except her mother would be home. Since she usually went grocery shopping on Saturday mornings, it was doubtful she would discover Vicki's absence until at least noon. Then, as Vicki had thought about earlier, her mother would be busy with all her Saturday chores, so this reinforced Vicki's feeling of a good head-start before anyone knew she was, in fact, missing.

Like pieces of a puzzle, circumstances fell into place as though one of the ancient Greek gods she enjoyed reading about had (perhaps out of mischief or just entertainment) looked down and decided to stir the pot of happenstance and see what happened. For a time, her interest in mythology had guided her reading choices and she had enjoyed the thought that "up there" were a bunch of mythical gods playing a giant game of "what if" with the humans below. Mythology fit right in with the vivid imagination Vicki kept to herself. It pleased her to imagine a group of magical gods living above, moving humans about like living chess pieces. Sometimes this was at odds with her intelligence, yet she felt it balanced her.

Although their town was just a small rural community, it was not immune to the larger world outside, but many of its' youth left upon completion of high school, either to a more exciting university setting or grown-up jobs but there was still a small hard group which believed in traditional values and not on board with a lot of change.

There had been no crime to speak of in many years and what there was of it tended to be petty theft, school truancy, and gossip about what went on behind closed doors of the families living there.

Occasionally some of the adolescents might get caught up in some vandalism, but if so, it was minor and short lived. Even the programs on television which showed exciting homicides and serious assaults or home invasions could be watched with a lot of skepticism. Did things like that really happen? Not in their little Tennessee town they thought.

Not once did the thought of someone stalking her, or trying to do her harm or take advantage of her even enter Vicki's mind. She was a bright girl and accepted such things probably did occur somewhere, just not here, in her little farming community. Being a salesman put her father in a white-collar class; as did her mother's accountant status. She certainly wasn't (and had never been) afraid of any of the bullies she had encountered in her school life; and was and had never been afraid of the dark or things that go bump in the night. She loved camping out; first in the backyard in a makeshift tent, and then with a youth group from church once. She had been one of the few who slept soundly throughout the night and had to be awakened the next morning. She was not dreading the nightfall, when it came, not even from any of nature's nocturnal residents, but certainly not from any unknown humans who might be sharing the forest with her. If she had some kind of special vision of home while walking along in the warm, soothing creek, she would have seen the perfectly normal activity of her mother. Her mother, Ann, had arrived back home after the run to the grocery store as predicted by Vicki and made a brief visit to the small local post office to mail a birthday gift to her sister in Wisconsin.

Her mother put the groceries away and answered Gus's entreaties for a new bowl of dog food and fresh water. She looked at the clock and told herself she would give Vicki an extra special Saturday by not requiring her assistance with the light house-keeping she engaged in on Saturdays.

Still…no one except Vicki knew she wasn't at home. Her father's business meeting went well, and he headed home. He decided to skip eating until he got home, and go by and pick the two young fishermen up first.

Vicki's mother went out in the backyard and watered her flowerbed and filled the birdhouse and Gus's outdoor water bowl.

Finally, she rolled the hose up neatly on the rack and took her shoes off, leaving them right inside the kitchen door.

Then she stood at the bottom or the stairs and called out, "Vicki, sleepyhead, time to rise and shine." She paused and when she heard no returning call, she called again, and then, with a small sigh of expiration, she started up the stairs. When she got to Vicki's door, she opened it, and peered inside. She took notice of the neatly made, empty bed, but the next puzzle piece on Vicki's scoreboard fell into place when she did *not* notice the envelopes on the bed. Who knows what kind of time would have been saved if she had noticed them and found out about Vicki's absence at that point, but seeing the made-up bed, and no girl, she jumped to the assumption that Vicki (as she sometimes did) had risen early and was out doing some of her neighborhood chores for her "regulars" like Mrs. Marshall?

Of course, her mother thought, *she might have talked to Mary-Margret, her best friend, on the phone or either gone down there while she had been at the store or out in the back yard. She was a little perturbed at the lack of a note. Vicki knew better and knew her mother expected her children to ask permission before leaving the house or yard.*

There was no fear…as yet.

She answered the phone as she noted it was her husband, Joseph.

"Hello, there. You need anything from the store? What have you got planned for dinner?"

"Wow, you got through early, didn't you? How did the meeting go?"

"Same old, same old. Want me to stop for anything except the two boys?"

"Oh, darn. I thought you would do us a favor and forget them. The long walk home would do them both good."

He laughed with her. "Can't do that, Hon. I want Tony to do the yard. I guess Vicki is over doing Mrs. Marshall's, isn't she? She only works where she gets paid. Maybe we should start charging her room and board so she would do any labor on our yard."

Again, they chuckled and then she said, "Can we cook something out on the grill tonight? I did the laundry and went to the grocery store and picked up some baby-back ribs that were on sale. I could fix up some kind of salad and baked beans."

"Sounds good. I feel I should get a haircut but maybe it can wait another week. It's always packed with kids on Saturdays, even in the summer."

"Actually, I don't know where Vicki is, I haven't seen her all morning."

"Well, maybe she got an early start on her chore list. Smart girl, it's supposed to be another scorcher today."

"I guess. Well, love you and see you in a bit."

As he hung up the phone the first inkling traveled her spine. Not a real anxiety just a soft fluttering as she again wondered why Vicki hadn't told her or left a note when she left the house this morning. She hated to let Vicki think she was being followed around and checked up on all the time. Vicki herself had complained about them still treating her like a baby and not realizing they could trust her without constantly checking up. She also told herself, Vicki was growing up and had never given them any cause to not trust her nor had she ever betrayed their trust by hanging with anyone of the local kids she disapproved of. She also acknowledged Vicki was heading towards those final pre-teen years which she dreaded. She wondered again *why parents had to watch out not to smother their girls while still allowing more freedom and less worry for their boys.? Because they just seem more vulnerable? And usually, their vulnerability was in many instances caused by boys who were given so much more individual freedom.*

In any case, she decided *What the heck, I'm going to go look for Mary-Margaret's phone number in Vicki's little pink address and phone book and call her. If she got annoyed with her, she would just have to get over it. That was one good thing about Vicki. She might get mad at a person but she quickly got over it too, and didn't nurse a grudge.*

She walked upstairs, opened Vicki's bedroom door and went straight to her little white vanity and desk by the window. As usual, unlike Tony's room, she had left her windows open a little and her ruffled pink curtains gently blew fresh air into the room. Ann looked on her desk, pulled out the center drawer and careful not to rummage through it carelessly, looked for the small book. Not there.

She opened each drawer on the sides, looking in and quickly gave up. Where could it be? Usually, she left it there on the desk. She knew Vicki would have her cell phone with her so she gave up on keeping up the subterfuge of not checking up on her, and went downstairs to get her own cell phone and see if she had saved Mary-Margaret's number on her own contact list.

Checking her contact list, she was disappointed to see she didn't have it. Again, a flush of frustration that she couldn't contact Vicki right away.

She folded laundry and then began going room to room putting everything away. This only emphasized her disappointment with Vicki's absence because she usually helped her mother with this weekly duty.

She put Tony's away, feeling further exasperation with the usual messy and disorganized room, realizing she was working herself into a cranky and grouchy mood, with everyone; not just the real cause which was Vicki's failure to arrive home and her inability to locate her.

She placed Joseph's and her own laundry away and then, fresh linens to the linen closet. Lastly, she went back to Vicki's bedroom and as she put her laundry away, her eyes took notice of the white envelopes propped up by her pillows.

She walked over and thought, a little guiltily after having been working up to a mild anger at her daughter's not having left a note, *well, she did leave a note. Evidently, she had left a note, just not in the usual place, on the kitchen table or under the magnets on the refrigerator.*

She saw one with Tony's name on one, she set it aside and quickly tore open the one for Joseph and herself. She read it and then read it again. She almost folded at the knees, her heart began to beat wildly in her chest and she was afraid she wasn't going to be able to breathe.

To keep from falling she sat down on the edge of the bed. Then she thought, *Joseph. I have to call Joseph. He will know what to do.* She sprang up and ran down the hall and down the stairs, ignoring the dropped basket still holding laundry.

Her cell phone was on the kitchen counter and she shakily dialed Joseph's number but the minute he answered she started crying.

This immediately raised a level of fear in him as he said, "Annie. Annie, what is it? What's happened? What's the matter? Slow down. Stop crying. I can't understand you."

As he spoke, he struggled to keep his voice calm and reassuring and he slowed the car down and pulled off safely to the side of the road out of the path of traffic.

Continuing to cry, but successful in slightly lowering the volume, Annie said, "Joseph, she's gone. She's gone."

"Who's gone?"

"Vicki. She's run away."

He was silent for a few seconds trying to absorb what she had said.

"Run away? Run-away where?"

"I don't know. She left a note."

"Where did she leave the note?"

"On her bed."

"When?"

"I don't know. I don't know. I just now went up there to put laundry away and found it just now."

"I'm on my way now. I have to grab the boys first but I will hurry. When you hang up, call the sheriff's office and tell them to come help find her."

"Should I wait to call him until you get here and we look a little for her first? Maybe she's just down there at Mary-Margret's or some other friends'"

"I don't care. Get him out there. And try and get hold of yourself, Annie. I'm scared, too. But we'll find her. I can't believe she did this."

"I know, Joseph. I know. She's our good child. Our low-maintenance child. This is totally out of character for her to do something like this and worry us so."

"I'm coming. I'm on my way, Annie. Hang up and call the sheriff."

"Joseph…" she interrupted him, "What if someone grabbed her?"

"You're not thinking straight, Annie. What about the note? No, no-one snatched her. Is the handwriting hers?"

"I think so…Yes, I am sure it is."

"Do you think this is some kind of hidden search she has been planning for a length of time?"

"What do you mean?"

"You know the stories about kids that are adopted sooner or later all want to know who their biological parents were and why they were abandoned…"

"No, no, that's not it. She even says so in her note."

"She doesn't have a secret boyfriend, does she?" Joseph asked.

Quickly Ann replied, "No, No, she hates boys."

"Okay, hang up and call the sheriff."

After she had called the sheriff and he was on the way, Ann sat down and thought about the day she and Joseph had finished all the extensive paperwork and finally picked up their new little infant daughter from St. Mary's home for unwed mothers and foundlings. They carried her home in a brand-new infant carrier and right from the beginning she was low maintenance. She rarely cried and when she did it was usually a quick "fix" with a dry diaper or fresh bottle. The administrators showed Walter and Ann a note which was found inside the blanket wrapping the baby. It read:

*Please take good care of the baby. I have no money I
Have no job. I have no home. I cannot take care of her. I'm sorry.*

At first, Ann had been a very apprehensive new mother. She worried constantly about doing everything right. After trying for a baby for so long, then so suddenly having been given her strongest wish, she was going to be as good a mother as she possibly could be. Joseph was careful not to tease her about this; such as her changing the baby's clothes several times a day.

Joseph was less anxious, and seemed to think babies could practically raise themselves and he was relieved when Ann began to relax a little in her role as new mother. By the time Tony was born, Ann had the mother role down pat. It was a totally different ball game. Part of this Joseph attributed to the new infant being a boy.

Ann's thoughts were interrupted by the arrival of the sheriff and shortly after that, Joseph and Tony burst through the door. Joseph clasped his arms around Ann and she started crying again.

CHAPTER FOUR

Vicki

Every time she felt a little tired, she considered stopping for her daytime rest stop; but she recognized the disappearance of the adrenalin from her start in the night. She thought her body was telling her she needed to conserve her energy and rest up for the evening when she would be trying to make the most distance in the cooler air.

She exited the creek on the other side (part of her plan) but first she squatted and relieved herself in the creek She also took her neckerchief and got it very wet. She traveled a little further until she came to a heavily scrubbed and forested area heavily loaded with blackberry bushes. Eating them did not appeal to her; she knew they were better in the earlier part of their season and she didn't like them warm. She liked them when her mom picked them, cleaned them, froze them on flat pans and then froze them in zip lock bags. Her mother said doing them this way kept the berries from clumping together in big sticky clumps. Vicki loved them cold and not sun warmed. The berry bushes grew up and thick around a big tree, and there was a nice little niche between the tree and the bottom of the bushes. She used her hands to scoop out the ground covering leaves, and dragging her backpack with her she put her back to the tree, and scattered leaves around on the ground covering her entrance into her little hidey-ho. She used her backpack for a pillow and after some rearranging, found a reasonably comfortable position. She spread the wet handkerchief across her forehead and bangs. Almost as soon as she was settled, her eyes, gritty and heavy with sleep, closed and she was sleeping soundly.

She woke late afternoon, probably a little after five, feeling sluggish and a little disoriented, as could be expected with a daytime nap in the heat of summer. Her shirt was sticky and sweaty, and the kerchief she had wet and placed on her forehead was completely dry. She felt scratchy and very low energy. To forestall some of these symptoms, she crawled out of her leafy nest and went down to the creek. She again rolled her jeans up, and walked out knee high. Then she took her shirt off and wet it completely, wrung it out and put it back on. Finally, she wet the handkerchief down and wrapped it, headband style around her head.

She splashed her face several times with water then walked back up to gather her belongings and move down to Creekside again. Sitting her things down she began to think of food and the rumble in her stomach reminded her that all she had eaten since yesterday was that one protein bar.

She was so hungry she began to feel temptation to eat more than she needed, and she tried to curb her hunger. It helped that she consumed some water from her canteen and let that settle for a few minutes while she kept her feet dangling in the water.

She remembered as a child when she and Tony would play the old word game, "If I won a million dollars, I would buy…" but instead, she thought, I can eat little sausages…I can eat bread…or I could eat the peanut butter sandwich; it might not be as good if I wait for it until tomorrow…I have tangerines…or more energy bars, an apple, I even have foil packets of tuna or chicken, peanuts, dried fruit and more. It was a representative of a huge smorgasbord of tastes and choices and it made her almost giddy to consider what to select. It comforted her to run her choices through her mind before making her final choice.

Finally, she did eat the peanut butter sandwich, anticipating the bread would get soggy and the sandwich less tasty if she waited to eat it. As a balance she ate one of the tangerines. Then she buried any traces of her dinner. Lastly, she decided to make good use of the remaining daylight by continuing her journey in the creek so would wait to put socks and shoes on until she went back to traveling on the land. She brushed the leaves and shrubbery back to as close as pre-nap as she could and checked for any broken branches, so she could disguise them and fool any trackers. She remembered every movie or story she had read where someone running from danger accidently tore their shirt on a thorny branch or dropped a scrap of paper or some other careless clue which gave them away. She was determined that she be smarter than that.

Of course, she made better distance traveling on land because she wasn't walking against the water's force and current; but she was still very cognizant about trying to avoid being followed and walking on the land would hold more chances of leaving a trail.

She had not mentioned it in her letter to Tony but she had also taken his compass. She wanted a way to check her direction now and then.

Especially when and if she was successful in leaving the state and moving into another. For some reason she has a strong belief that moving to another state would add to her chances.

To vary her steps for a while she softly sang some of the marching Army cadences, she had heard Tony's scout troop sing as they practiced for a demonstration or holiday march.

Her top two favorites were:

We are marching By
Let 'em blow let 'em blow

Let the four winds blow
Let 'em blow from east to west
The US Army is the best
Standing tall and looking good
Ought to be in Hollywood
67th Platoon is marching by
Hold your head and hold it high.
Sound off, one, two,
Sound off, three, four,
Sound off one, two, three four!

The other favorite was:

Tiny Bubbles
Tiny bubbles
In my beer makes me happy
And full of tiny cheer.
Tiny bubbles
In my wine
Makes me happy
All the time!

Randomly she wondered in her brother Tony would eventually decide to go into the military?

Each time a foot came down, she did it with a stomp; it was more fun in the creek with the splashing; but when she had her hiking boots on land there was an equally satisfying, emphatic thump to it.

Her mood was remarkably upbeat and though she had not slept as long as usual, she did feel confident and optimistic. Physically she wasn't really tired, and she was also looking forward to the cooling of the approaching night. Presently she didn't dwell on what was happening at her home or with her family; rather, she was focused on covering as much distance as she could during the night. She did note a small sense of urgency, but used this to keep up a good pace. She acknowledged to herself that by now the alarm was out and briefly felt a little sense of shame and regret that she knew she had left worry and genuine concern in her wake, but this did not make her sorry for embarking on her adventure. Along with this feeling of guilt, there was an exhilaration and excitement she welcomed. She felt these feelings added to her stamina and her determination for success.

The noises of the forest were muted and not frightening to her. Once, when she had voiced her extreme fear for snakes, her father had explained to her that other than to take a sensible caution when out in the woods, for the most part creatures living there were more afraid of the humans who crossed their path than the humans should be. He had put it, "Remember, Vicki, these animals are more afraid of you than you are of them."

She did not necessarily agree with his interpretation of any rule of nature, but if true, she reasoned, that was at least somewhat comforting.

She was glad to be able to identify some of the sounds as harmless, and move a little faster past those she could not.

As the dusk began to fall, she went to the creekbank, dried her feet and lower legs off with her handkerchief, rolled her jean cuffs down, put her socks and shoes on, rubbed her exposed skin sparingly with bug and mosquito roll on protection and began her land travel. As the light departed and the dusk moved in, she did not need the flashlight she had in her backpack. The moon was full and beautiful, and her sense of well-being continued unabated.

Slowly she recognized that she was beginning an upward movement to her march, indicating she was getting closer to the foothills of those beautiful mountains which had stood guard over er the valley below and her little farm hamlet. This increased her hiking efforts, and yet spurred her forward with enthusiasm because she knew this was following her intended plan.

Briefly, as the walking got more difficult, she wished she had found a good walking stick when it was still light enough to spot one; and made a mental note to get one the next day. Having a walking stick to push off with one hand and arm and the other hooked through the strap of the pack would be extremely satisfying.

Although she had thought of and taken into consideration that the uphill part would be slower and more difficult, she hadn't really expected her body would complain as much as it was. It made her try harder to keep her speed up, there was no more singing of Army Cadences, this took too much of her breath which was valuable. She made herself keep her mouth closed to keep it from drying out, and tried to breathe more deeply because the shallow breathing seemed to wear her out. She focused her concentration on keeping a level balance of caution of where she put her feet down; there were rocks scattered which could cause stumbles though she thought the slippery consistence of loose pine needles might have presented more danger of falls, and more trees (both upright and lying on the ground) to pick her way through. The trees were getting sparser now, with even a few gaps of fields, some surrounding small ponds or lakes. She made a huge mistake in judgement when she stopped briefly at one of the small lakes, and sitting on a rock stuck her feet into the water. She closed her eyes and rested briefly but was horrified when she pulled her feet out to see what she thought were blood clots; but discovered to be leeches. She tried to pull one off and it broke in two so she then got the matches from her back pack, and would light and hold the flame close enough for the warmth and smoke to cause them to curl up and drop off. Luckily, she had not placed her feet in much above the ankles. She shuddered and felt nauseated She moved up the hill further; although she convinced herself that leeches needed to be in the water. She prayed this was true. Vicki noticed and had already taken into account the fact that being in any close proximity to the rather still movement of water in lakes and ponds might present the most problem with insects, including the hateful mosquitoes; but had not considered the possibility of leeches.

The running water of the creeks would be another story. In the future she firmly committed herself to moving water only.

* * *

Vicki thought she knew her other family members better than they knew her, and better than they knew each other. This did not come from her own ego or her judgement of their behavior but from her habit of close observation and her listening skills.

Based on her knowledge of them and their past actions and opinions, she reasoned Tony wouldn't give her credit for any special courage or abilities for such an adventure as this. He would venture an opinion that she would choose the easiest path possible; that she would give it up pretty quickly and come home with her tail tucked between her legs, calling "Uncle".

Her mother would most probably agree with his opinion. Her mother still thought of her as her ruffles and lace, pink and pretty daughter and even had been against her going fishing or hunting, and having her little neighborhood chore business.

Her father-now that *was a different story.* He would be the one who knew her best; who thought out what she might attempt. He was knowledgeable about her general fearlessness, equal certainly to Tony's; sometimes surpassing it even. He knew her focus and concentration skills were superior to other children her age and her determination on never quitting and admitting failure was extremely strong. She held her own in an argument and never just said what she sensed her opponent wanted to hear. She could fight hard for her beliefs and other sometimes found it difficult to persuade her to change her mind; certainly not just to end the argument. She worried that her father would ignore Tony's view, and would know she would follow the path more likely to succeed or which would discourage those who would try to track her. Her father was sort of in the middle; encouraging the developing of the pretty in pink little feminine daughter Ann saw in her; and the brave, adventurous, risk-taking athletic daughter he saw.

Although she did enjoy the varies distractions to her trudging pace such as the many squirrels who chattered their questions at her, and the beautiful colorful birds who either ignored her, or startled, flew quickly away, she let her imagination run wild.

She thought of herself as an explorer and what it must have meant to those who had gone before and she had studied in school. How excited they must have been! She knew many had gone this same path as she was now following, she could imagine how it must have appeared to those long ago who dared to go where no one else had ever been before. Imagine the first space flight and Armstrong's step on the moon. How exhilarating! What an honor he must have felt.

When wading in the creek she noticed some of the smooth, almost symmetrical rocks which may have been there since even before she was born. She noted how some of the trees, while reaching as high as possible seemed to almost be nudging each other out of the way in order to get their fair share of the sunlight so far up. She saw animal tracks; those of deer, the rabbit pellets and even bits of fur caught on thorns or branches, in silent testimony of a rush to escape a threat. She heard the loud, throaty songs of bull frogs and occasionally saw their splash into the creek from a log or the shore line. She had been frog-gigging with Tony and J.R. once, but only once because she hated to see them use the pronged gig stick to kill them and later refused to eat the fried legs that Tony claimed tasted like fried chicken. She vowed to never go watch that again. Their teasing about her being a sissy-and squeamish girl did not bother her in the least.

During the heat of their teasing, she had said forcefully, "And you would probably have been a couple of the first to resort to eating friends if you had been on the Donner ill-fated trip west who got snowbound crossing the Sierra-Nevada mountain pass and resorted to cannibalism to survive."

Her father had chastised her for her remarks, and her mother had frowned in disapproval, but Tony had quickly replied, "Well, you wouldn't have had to worry-you'd have been way too tough and skinny to eat."

Her father had told her there were coyotes in these woods, and even wolves, and that there used to be wild boar and big cats but humans had mostly driven them out. Again, he had emphasized that most wildlife will fear humans far more than prey on them. Maybe that's why she wasn't afraid of the night. Wistfully, though, she wished she had some of those "night-goggles" she had heard Tony talk about. Meanwhile she was grateful for the moon's steady guidance.

Second night out, she thought. She stopped to take a drink from her canteen, and moved another energy bar from the backpack to her pocket to eat later. When her thoughts traveled back to her family and the probable anxiety and worry, she was causing her family and others, she determinedly pulled her thoughts into another direction. She regretted causing them pain, but did not regret her adventure. She had brought her cell phone; fully charged, and the charger but vowed this was strictly for emergencies only-like something requiring hospital and medical assistance. She had also turned it off before she started her journey, to conserve the battery but also to keep from hearing and acknowledging the continual calls she was sure she was getting by now.

This night went by more slowly than the first but she had expected that to be the case, with the change in terrain, and altitude. She was not disappointed. She was still alternating her land progress with water, to assist in evading any trackers, even during the night.

Vicki was surprised to find herself covered with a fine mist of sweat, even though the sun was gone and the night air felt cooler. She attributed this to the extra energy it took to be climbing up instead of the former almost level path. Occasionally she would wipe her face with her handkerchief, but the sweat returned almost immediately. A couple of times she wet her handkerchief and again tied it around her head like a headband. She remembered her mother buying headbands with some kind of liquid inside them. Her mother had purchased; one for each of them and they were more effective than one would think. These were kept in the freezer, and then taken out to tie around heads and keep them cooler. When they had defrosted completely, they were put back in the freezer to restart the process.

When the sun broke the night with a beautiful painting of color, she stopped earlier than the previous day for her daytime rest. She had once heard that new exercises or unaccustomed work on one's body did not show it's stressed the next day, but two days later. She believed this. Her sturdy small body ached in her knees, her back, even her neck; not dramatically so, but certainly noticeably.

She searched for what seemed a well-hidden "nest", arranged the leaves and backpack to her liking before removing her socks and shoes and then, with a sigh, found a comfortable position and after consuming the energy bar from her pocket and another tangerine, she closed her eyes and was almost immediately asleep. It was in her plans to eventually swap her resting and walking back to the normal night for sleeping and day for making progress in her journey. For one thing, she realized she slept better during night hours, and could face any surprises or threats during the day when her sight was unlimited. But first, she wanted to make a good amount of distance.

CHAPTER FIVE

Watermelon

Vicki was surprised when on her next day she woke before noon. She reasoned it was because of the building heat, and she had forgotten to spray herself with insect spray and had fought off bugs and mosquitos all morning long. She had made sure she wasn't in an ant pile, but it seemed to just have been an all-out attack by mosquitoes. *Maybe*, she thought, *it was time to wash her body of sweat and dirt; and freshen herself up a bit.*

In her backpack, in a plastic soap container for travel, she had encased a bar of soap, unscented and no claims to beauty restoration, but usually bland enough for even infants. She navigated a path to the edge of the creek and stripped down to her underwear, and took down her braids. Then she eased out into the cool, but sun-lit water and wet herself down. She soaped a good lather up and thoroughly washed and rinsed her hair. Sitting in the sun, she combed out her hair and re-braided it.

She immediately felt renewed and fresh. She was glad she had done this. She washed her shirt, rinsed it, and put it back on. Then she did the same with her jeans.

She alternated creek sides once again, and ate all six cheese and crackers in a packet from the backpack. She debated about the safety of drinking from the creek, but it looked fresh in its' bubbling journey over the rocks. She decided the risk was worth the fresh water to rid her canteen of the stale, metalized taste it had acquired.

She finally repacked everything and resumed her walk. After a few moments she heard the noise of helicopters but it did not alarm her. She had expected that they would utilize every source they had to hunt for her. She knew since she had built no fires, not even a small one, and there was such a thick canopy of trees overhead, there was little likelihood of being discovered from the air. Also, her choice of clothing was taken carefully into her planning; she wore camouflage, olive greens, dark grays, browns tans and other bland and ordinary colors which blended in with the forest colors of bushes, leaves, barks and other foliage.

However, she also was aware that there was probably an enormous number of volunteers, as well as law enforcement and even the forestry service searching. Briefly she felt the twinge of guilt at the pain and worry she was causing, but felt it was way too late to turn back or dwell on what the possible consequences for her action would be if and when she was found.

She rounded a log, sloping curve in the road; not following the road where she would be seen, but enclosed by overgrowth and shrubby just inside the road border. As she rounded the curve she stopped, and silently gazed at the scene before her. There was a small cabin designed and somehow appearing as though painted there on a larger canvas. There was no smoke coming from its' small chimney nor any other sign of occupancy. There was a small porch the length of the cabin front, and radiant vines of blue Morning Glories almost walled off the width on the other end. To the side of the cabin was a neatly kept small garden, and under the water spout was a barrel to catch rain. Although there were two rocking chairs which occasionally moved minutely with the breeze, no sign of the human inhabitants.

Vicki stayed safely out of sight, but still surreptitiously keeping her eyes on the cabin, mulled over her options. Finally, she slowly advanced, but rather than move towards the porch, she moved towards the garden. She took notice of the old truck parked at the side of the cabin. It might very well have a dynamic and smooth-running engine; but its appearance was one of neglect and raised feelings of sympathy for anyone who had to depend on it for transportation for any distance. *If it's true,* thought Vicki *we should look for a person's character inside and not their outward possible beauty; then certainly this truck's owner must spend more time caring for its engine than its outward appearance.* Her description, *if asked,* would certainly have included the word "Junk".

As she approached the small garden, she saw a wealth of beautiful red tomatoes, green toppings of what could be either carrots or onions, and even gourd-types which may have been cantaloupe or watermelons.

When there was no alarm given by the birds around the cabin or field, nor any real sign of life, Vicki carefully picked a couple of the red tomatoes, two or three of what turned out to be carrots and several green topped onions. She wiped the excess dirt off with her hands and on the side of her jeans, then carefully placed them on top of the contents of the backpack, being careful to use caution with the tomatoes, to keep them from being mashed or opened.

She dusted her hand off and was almost back to her coverage in the woods when a loud, strident voice called, "Hey, you! Girl!"

Vicki's voice stuck in her throat; her body frozen in place.

"Come on over here, hear me?"

Vicki turned slowly and not seeing any alternative, began her slow walk towards the figure on the porch. It was an older woman, who could have been anywhere from fifty to a hundred. She had ample girth, and wore a faded floral dress which covered her from throat to toes, and an apron on top which may have been white at one time or other but was now slightly yellowed with age. She was standing by the side of a small wicker table which sat next to one of the rockers. One hand on her hip, and most frightening of all, one holding a large butcher knife.

The sight of the knife certainly slowed Vicki's progress towards the porch, and when the old lady noticed this, she let out a laugh and put the knife on the table before she said loudly, "Hey, don't let this old knife bother you. I am totally harmless. Not like the old witch Hansel and Gretel ran into in the woods. Look up here," she pointed as she said this last.

On the table was a round green watermelon, resting on a towel, and dripping water as though just freshly washed.

The old woman said, "I was just about to cut into this little beauty. Come on up and have a piece with me."

Vicki gave a tentative smile and climbed the three steps. She went to one of the rockers, placed her backpack down and sat. She almost laughed, thinking of the old childhood story of the witch in the woods who tricked Hansel and Gretel with a house made of candy. But this old lady had a look of kindness and acceptance.

The old woman cut into the melon and exposed the red, ripe interior. She sliced a round, then cut it; first in half, then in quarters. She handed one to Vicki and kept one for herself and there was silence except for Vicki's "Thank you."

After she took a couple of bites, the lady went inside and returned with a folded clean face towel and she handed this to Vicki and said, "Here, use this for the juice and mess. The juice will be sticky when it dries." The towel had been dampened.

Again, silence for a few moments then the woman sighed and said, "Ah, that's sweet. Just spit the seeds over the porch railing. Last year I did that and two or three of the hardy ones took root and grew. I already ate them."

Vicki's mouth was full so she just nodded.

"So, who are you and what are you doing out here? Are you lost? I can probably take you somewhere if the old truck fires up; and it hasn't failed me yet, but I don't have any phone. Never had anyone to call no how."

Vicki was beginning to get her courage back, as well as her voice; she said in what she hoped was a believable and confident voice and with a smile, "Oh, no, I'm not lost. I'm with a Girl Scout Troop camping and hiking. We're being tested for our explorer badge to go on our badge sash. We have to prove we can use maps and our compass to reach each check point. We all were sent from the same starting point, but were given different routes to take to the finish. We will have achieved out navigator badge for our badge sash. It will be my 37th badge."

The old lady shook her head and said, "I never got to do things like the scouts when I was a girl growing up. I guess there was such a thing but I was lucky to even get to attend school; and that was only when I wasn't helping get the harvest in. I probably would have been good at it. I used to have a brother, he's passed now, but I was better at all kinds of outdoor things than he was. I could chop wood better, tinker the tractor back into life when it gave out; even a better hunter or fisherman than he was."

When Vicki, mouthful of melon just nodded, the old later continued, "Now, now, now; isn't that something? Lots of people think I'm crazy living up here all alone but to tell the truth I've never liked a lot of people. My husband and I built this cabin a long time ago and even after he went to his reward, I didn't see any reason to leave my home. I had discussed these things with my husband when he was still with me and his last advice was to do what I wanted and not to let anyone else force me into what they thought I should do but to make my own decisions."

As she spoke, Vicki noticed two deer slowing munching grass and walking closer to the porch and the old lady slowly stood and said, "Excuse me just a minute. They are here for their lunch. I always throw them corn and I'm late today. One of them has a little fawn, but since you're new to them, she has left her in there in the woods, safe until she feels you are not a threat."

She rose, slowly so as not to spook the two, and from right inside the screen door she brought a pan with corn kernels. She gently threw some out to the deer and they began to eat it.

Vicki was enthralled. They were so beautiful and graceful. She wondered at their ability to support their body weight on such thin legs and this surprised and pleased her. The old lady looked at her and acknowledging her interpretation of Vicki's admiration she said, "Yes, they're beautiful, aren't they? It's only part of my menagerie. I have rabbits, squirrels, possums, foxes, as well as all kinds of birds. Me and God's creatures. We share the bounty of the earth and forest."

Nodding her understanding, Vicki asked, "Do you have electricity?"

The old lady laughed. "No, but I do have oil lamps and when I once in a great while go into town for supplies and check my mail, I replace that so I always have some on hand.

"How did you keep the melon so nice and cool? If you don't have electricity or ice, I mean?"

I laid it in the creek bed, it kept it very cool. I wash my clothes in water I heat on a fire, then rinse them in creek water. Don't feel sorry for me, I love the way I live. I wish young people would be taught how to live without all these so-called modern inventions. I bet you've never had squirrel gravy on homemade biscuits, have you?

Vicki remembered Tony and his frog legs as she said, "No, I never have. Is it good?"

"The best! Come back and visit sometimes and I will make you some. Any other questions?"

Vicki stood and said, "No, but I better get going or I will be the last one on my team to reach our check in point. I sure appreciate the watermelon. It was wonderful. The rest stop was good, too."

The old lady looked closely at her eyes and said, "Are you sure you're okay, my dear, and don't need any further help?"

Vicki tried very hard to present a natural smile and she said, "Yes Mam, I am fine. We're not supposed to accept help on achieving this badge, but I don't believe having a chat and eating a piece of watermelon would disqualify me in any way."

"I don't believe it either," she said, "And I wish you luck in being of the first to reach your destination. God bless and keep you, my child."

She came to give Vicki a quick hug and pat on the back, and then stood on the porch to give her a quick wave as she reached the spot which would take her out of sight.

Vicki walked about another twenty minutes before she again walked down to the creek, removed her shoes and socks and resumed the middle of the creek progress. As she walked, she mused over the old lady. First, her kindness and her sharing of the cool watermelon, and then her willingness to accept her story; even though Vicki could not help but believe she may have seen through it. She felt the old lady had known that it wasn't the truth; yet after judging her mete and ability to follow her goals, decided not to try and interfere. Maybe her own admitted acuity with outdoor survival activities allowed her to credit Vicki with such capabilities? Vicki had sensed a feeling of approval in her goals and faith she could accomplish them. Almost as if she had seen something of her own personality as a child in Vicki. Vicki could easily see this old lady as a child seeking such an adventure on her own. She was not worried about her contacting anyone and putting a stop to her adventure, feeling her contribution may have included at most a prayer for her safety and success. For several reasons; first, she had no phone, but secondly, she seemed to be someone who minded her own business. Vicki felt the old lady had prodded just enough to reassure herself she need not interfere with Vicki and that Vicki was not in any kind of trouble.

While the old lady readily admitted she lived off the land, obviously she used only what was necessary for survival; it was clear the deer were not intimidated by her presence and used to seeking food from her. Unlike many elders she had observed and dealt with in her neighborhood and family this elder showed no signs of stress, unhappiness in her living situation, or seem to long for anything she did not already have. There was a contentment to her explanation of her life which Vicki admired.

Vicki thought, again showing her maturity, *I'll bet she doesn't have high blood pressure like Mrs. Marshall, or ulcers like Uncle Mike. She doesn't seem lonely, but seems comfortable with just her animals and nature. Lucky her.*

Vicki thought, as well, how she would love to live like this; at least temporarily. She did realize, unlike the old lady, she would *eventually* want to go back to what she was used to; the modern inventions, the future of space travel and future exciting things likely to be discovered.

She wanted to learn to drive and have her own car, she wanted to go to college, away from home and have her own space and make her own decisions. How she could reconcile her adventure of the behavior of the moment, her running away and these other recognized goals she refused to mull over; preferring to live in the moment right now and push off to the future. Vicki was thinking less and less of home. She had no sign of homesickness or regret, but instead tried to imagine what other surprises awaited her like the old lady. Since she had used up some of her daytime napping, she decided she needed to find a place to safely hide and sleep so when she noticed a slight indentation in a nearby rocky wall, she carefully checked it out inside, and found there was enough room for both her backpack and herself. Again, she wet her handkerchief for a headband, and even removed and replaced her shirt, after wetting it thoroughly. Remembering to carefully brush her entrance signs away, she crawled inside the small space, and moved until she at last found a space where her body did not complain; closed her eyes and as in the past few days, fell almost immediately asleep. She was oblivious to the sounds of birds, squirrels and other creatures, even to a snake which didn't enter her space but moved slowly and smoothly across the front of her opening. Had she been awake to see this she might have been able to ignore it as it went on its way, or she may have panicked a little. But she was sleeping deeply and did not see it.

When she woke, she was surprised to find it already dark, but reasoned her body must have needed the extra sleep and she was not upset. She yawned and sat up, listening to the night time sounds of the nocturnal world around her. She thought of the earlier watermelon and her mouth watered and she realized she was hungry. This reminded her of the tomatoes and carrots she had from the old lady's garden and she carefully spread the opening of the pack until she found them. One of the tomatoes had split, but she carefully removed it from the pack, along with the carrots and walked down to the creek to dip and wash them. The she bit into the tomato and let the juice run down her chin. She savored its' ripeness and then cupping her hand, washed her mouth and chin clean with creek water. She washed the dirt clinging to the carrots and put them in her pocket with the peanuts. She let her mind wonder through her store of edibles in her backpack and decided she would retrieve the other tomato and eat it now, then pack up and prepare to take up her journey. She would make up for any lost time. She would take a small bag of her peanuts and a tangerine; maybe even some of the dried fruit, stuffed in her pocket. She would start out on this side of the creek shore on land, and wait until almost dawn to go back in the water. Meanwhile, the fresh morning dew and the early sounds of night had swapped places with the scorching heat of the summer day just passed and she welcomed the cooler air. She took the two squares of toilet paper she had allotted herself and walked out from her sleeping nest to find a place for her morning toilet, digging a hole in which to buy it when she was done.

She was beginning to lose track of the days and nights and this worried her a little. She pulled out her fresh new notebook from her pack, and turned to the first, clean and blank page. She rummaged until she found her pen and she dated the top with: Fourth Day, evening. She carefully detailed her visit with the old lady she labeled "The Watermelon Lady", She made note of how she was getting acclimated to reversal of her nights and days, and that she sometimes dreamed of food she missed; hot-dogs, scrambled eggs and bacon, and iced tea. Still, she noted she wasn't hungry, or hurt, or homesick. She wrote she missed her family but still was content with her decision to make this journey.

She repacked her backpack, placed the bag of peanuts and the tangerine in her pockets, and as she walked, she realized she felt at home in these woods. When her footsteps gave warning and startled three deer calmly standing in the moonlight, they did not run, but continued chewing and merely looked at her as she walked slowly by. She was far enough away so they seemed to accept her into their forest as though she, as well as they, all belonged. This thrilled her.

As she soon passed from their sight, she thought of her father and brother hunting these beautiful animals, and then; further, eating them, she wondered why she was so different in her feelings about these things. She did accede that Tony so badly wanted to be just like their father, and thus what he thought of as a "man's man", it made sense he would try to mimic his dad in every way. Vicki dearly loved her parents as well, but did not want to be like her father and, even not like her mother. She did view her household and two distinct sides; the females versus the males. She knew her parents used two different standards and rules for males and females. Neat, but strong boundaries for behavior. She had no aversion to dressing up "like a girl" on Sundays for church, but admittedly felt more at home in shorts or jeans and was as likely to climb and hide in the clustered leaves of the big china-berry tree in the back yard as she was to sit docility and drink iced tea with her mother and grandmother on the front porch and discuss the latest gossip or plans for upcoming social events.

Vicki did not feel this made her easily manipulated by others, rather that she was willing to examine and admit a difference of opinion with others, even those she loved. She knew her mother and grandmother saw and wanted to see in her a pink-ribboned and lacy polite lady-like girl and she accepted this, but she also courageously held her own with any strong beliefs she had that differed from theirs. She knew her father loved her, but he felt her mother should set her path, and he generally meant it when he said, "Ask your mother" and preferred to allow her mother to make decisions in regard to Vicki while he felt in charge of Tony.

Occasionally Vicki would again hear and see helicopters above her but this was only during daylight hours and the forest was even more densely populated with brush and trees as she got further up so it did not alarm her.

She munched the carrots as she walked and this made her remember the bunny her parents had allowed, she and Tony to have. They had named it "Hoppy" and was brown fur with pink inside the ears and white fur on his belly. They shared in the care of the bunny but shortly after getting him, Tony lost interest. He had wanted a pet snake or a Gila monster; something more" dangerous and manly" he said, indicating Hoppy was too much of a sissy. They had had Hoppy for three years until he developed a goiter which was cancerous and he had to be put down. She had cried for several nights, and Tony did use his wood burning kid to make a cross and burn "Hoppy" into before burying him in the back yard, under the big old Chinaberry tree. Thinking about it now, Vicki realized *she had never seen Tony cry. Never. Not for any reason. Even when he fell from his bike, jumping ramps once and had to have several stitches on his calf. He viewed the scar this left as sort of a badge of honor, and Vicki had cried for him even when he didn't cry for himself. She idly wondered what it would take for him to cry? Was he crying in her absence now? Was he really worried? Did he really miss her?*

She finished the carrots and peanuts topped them off with some of the dried fruit. She was still very careful about leaving any evidence of her passing along her trail; even burying the carrot tops and small peanut bag.

It must have been a good three hours later that she decided to take a brief rest. She took the boots and socks off once again as she planned to restart her trek in the creek once again. Then she reviewed her choices for a snack, and pulled out another packet of dried fruit.

She rested there for a few minutes, and then after a few minutes of star gazing, she gathered her things and waded out to the center of the creek, enjoying the feel of the water, began walking once more.

As the night began to wane, and she could see the very beginnings of a sunrise she began to sense something different. There was a feeling of being watched. She tried to shake it off, but it wouldn't go away. She tried to laugh at herself, but then heard something she could not discount: the sound of a twig. It was a sharp noise, totally out of place and foreign. She stopped moving and waited, frozen in place, breathing rapidly increased. The more she tried to still her apprehension, the more she felt something was wrong. She could not dismiss her feeling of alarm and no amount of mental persuasion could return her usual feeling of being at home with her environment; instead, the feeling grew. Finally, feeling if their danger she would be better off if she had her shoes on. If she had t suddenly run from something, being barefoot would definitely be a disadvantage.

She walked to the creekbank, left the water slowly. She looked cautiously around, but saw nothing out of place. She tried to reassure herself by the small noises she usually took for granted, and by the squirrel she saw make his rapid run up a nearby tree. It wasn't just that it was suddenly more quiet than usual, it was a different kind of quiet. She felt herself waiting for someone or something to make itself (himself? herself?) known. She felt on alarm and decided, once she got her socks and shoes on, to walk a bit more, on land.

She walked a few minutes, feeling somewhat more at ease but found herself taking large breaths, holding them and listening for any unusual sounds, then holding still and not moving and finally starting again. Whatever had started this feeling of distress did not disappear, but, in fact; began to get stronger.

Trying to gather up her courage, she finally said out loud to the forest, "Who are you? What do you want?"

She walked several steps now, paused when she heard the rustle of leaved and undergrowth. Who or whatever it was seemed to be growing stronger? Its gait changed too, as well. She walked; the noise followed softly in her footsteps. There seemed to be a regularity to it. She moved about six feet; then paused and listened. "It" about six feet, then stopped when she did and seemed to listen.

A definitely creepy feeling was on her back as though whatever was behind her was merely waiting a chance to lunge on her. It was akin to the feeling one gets when threatened by something unknown and the hair on the back of the neck rises up. She remembered her father telling her that while he doubted there were many dangerous creatures in these particular woods, he did believe an occasional bear had been reported, even going so far as to be seen rummaging in trashcans in some neighborhoods. They seemed to be afraid of humans and ran quickly away when discovered. He had also said there were fox, rabbits and an occasional mountain lion or other big cat.

Suddenly she became aware of the possibility of being hurt; perhaps with no one ever knowing what had happened to her. Her breathing quickened and she discarded her inclination to run. For one thing, her backpack was heavy and bulky, and she was afraid if she broke out in a run, whatever or whoever it was could be driven to also increase their speed in order not to allow her to escape.

Now she knew this feeling of danger and the unknown was not going to just stop, she stopped in her progress, and choosing a huge pine, she sat down in front of it, with her back firmly pressed up against. She knew the limits of its size and capability, but she rummaged in the backpack until her hands closed around the comforting feeling of the Boy Scout utility knife. She brought in out and opened the longest blade and held it loosely in her lap. Rotating her gaze all around the diameter of a large circle she continually searched and gasping a big breath, saw two glowing eyes at the edge of the creek. It made her think of a vampire from one of the horror movies she and Tony so enjoyed, but her mind made this observation and instantly dismissed it as the absurdity asserted itself.

She tried to strain her eyes a little better, trying to make out what it really was and tentatively told herself it looked like some sort of wolf. Could it really be a wolf?

It sat still for a while and then abruptly lay down, watching her intently.

Trying to keep her voice calm, and steady she said, "Hello there, boy. How you doing? Where you from?"

The animal, of course, did nothing but lay there, mouth slightly open, and gently panting.

It kept it eyes on her, but didn't move from his spot, except once or twice to lick the bottom of its paws.

"Oh, I see," Vicki said softly, "You're like the lion in Aesop's Fables…the one who had a thorn in his paw and a little mouse helped him get it out. Only thing is you're very definitely not a lion and I am not a mouse."

The dawn began to break ever so slowly off in the distant mountain range. She could see while this animal *could* be a wolf, it was more and more likely to be a large dog. Maybe a mix of some kind of Labrador and Sheppard. She began to stand up and when she did, the animal did as well.

She felt a flurry in her heartbeat, but as she braved a small step forward, the animal began to wag its tail.

She thought, *I don't believe you'd be wagging your tail if you meant me harm.* Then she said out loud, but in a soft and non-threatening tone, "Hey there, boy. I don't know where you came from, but if you're just looking for a friend, I volunteer."

When she reached the animal, he sat back down and willingly allowed her to pet his head softly. She noted he was very, very thin and his fur was matted here and there.

There also appeared to be several places he had been injured, with traced of dried blood and one of his ears even had a notch when something had taken a bite during whatever aggressive encounter he had gone through. He had been attacked and from his injuries it must have been a vicious and hard-fought victory. And if not a victorious one on his part he wouldn't be here. He very defiantly could use a bath and probably some food.

She scratched his ears, and then she opened her backpack. He watched her carefully, but did not either advance further, or retreat. He didn't display any aggressive behavior; just a sort of curiosity. He watched her every movement but made no move to advance on her further.

She found a small can of Vienna sausages and brought them out. She left her backpack sitting there, and opened the can. The dog flinched with the "pop" of her opening the can, but raised his head and sniffed the air when he smelled the food. She turned towards her earlier seat at the bottom of the tree, and the dog followed her. She sat her backpack down and then sat down, carefully holding the sausages out of reach of the dog. He never let the can get out of his sight but followed it with his eyes.

She didn't really want him standing so far above her, though now she felt he wouldn't be aggressive; if he was, she thought he would be a formable foe, he must have weighed 85 pounds or more.

She said, in a slightly firmer voice than her earlier comments, "Sit."

She was a little surprised (but pleased) when he promptly sat down and looked at her expectantly.

One at a time she broke the little sausages into small thirds, and gave them to him. He did not even pretend to chew, he just seemed to swallow them. When she held the last piece out, he ate it and before she could pull ither hand back, he licked it. She laughed and then got up and walked down to the creek to wash her hands.

She was really tired all of a sudden and she credited this to the adrenaline which had flooded her body when she was so frightened and had left her now that the alarm was gone. When the dog saw her intent to brush out a spot and then lie down, he immediately came closer and lay down beside her.

He was close enough for her to place one hand on his back and he accepted this and did not attempt to move from her touch. She closed her eyes and very quickly fell asleep.

CHAPTER SIX

Rusty

When she woke that next morning, the dog was laying close to her, and she had one arm thrown over him. He raised his head and looked at her briefly and then got up and shook and stretched before going off into the deeper forest. She had a momentary worry he was leaving and she didn't want him to; but while she walked down to the creek edge and splashed water on her face, hands, and braids, he returned; after having finished his morning toilet. She called him closer to her, until he was standing in the water at the creek's edge, and she began to splash water on him. She didn't know if he would accept this, but he made no complaint and didn't move away. Perhaps, Vickie thought, *the lukewarm water felt good to him.* Being careful to be gentle in her ministrations, she was able to free his fur from the worst signs of his recent injuries, but not to avoid the shower of water when she stopped and he came out of the water to give vigorous shanking which made her laugh.

She scratched his ears again upon her return and said, "Well, I guess I have a partner now, don't I? What shall I call you?"

She watched him for a few seconds and then she said, "Rusty. How does that sound? You are a Rusty color and it fits."

The dog cocked his head to one side as though considering her words then stood, waiting. Vicki thought he probably was dreaming of something to eat. She got out a little red box of raisins for herself and a stick of beef jerky from its packaging. Again, when she told him to sit, he quickly complied. She would have thought the toughness of the jerky would slow him down in his ability to chew and swallow it, but this was not the case. He laid down, holding the jerky between his two front paws, snapped and broke it into smaller pieces which he quickly devoured.

Vicki said, "That's all we have for now, Rusty. We have to ration our food; especially now that there's two of us." She put her backpack on, and started off walking. The dog quickly fell into step, walking along aside her primarily, but occasionally venturing off here or there in the woods, but returning right away. Sometimes he would wade a little in the creek, and drink but she was pleased when he always returned.

It was two days later, and she and Rusty had slipped into a complacent and routine pattern when the dog stopped one afternoon and sniffing in the air, looked at her and then off in the distance ahead. He sniffed again and then, almost as though he wanted to draw her attention to something ahead, he put his paw on her thigh and gave a small, unexpected and soft bark. It was the first time he had made any noise and it immediately put her on guard. She looked ahead, and in a distance, she saw a very small column of smoke slowly curing its way upwards as though to join the few cumulus clouds circling the indigo blue sky.

She was not on a road to speak of, but there was a well-worn path a few feet away from where she and Rusty were.

"What is it, boy? What do you smell?"

The dog looked attentively up at her and then, almost as though to reassure her, he began his forward march, this time a little ahead of her, instead of his former "alongside" position as if he were encouraging her to continue. He wagged his tail and reached over to lick one of her hands.

"Okay, if you say so," Vicki murmured to him, "I trust you."

The slow, wind-driven column of smoke was deceptive in his closeness and it took almost two hours to get close enough to decipher where it was coming from. She began to hear a distinctive, almost rhythmic loud, powerful noise repeating itself over and over. Staying hidden among the trees and overgrown shrubbery the dog and the girl peered out to see a small, rather depilated cabin. There was a distinct "cracking" sound to it which was explained by her vision of a thin, dark-skinned boy in overalls and bare feet chopping wood a few feet away from the house. He would take a good-sized chunk of wood, balance it carefully on the big stump, and hit it with his ax. Then he pitched the smaller logs onto a pile several feet away from his big stump.

Her first thought was admiration at his total disregard of what seemed to be a dangerous task. He swung the ax in an expert fashion, in what looked like the exact place he aimed it; without seeming regard for either his bare feet or legs. She had cut wood at home sometimes for their living-room fireplace but her father had demanded she have her hiking boots on, and that she only do it when he was home, just in case. When she had questioned her, "In case of what?" he had always answered the same, "In case you chop your toes off, that's what!" They had both laughed, but still she did accept it was a dangerous chore.

There was a woman by a large round tub, with a stick, stirring what appeared to be clothing or some kind of material. There was a residue of some sort of suds on the top of the water and steam showed the fire beneath it was keeping the water very hot in the tub.

"Boy, what they need is a good washing machine. Behind them, to the side of the cabin were several clotheslines, with various articles of clothing and other linens hanging and blowing gently in the wind.

The dog seemed to be trying to indicate their entrance into the yard, but she hesitated. These people might not appreciate her invasion of their property. She did not believe they would have any phone; as the old woman hadn't, either; but still she did not want to intrude where she and the dog would make a lasting impression which would be remembered if they were ever questioned about them. Briefly she remembered watching the old movie "The Hatfield and McCoy's'". Hopefully this cabin was not housing a bunch of violent hillbillies.

She thought the dog's eagerness to make himself known might have had something to do with the smell now wafting on the breeze and mixed with smell of the fire and the boiling clothes. It was the smell of cooking food and it made her mouth salivate as she, too, smelled it.

Finally, slowly; so as not to startle the woman or the boy, she and the dog began to emerge from the woods into the yard. Vicki didn't know if there any other people in the cabin or nearby; surely there was a father or older brother or some other male on the place, not just a boy and his mother or grandmother. When they had come out into the dried dirt of a front yard which had probably never seen weeds, much less grass growing, the boy stopped swinging his ax, and removed a kerchief from his picket and wiped the sweat off his forehead.

Two things happened then, the cession of the ax sounds caused the woman to turn around and look towards the boy in an effort, Vicki thought, to reassure herself he was okay and the boy looked over and saw her and Rusty.

"Hey," said the boy.

"Hey," said Vicki.

The woman stood quietly at first, not speaking, just observing.

"Nice dog," said the boy, nodding his head towards Rusty.

"Thanks," Vicki said, "His name is Rusty."

"Does he bite?"

"No, never that I have known of. He might if he thought someone was going to bother me.:

"Well, that's a good thing, isn't it?"

"I used to have a dog. I mean, my family. His name was Trouper. But one year he got snake bit and we didn't have no way to get him to town and the vet. My dad works for the railroad and he's gone awhile and then home awhile. I sure miss that old dog, though."

"I'm surprised you still go barefoot. Aren't you afraid of getting bit by a snake too?"

" Naw, but I *am* more careful where I walk, especially if I go hunting or fishing."

"When your dog got bit, did you lance it and try to suck the venom out?"

He looked at her and started to grin before he said, "Aw, there ain't no truth to that old wives' tale." He paused and then he added, "If I thought there was, I'd have tried it. I loved that old Trouper."

"Oh. I always wondered about that," Vicki said.

"Can I pet your dog?"

"Sure," Vicki said, hoping Rusty would have no objections of his own. She needn't have worried. The boy walked over, and Rusty sat down and reached out to lick the boy's hand as he reached out to pet his head.

By this time the woman had walked over and, putting one hand on the boys' shoulder she said to him, "Where's your manners, boy? Did you introduce yourself to the girl?"

The boy flushed a little, and then, he wiped his hand off on his overalls and reached out a hand to shake with Vicki.

She, herself, wasn't used to being offered a hand to shake but she gamely reached out a hand and they shook and the boy said, "Jeramiah; my name is Jeramiah."

"Vicki," she said, "Mine's Vicki, proud to meet you. And this," she said, putting her hand on Rusty's head, is Rusty. Say hello, Rusty."

To her great surprise, Rusty held out his right front paw for Jeramiah to shake.

"And I'm Marybelle," the woman said.

"How do you do?" asked Vicki.

"Just fine, young lady. I was just fixtin' to call a break and have some lunch. Would you like to join us?"

Quickly the boy said, "Yes! Yes, have lunch with us. We don't get much company. Please stay."

Vicki grinned at his excitement. She looked at the woman, "I wouldn't want to be any problem...Are you sure it would be okay?"

She nodded affirmatively and said, "Always room for one more. You stay, young lady."

Vicki was gathering thoughts about this woman. Though most of her hair was already gray, there were few lines on her face, and her body appeared sturdy and strong. She wondered at her age, but it was difficult. She moved with a strength of perhaps someone in her forties; yet the gray hair…

She turned her head towards the boy and asked, "Have you done your homework for today?"

"Homework?" Vicki asked. "Do you go to school?"

"My Ma teaches me. She used to be a school teacher. She's a good teacher. I'm pretty smart, huh, Ma?"

She laughed as they went up the porch steps and tousled his hair. "You sure are," she replied.

As they walked to the porch Jeramiah said, "Come on and I'll show you where to wash up. Rusty can come inside, too, can't he, Ma?"

She smiled and said, "Of course he can. Maybe we can even dig that old hambone out of the pot of beans and let him eat it."

On the porch the woman went inside and Jeramiah guided her to the small table which held a tin basin and a thin bar of soap. There was a towel hanging on a nail above the washbasin. Jeramiah waited until she put her backpack down on one of the rocking chairs and he allowed her to pour water from the pitcher sitting there into the basin and wash her hands first. She stood, waiting until he had dried his hands and then they went into the large room. There was an aura of disbelief Vicki felt about out the entire scene and an almost dream-like sequence she expected to wake from any minute. There was a wonderful smell of food cooking and Vicki felt like she had gone back in time when she saw a fire in a fireplace, with an old black iron pot hanging with food filling the room with mouth-watering odors.

Rusty stood, watching her and when Jeramiah showed her where he wanted her to sit, and once she had sat down, he came to lay down on the floor by her side.

Jeramiah sat at the closest chair and said, "Look, Ma, can I sit here?"

"Of course. I'll sit down at your place."

The two children stayed seated while the woman used a folded towel to wrap around the handle of the black pot and another for it to sit on in the middle of the table.

"That's very hot, you two. Don't go and touch it, now."

She returned to the hearth and, again using the folded towel, placed a black skillet of what appeared to be cornbread on the table. She then placed three tin plates at each of their places and added forks, spoons and knives.

"Don't have butter for the cornbread," she said, "But there's honey in this jar."

Finally, she placed a bowl containing steaming corn on the cob, and a small plate with sliced tomatoes and onions.

Jeramiah jumped up, saying, "Forgot the cups, Ma. I'll get them."

The woman filled a pitcher with water from a bucket with a dipper; sitting on a small table by the back door. She returned to the table and filled the three cups Jeramiah had placed by the plates.

The woman brought another tin plate and carefully fished a big hambone from the pot of beans and carefully replaced the dipper in the pot and bending down by Rusty placed the plate with the bone in front of the dog.

"He won't burn his mouth, will he, Ma?"

She laughed gently, "No, Jeramiah. Animals are smart. He'll sniff it but he won't try to eat it until he knows it's cooled off enough."

The woman went to the third plate, and sat down.

As soon as she sat, Jeramiah reached for Vicki's hand and from the other side, the woman reached for her hand. Vicki realized this gesture signaled prayer. All three bowed their heads

The woman said softly, "We thank you for this food and we dedicate it to the nourishment of our bodies, Lord. Thank you for this nice young lady to share our bounty, and place her under your protection when she continues her journey."

Quickly Jeramiah added, "Yes, Jesus, and thank you for Rusty's company, too."

Both Vicki and the woman smiled.

After asking each one for their plates, the woman filled them hot beans, an ear of corn, and a square of still warm cornbread.

Jeramiah passed the honey jar to Vicki before dousing his cornbread with it.

"Have a little cornbread with your honey, why don't you, Jeramiah?" The woman smilingly asked.

"Sorry, there's no butter for the cornbread. We do have a cow, and milk her daily but today I was fixated on getting that laundry done. Sky looks like rain coming to me. It takes me a long time to churn butter. I do have milk from this morning, if you want some to drink."

"Oh, that's okay, water is fine. Everything is wonderful! It's all so good."

Jeramiah peeked under the table and reported, "Hey, Vicki, Rusty likes the bone. Look at him go on it."

She looked down to watch Rusty for a few seconds, holding the bone steady with his two front paws; he was scraping any left-over meat and gristle off the bone.

"Guess you're both really glad when it's time for your husband to come home, aren't you?" Vicki asked, looking at the woman.

Jeramiah said, "Oh, yeah. He always brings us a surprise."

"And he always brings me a new bag of sugar and cornmeal," his mother said.

"Our grandma used to live with us, too," injected Jeramiah. "And guess what?"

Responding to his enthusiasm, Vicki said, "What?"

"She used to be a champion checker player."

"Really, now?" Vicki asked.

"Yeah. We would go once every year to the town Fall Festival and she would always enter and would win, too. I could never beat her."

As the woman first tried to urge more food on her; and then began to clear the table, Jeramiah asked, "I don't suppose you would play me a game of checkers, would you?"

Vicki paused and then she said, "Well if you don't mind putting up with me and Rusty a little longer, I will take your challenge."

"Can we play? I promise to chop the rest of the wood before bedtime tonight. I promise. And I will help with the laundry."

He looked up at her with such a longing his mother had to laugh. "Well, I've certainly heard that before, have I not? Go ahead."

When she finished clearing after the meal, Jeramiah got out a checker board which had obviously seen a great deal of play, and he set the checkers and board up on the kitchen table.

He grinned and said, looking at Vicki, "I'll even let you choose your color, Vicki."

She chuckled, and sat down across the board, choosing the red checkers.

The game roused a lot of laughter and cheers from both the players, but eventually Jeramiah won handily.

Vicki had not allowed him to win so she was generous in her congratulations.

"Yea," yelled Jeramiah, holding one fist up in the air.

"Let's play again," he said hopefully.

"No, afraid not," Vicki said, standing to help him collect the checkers and place them in the little tin box which had housed them before.

She continued, "I've got to be moving on, but this sure has been fun and the lunch was absolutely wonderful.

Jeramiah said, "But look, Rusty is not done with his bone yet."

"That's okay, we can take it with us and I will let him eat it later."

"Vicki, will you be coming back by here?"

"Probably," she said, to soften his let-down look.

"If you do, will you come play some more checkers?"

"I wouldn't miss it for anything," she answered him.

Jeramiah walked her to the porch and he called his mother, "Ma, Vicki is leaving now."

His mother said, "Hold on, young lady."

She walked back up on the porch and into the kitchen as she said, "Wait just a minute. I want to give you something to take with you."

When she came back to the porch, she handed one package wrapped in a clean cloth and tied with string to Vicki and said, "This is some more cornbread for you to eat later," she paused and added, "and this is Rusty's unfinished bone for more enjoyment later." She handed another package, this one wrapped in some obviously older brown paper probably salvaged from an earlier visit to town or perhaps from her son's return from the railroad on one of his trips home over to Vicki.

"Thank you so very much. You have been so kind to me." Vicki took both packages and worked their way into her backpack.

Then, the woman said, "It was a treat for us both. We hope you return one day." She paused and added, "I don't want to be nosy, but is there anything else we can do for you? We don't want to pry into your journey or life, but…we will pray for you. Be careful."

Vicki said simply, "Thank you. I appreciate the wonderful lunch, the checker game, even though I lost, (Jeramiah giggled at this) and I will think of you often."

She snapped her fingers at Rusty and he quickly followed her down the porch steps and across the yard. Before she got very far down the packed dirt trail, she heard the resumption of the ax snapping through the wood. *Jeramiah was back at work,* she thought.

She took an unusual look at one of her watches and noted it was 3:30 p.m. *Not too late*, she told herself. *I must try to do some make up time here. But I must try to make up some time here before dark.*

As Vicki walked, she curiously mulled over the fact that *Jeramiah and his mother did not try to pellet her with questions as to where she was from, where she was going, and the why behind it all. Was this the way hill people reacted in their responses to outsiders? Or was it truly that Jeramiah and his mother felt it was not their business? Was its fear of some unknown consequences they might encounter later if they knew more than was necessary about her reasons for this journey? They had merely accepted her as she was, noting she was on the move as a young girl, alone and certainly up to the possibility of danger or harm. Certainly, they did not accept her journey, alone, and unprotected as something common and usual; but again, they felt she had her own reasons and it was simply it was not their business. There was no doubt they truly would pray for her and she welcomed the idea that she had someone on her team besides her clueless parents.*

The terrain had most definitely changed; often now she was reduced to bending over, using her hands to help make her way up. The few times her path was level did not last long, and she was now wearing the gloves from her pack to protect her hands for the roughness of the rocks. There were occasional ledges of a sort which allowed her to come to a semi-standing stance so she could look below for a long distance. Far off behind her and to the right she could see the very distant small ambling column of smoke of Jeremiah's home; even though the details were not clearly still visible. Others might have seen this as the smoke from a small campfire. This part of her journey definitely favored Rusty's capabilities; he seemed to scramble easily over the rocks and around boulders while she was making much less headway that the previous days.

If he got what he designated as too far ahead of her, he would pause, even occasionally lying down to wait for her slower progress. She drank more water and when her path seemed to pull her away from the nearness of the creek and water, she readjusted it, because she did not want to move away from her access to water. When she heard the difference in the sounds of the water, she realized she was coming up on a real sight; entrenched in the side of this low mountain was a good-sized waterfall, which ended below in a beautiful small lake. Hoping to be able to cross to the other side, perhaps above the beginning of the water tumbling over and over down to reach and end in the foaming and bubbling white droplets, she continued upwards and eventually reached what appeared almost in a dam of sorts, which displayed rocks across from one side of the creek bank to the other, with a surprising shallow covering of water before; in its then change from an almost serene flow of water into a building, noisy, powerful, crushing, crashing and fearsome waterfall into the pond below. It was easy to see when the water then slowed moderately to a smaller developing waterfall further below.

Vicki was awestruck by the scene and she sat, next to Rusty, just watching and listening to this impressive show of nature's powerful changes. Vicki looked carefully at the rocks forming a span from one Creekside to another and had no false preconceived belief she could cross this; what had gone from a small creek into a real river; safely. Those rocks would be slippery and dangerous.

She knew she would have to continue her land journey until somewhere below, where the river slowed down in its travel and she could wade across safely.

She noticed Rusty's sniffing interest in the backpack and she said gently, "No bone yet. You can have it tonight. Here, I'll give you something else."

She put the backpack on her lap and pulled out the package of cornbread for herself. She opened another small pack of jerky and gave a good-sized piece to the dog. Immediately he lay down beside her, and used his front paws to hold the jerky while he chewed on it.

Vicki and Rusty made good (but even a little boring) progress over the next two days. She had located a great hiking stick and this aided her upward climb considerably. It was on the third day after the visit with Jeremiah and his mother when they reached a point long past the awesome waterfalls when they were walking, following a slightly less strenuous upward progress that she once again began to think someone was following them. The first sign was the one she trusted the most: Rusty was definitely restless. He would whine a little, then look at her, and though she talked softly to him, trying to calm him down, with no real effect. He then began to leave her side, and walk further back, seemingly to check their past route, and in a few minutes, come back up even. He tried getting her closer attention by licking her hand and finally, he even took a bite of her jeans, and attempted to pull her back on their recent path.

After saying, "What is it, fella? We don't want to go back; we want to go forward. Then she mentally acknowledged the futility of trying to communicate verbally with a dog. She tried to use a firmer tone with him and said, "Come on, now, we're not going backwards." When he looked at her, with what almost seemed a pleading look. She tuned him out deliberately and turned her back on him and began to continue forward; she hoped he would just docilly follow. *Perhaps*, she thought, *there was a particularly obnoxious (to him) creature which was causing his anxiety.* She grinned as she thought, perhaps even a skunk. Wouldn't that be great? She decided to leave whatever was bothering him behind them. She felt he would eventually give in and follow her or stop and go his own way.

The dog did not cease with signs of his unease, but almost seemed like a reluctant child, giving in to the adult because he had no choice, other to be left behind; and she was sure he would not want that.

So, they continued and briefly Rusty seemed to give up, he trotted along by her side, only occasionally stopping and looking behind them.

Vicki reasoned that he would have been more persistent and unwilling to give into her insistence of moving forward if it were anything really serious or dangerous. If it was a large cat, or, very unlikely (even a bear) she thought Rusty would act much more desperately in his desire to get her to let him lead.

CHAPTER SEVEN

The Boyfriend

Although Vicki was on a higher alert than normal, because of Rusty's strange behavior, she was still taken by surprise when there was a loud shout, and someone or something leapt from the bushes behind them and landed right beside them. Immediately Rusty growled and all the fur on his back stood up like some kind of weird mohawk haircut. Rusty moved closer to her, providing a barrier between Vicki and the intruder.

Vicki was immediately frightened but probably would have been more so if the intruder had not yelled, like a child, "Boo! Got you!"

She jumped and screamed, holding her heart, which was beating very rapidly.

"Oh, I'm sorry. I didn't mean to scare you."

"Well, you did", Vicki said, angrily and too mad to be afraid now that she had gotten a closer look a closer look at the apparition which had come at her from nowhere.

Not really listening to his words, she took a look instead. He was much taller than her, and had dirty bare feet, uncombed and again, dirty, brown hair, which had some signs of a long-ago haircut which was very grown out and ragged now. She was reminded of the old fashioned "bowl cuts" that were popular at one time long before crew-cuts, and styled cuts. He wore no shirt, but a pair of worn and dirty overalls, one strap unfastened and hanging down. The more she looked at him, the more her sense of fear began to dissolve.

His face was the one which mirrored fear and distress; and she felt sorry for him. She felt absolutely no alarm and even wanted to reassure him she was no threat and that she wasn't upset with him for frightening her.

"Who are you?" Vicki asked, noticing that Rusty had sat down at her side, and other than keeping eyes on the intruder, had relaxed. Even his fur had laid back down. Not that he completely dismissed his curiosity, nor let down his guard, but just seemed to admit this was no real threat to her.

"Herman," he said, and he almost had difficulty in getting it out.

"My name is Vicki," she said.

His face relaxed a tiny bit. He paused and then, rather in a jerky manner, stuck out his hand stiffly as though he had seen someone else do this and felt it was the proper thing to do.

She shook his hand, making a mental note to be sure and wash her hands at the very next possibility.

"Where did you come from?"

"Over there, yonder," he said.

He pointed off, from where they had come.

"Is your home there?"

He nodded and said, "Yes."

"Who lives with you?"

"My Grandma and my brother."

"I met a young man named Jerimiah yesterday, do you know him?" asked Vicki.

"Sure, I know Jerimiah. He's my second cousin."

"He beat me at checkers," said Vicki.

Herman laughed. "That's no surprise. He beats everybody. His Grandmother was a champion and she taught him how."

All of a sudden came a loud, very shrill whistle."

He jumped and then, turning he said, "I gotta go. That's my brother."

"Wait," Vicki said, hoping to get more information from him and perhaps trying to see if she could get him not to talk to anyone about her, but very rapidly he was gone from sight.

Rusty looked up at her, then sitting down, began to lick his paws.

Vicki had an almost irresistible urge to giggle. *Where in the world did, he come from? Did she fall down a rabbit hole? Was she in the hills of Kentucky or Tennessee? Or was she still outside the hills of Big Ben National Forest or where? Or was she dreaming? Feeling slightly disoriented, she and Rusty made their way further forward until they had a relatively clear view and path down to the river bank where she washed her hands and face and Rusty drank.*

She was worried "Herman" might return with his brother, so she then picked up her backpack and resumed their journey. She walked further than she had intended, because of this worry, and it was almost completely dark; at least too dark to see very well, before she and Rusty finally stop and carved themselves a sleeping niche from an indentation in the bottom of rocky cliff. Her muscles ached more than usual which was an indication that she had pushed herself further.

Vicki ate a small treat size box of raisins and then, in response to Rusty's seeming expectation and her own curiosity as to whether dogs would even *eat* raisins, she held out some in her hand. He sniffed them at first, then licked them off her hand and patiently looked at her once again. She was more than a little surprised. *He must be really hungry,* she thought. I don't think he regularly eats raisins. She shared another box, and then once again, brought out the now practically bare and white bone from Jeramiah's house with no seen nourishment left on it. Rusty took it with good grace, seemingly glad to have it back, even though it seemed totally lacking in more gastronomical value.

She gently scratched his ears as he lay down beside her, smelling the bone and turning it this way and that to find perhaps some hidden gristle or marrow.

"I know, old guy," she said softly. "We'll take a chance in a day or two and go down the hill to the nearest little settlement and maybe even use some of our money for the first time."

The two of them slept close, and for the first time, Vicki turned her thoughts to her family. *Were they still looking? What were they saying? Had they gotten any clues? She* turned from her questions, and fell asleep with one arm thrown over Rusty and the sounds of his work on the bone in her ears.

The next morning after they walked to the bank of the river; and it was a real river now, having grown from the creek close to her home, to this (for the most part) slower moving and more placid river. She did more of a real wash up, even changing from her jeans to some safari shorts, and a clean shirt. She put her shoes and socks on, and then, after choosing some beef jerky for Rusty (the last of it, unfortunately) she pulled out a small packet of dried fruit for herself.

They had only walked about thirty minutes when she began to hear signs following, seemingly trying to catch up to her. She rightly accredited it to an upcoming vision of Herman. She was disappointed, especially when she thought of the extra efforts yesterday to try and be beyond his reach.

She paused and pushed Rusty down to a sitting position. He looked backwards as she did, but did not growl or bark.

When she estimated he was very close and she saw the vegetation begin to wiggle with touches from someone else, she gathered herself and her breath and leaped towards the bushes, hands out, and she yelled, "Boo, got you!" as he had that first day, she met him.

When his head popped through into sight, his eyes were absolute wide with something which could only be delight. He was thrilled about her entrance into the game. This made her feel a little bit ashamed at her earlier wish to be rid of him, and wonder at his persistence to come each day to interact

He exploded into laughter and though it was more restrained with her, so did Vicki.

"I wasn't expecting you today, Herman. Isn't this getting a little far for you to come see me and still make it back to your home before your brother whistles?"

"Oh, I have to see you. I have something to ask you."

"Really?"

"Yes. Will you be my girlfriend?"

She was extremely surprised at this question. Where had it come from? Was it something she should be concerned about? Her thoughts whirled, or was it because of his capabilities? She had almost at once after meeting him realized he was what others would label as "slow". Some of her classmates were good with others like Herman; being patient and kind; some were rude and judgmental; even cruel. in their treatment of such. She didn't want to hurt his feelings, nor did she want to risk herself to any unwanted attention until she knew what he considered by the label "girlfriend".

She dodged the question at first by asking, "girlfriend? Don't you already have a girlfriend?"

He scuffled his feet and that's when she noticed he was wearing worn army boots; gone were the bare feet.

"Nope," he said, in answer to her question.

"Well, what does a girlfriend have to do? Does she have chores? Because you know Rusty and me are going on a journey and we can't stop our journey."

"Where is your journey going? To your family?"

Thinking it would be easier for him to be satisfied with this answer, she nodded and said, "Yes."

He nodded his head and said, I know that's an important kind of journey and you could still do that." He paused then, thinking it over, then he said, "Mostly it would just be that you are my friend and I could tell my brother I have a girlfriend, just like him."

Vicki felt a twinge of worry at the thought of Herman telling his brother about her existence.

"Well, Herman, sometimes being girlfriend and boyfriend means having a secret. A big secret. It means not telling your brother you have a girlfriend, but keeping our friendship a big secret. Can you do that? Are you good at keeping a secret?"

Vigorously he nodded and said, "Oh, yeah, I am really, really good at keeping secrets. My grandmother tells me secrets and I never, never tell."

Vicki nodded while her mind began to try and measure the danger which might lie in this new development. At the same time, she noticed he was holding a cloth-wrapped package to his chest. Rusty seemed to have a great deal of interest in this package. Curiosity got the best of her and she said, "What have you got there, Herman?"

He looked down at his arms, folded across his chest. Then he smiled and held out a folded cloth to her.

"Here, Vicki, is a surprise for you."

"Thank you," she said.

She carefully opened the folded cloth and revealed some sort of flatbread; or a version of a tortilla. It appeared like it was sprinkled on top with a little sugar and perhaps cinnamon or nutmeg spices.

"Oh, how nice! May I go ahead and taste it?"

"Yes," Herman said, flushing a little bit. "My grandma makes them for me. It's my desert for cleaning my plate at supper. I saved mine for you today."

"May I give a little bit to Rusty?"

"Sure."

Rusty was wagging his tail and Vicki inhaled a sweet, cinnamon odor coming from his offering. Her mouth started watering, and she thought this a good sign it was safe. Rusty quickly goggled up the piece she gave him and sat, obviously begging for more.

It did have the texture of a tortilla, but she could also taste a dab of honey and the easily recognizable cinnamon.

"This is so good, Herman. Thank you so much."

A little embarrassed, he said, "You're welcome."

"I wish you didn't have a journey to go on anymore," Herman said.

"I know, but it's something I have to do."

"Yeah, I understand, but today is my last day to see you."

She hesitated in replying to him, not sure if she understood what he meant by his words.

"Do you know why?" he asked her with a serious expression.

She shook her head negatively and waited for his explanation.

"'Cause this is as far as I can go to get back home before dark and I will be in trouble with Buster if I don't get home for dark."

"Who is Buster?"

"My brother. He gets really mad if I don't do what he says."

She wondered if the sense she had of a big, bullying and abusive older brother were true. How sad Herman had to figure out exactly how fast and how long he had to go to keep out of trouble.

"Will you ever come back, Vicki?"

"I…I'm not really sure, Herman. Maybe and maybe not. I will miss you though."

"I will miss you too. Will you remember you have a boyfriend here?"

She smiled. "Yes, I will."

He looked over at the sun in its path sinking lower in its scheduled way to late afternoon.

He was beginning to get anxious and you could see that anxiety.

He then said, "I gotta go. I gotta go so I will be home before Buster gets home and before it starts to get dark."

She wanted to give him something to mark their friendship and see him smile again. She thought about what was in the backpack which might be suitable.

"Just a minute," she said, and began rummaging through the backpack. Her hands came across the wrist watch she had brought with her; and had yet to use. She would still have her grandfather's pocket watch. She pulled the watch out and holding it out to Herman, said, "Here, Herman. Do you already have a watch?"

His eyes showed such astonishment she wondered if he ever had anyone in the family with such a treasure.

He reached his hand out tentatively and said, almost stuttering in his excitement, "A watch! A watch! Even Buster doesn't have a watch! Are you sure? Are you sure? And I can keep it?"

She smiled and replied, "Yes, very sure. Every time you look at it, you will remember your friend."

"My girlfriend," he corrected, holding the watch with almost reverence with both hands.

"Yes, your girlfriend," Vicki affirmed.

He was trying to fasten it on his wrist.

"Here, let me help you. When Herman held out his arm, Vicki threaded the small bar through the ring and fastened it. "Just like a belt, only for your wrist, see."

She was worried he might be so moved he might cry which is something she most definitely did not want.

He looked at her. "I will take really good care of it. I will hide it from Buster, too. He doesn't have one and he might try to take it."

She said mentally, *I really hope not. What a cruel travesty that would be.*

"Okay, then. You better get going so you won't be late getting home."

"Oh, yeah. I almost forgot. Bye, Vicki."

And with that hurried, rather short goodbye, he turned and disappeared into the woods. Rusty looked up at her with a look she credited as a very human expression; that of sadness.

She sat on the closest suitable rock, and shared the rest of the sweet treat Herman had given her with Rusty.

Since she had (for the most part) traded her night traveling for daytime, she drank from her canteen; and having lost her fear of infection from creek water, refilled it.

Then she picked up the backpack and began her forward progress once again. The rocky up-hill progress limited her speed during this stretch, but she was thrilled to notice how close she was to the top of this, the smallest, and lowest of the mountain range. She imagined the view she would have when she reached the top.

Her thoughts returned several times to Herman. Again, she hoped his bully of a brother did not take the watch away from him. She also thought of what kind of future Herman had ahead of him. She wondered about his grandmother's age. You could tell he loved and trusted her; and Vicki imagined the grandmother protected Herman from any abuse Buster may have attempted to subject on Herman.

When she next stopped for a brief rest and water break, she sat Creekside, removed her socks and shoes and dangled her feet in the wonderful water. She ate one of her last two energy bars; sharing it with Rusty. After a long drink, he sat beside her, resting his head in her lap.

She realized she had not written in her journal for several stops now; so, she pulled it and a pen from the backpack and; beginning from where she left off with her pleasant visit with Jeremiah and his mother, she brought her story up to date. Reading it back to herself, she made a couple of corrections and then, satisfied, replaced it in her backpack.

It wasn't more than fifteen minutes later that she again to begin to hear noises coming up behind her. These were totally different noises than the ones before which had been, for the most part, stealthily, these were loud and noisy and seemed to come without any attempt to muffle them.

Mentally she quickly dismissed the thought it might be Herman again; though she had come quite a good distance since she last saw him; and at that time, he had told her his final goodbye.

Rusty immediately went on full alert, growling and beginning to bark loudly; something he had not done before. His fur was standing up again in the "mohawk" on his back. She attempted to quiet him, to no avail. He was loudly, and aggressively straining towards the noises. Finally, trusting his sense of danger, she removed her hand from his furry neck and released her efforts to any attempt to restrain him.

Suddenly, bursting through the weeds and brush, coming almost at a run through the trees blocking his way, she saw a huge brutish man running towards her. When he was almost on her, she couldn't help it; she screamed.

"So! The monkey wasn't kidding. Are you his little girlfriend? How about a watch for me too? What did you trade him for that watch, girlie?"

She became immediately aware of two things simultaneously, there was someone else coming rapidly behind him, and whoever this was welding a branch which had been carved into somewhat of a club.

The man stopped a few feet from her and snarled, "I thought he was imaging things again, but for once I guess he wasn't. Who are you? Where you from? What are you doing out here? Are you alone?"

Later, Vicki wondered *if she had thought quicker and told him her family and herself were hiking and they were up ahead and would probably come after her screaming; would that have changed things any?* Probably not. *People like Buster never listen to reason. They act without thinking with any rationality; and they only resort to physical means to get their message across.*

Rusty threw himself towards Buster's throat,

Before she could assimilate what was currently happening, or answer any of the rapid-fire questions he was throwing at her, Herman came busting through into the small clearing, right on Buster's heels.

"No! No! Don't hurt her! Buster, leave her alone." Herman was yelling, his eyes wide with fear, but also a determination to protect her. As he strove to throw himself at Buster, to Vicki's horror, Buster raised the club and hit Herman right on the head. The blow was hard enough to lift the boy off his feet and toss him into the nearby bushes where he lay, quiet and still.

Vicki ignored Buster and his club and ran over to kneel down to Herman. He had a trickle of blood already running through his hair, turning it a bright red.

She leaned over him, gently trying to raise him to consciousness; and being unable to do so, she screamed at Buster who seemed completely unmoved by Herman's still body and her anxious calls to him.

CHAPTER EIGHT

New home, New family, New Life

The first thing she was conscious of was that of darkness, and of pain. Her head was throbbing and she could identify nothing in the extreme darkness which surrounded her. She closed her eyes and immediately slipped back into the unnatural and frightening unconsciousness.

Noise was what awakened her next time. It was as though she had been in a long dark tunnel and now could see (from admittedly a very long distance) a slight glimpse of light. The noise came from two sides. One side was the sounds of someone using kitchen utensils as in a kitchen. This sound fit with the smells of food being cooked. She could distinguish most strongly the scent of bacon frying and coffee brewing. On the other side she sensed someone patting her hand gently and heard someone softly speaking to her.

"Vicki, wake up, Vicki. You're going to be alright. Grandma will take care of you. Wake up, Vicki."

If only her head didn't hurt so bad, she thought, *she could make sense of where she was and whose voice she was hearing.* She thought she should recognize the voice, but trying to ignore the excruciating pain in her head kept her from the answers she sought.

Suddenly the voice which had been calling her to wake up changed, both in content and volume.

"Grandma! She moved. She's holding her head. Come see."

Now something clicked to Vicki. The voice was Herman's. She tried to open her eyes, but somehow it seemed too difficult and too painful and so once again she escaped into blank and dark "nothingness".

The third time she woke, she opened her eyes to full light and though it hurt to open them, she forced it. Immediately the person on the right side of her excitedly said, "Grandma! Grandma, her eyes are open. Come see!"

She said tentatively, "Where am I? Is that you, Herman?"

"Yes! Yes, it is, Vicki! It's me."

She turned her head and immediately felt the pain return in full force.

"Ow, that hurts," she said.

Then she felt the comfort of a cool rag across her forehead and saw the shadow of another person across from Herman.

"Here, let us help you sit up just a little. Here's something for your headache. Do you think you can swallow it?"

Vicki foolishly tried to nod and immediately the pain intensified.

She tried to reach one hand up to her head, but hands on both sides reached out, and took hold gently of her shoulders and arms to assist her in rising up to a semi-sitting position.

Once up, the hands on her left side held out what appeared to be an aspirin tablet.

"Do you think you could take this for your headache?" the voice asked.

"Yes, I'll try," Vickie croaked out with her raspy voice.

She was able to grasp the small tablet and place it on her tongue. At the same time, Herman said, "Here, Vicki. Here's some water."

She eagerly reached out for the glass and the wonderful, cool, and most welcome water rushed down her throat, with a glorious soothing feeling.

She took several long swallows and then the grandmother's voice said, "Slowly, now. Slowly."

Immediately Herman withdrew the glass.

"More," she croaked out, reaching for the glass.

"Wait just a few minutes. You don't want to get sick," Herman said. "Grandma says you have a cushion."

There as a chuckle from the old lady and she said, "Not cushion, Herman. A concussion."

"Whatever," Herman said, impatiently. "Anyway, you're still hurt."

"Where am I?"

"You're in my house," Herman answered with an obvious sense of pride."

"How did I get here?"

"Buster brought you. You were knocked out."

"I don't remember that."

There was shame in the old woman's voice as she said, "I am so sorry he hit you. He is sorry, too. Your dog really scared him. He knocked the dog out, too. He just has a short fuse on his temper sometimes. We had no way to get you here except if he carried you. No one else is strong enough."

"He hit me, too," Herman interjected. "I was knocked out. He threw water on me and I woke up."

"How long have I been here?"

"Almost a week," the old lady answered.

"A week!" Vicki said in surprise and dismay.

"Yeah, Grandma took good care of you, though."

Vicki was stunned. She had been here an entire week? How was that possible?

"Yes, do you remember me feeding you soup?" The old lady was changing the cloth on her forehead as she spoke.

"Barely…"

"She took care of me, too. Look, I still have a great big bump on my head." When he said this, Herman bent his head over and taking Vicki's hand, laid it over a large lump on the back of his head. He even said, "Ow, still hurts."

The old lady asked, "Think you could eat a little bit now?"

"Maybe. I think maybe so."

"Some soft scrambled eggs and toast?"

"Yes…and could I please have a cup of coffee?"

"How about warm milk instead?" the old lady asked softly.

Vicki smiled at this. This gentle, caring, sweet old lady was trying to take good care of this child, this youngster who was friends with her very needy, and almost helpless own grandchild. A strong feeling of gratitude and acceptance of this woman's possible sacrifice in her behalf swept over her.

"I thought maybe the coffee would help me wake up but whatever you think is best," Vicki replied.

Another smile from the old lady and she said, "Okay, half coffee and half milk."

Herman said, "Aw, no fair, Grandma. You don't let me drink coffee."

Vicki grinned and the old lady did, too. "Well, maybe just this once," she said to Herman.

"Where's Rusty?" Vicki said, suddenly anxiously looking around the room.

"Don't worry. Don't worry," said Herman. "He's gonna' be okay. We had to lock him in the barn in a stall because he wanted to keep running around and Grandma has to nurse him, too. He had some broken ribs," the old lady said, "and I had to tape him up really good. He won't heal if we let him run around."

"So, you were a nurse for all of us," Vicki said, gratefully.

"Well, I guess so. I've done a lot of doctoring in my lifetime. Wasn't any big deal or anything I haven't seen before."

"Can I see him?"

"In a little while. Maybe I can let Herman walk you really slowly out there; but we can't take things too fast. Or maybe put a rope on the dog and bring him in here to see you. That might be the best way to do it. You have a long way to go. Besides your head, you have a badly sprained ankle. It's not broke like I thought at first, but sprained really bad. I have it wrapped up, but you shouldn't be putting any weight on it. Not at all right now."

Vicki was surprised at good the food tasted, and she managed to eat all of it. She drank the half and half coffee-milk and afterwards, listening to Herman recount the entire attack by Buster and the subsequent takeover by grandma, helplessly closed her eyes and fell into an immediate new deep sleep.

When she woke and groggily looked around it was silent, and Herman was no longer in the room. The old lady seemed to be on the porch, rocking and preparing snap green beans; probably for supper later that evening. She heard a thumping on the porch floor and then a whining which she recognized as Rusty.

"Alright, alright; hold your horses, dog." She heard the old lady say. Trying to push herself up a little in the bed, Vicki's eyes fastened on the door. She saw the old lady put the pan of beans down on the table, then undo the rope she had tied around the whining, whimpering and wriggling dog. Unable to wait another minute, the dog pulled the rope from the old lady's hands and leapt on the screen door, almost busting through the screen.

Watching the ball of fur come bounding in, she inhaled and held her breath, bracing for his weight. One final bound and his front paws were on the bed, tongue licking big swipes across her face and hands. The dog was making noises, as though trying to talk and she laughed and clasped his top half in her arms, lying her head on his shoulders. The dog's midsection was wrapped in white adhesive tape, making it look as though he wore a white saddle.

Rusty kept trying to pull himself completely up on the bed and finally, giving up, she allowed him, wrapping her arms around his upper body and trying to assist him. She was worried he might hurt his ribs trying to get up there.

"Oh, yes, yes. Yes, boy, I see you. You're okay, aren't you now?" Vicki kept rubbing him and talking to him and finally he began to settle down.

"Don't let him wallow on your ankle now," the old lady warned. "He's heavy. I think he's put on some weight since the accident."

Accident? Thought Vicki. *Is that what we're calling it?*

Herman came hurrying in, carrying a milk bucket, splashing it in his speed to join all the fracas.

"Hey, just look at that old dog, Vicki! Look how happy he is to see you."

She laughed along with Herman. "Seems like it, doesn't it?" she asked.

Slowly, as though just remembering (or noticing) her injuries, the dog began to gently crawl up towards her until his paws were on the pillow next to her, and his head resting on his paws. The dog let out a huge human-like sigh and moved his big head under her hand, giving notice he was ready for some extended affection from her. Seeing his struggles, Herman came over, and lifted the dog's bottom half so even though he was crowding the bed, he was at least up *on* the bed with Vicki. And relishing his nearness to Vicki.

Vicki was surprised to feel tears in her eyes and looking over at the old lady she saw the same there.

"You big ole' baby!" Vicki said to the dog as she hugged him close.

The old lady cleared her throat and said, turning towards the stove, "Think you could eat a little oatmeal and a biscuit or so?" she asked Vicki.

"I sure could," Herman said.

"Oh, you! I know you could. You can always eat. Sometimes I think you never fill up."

After fixing Herman and Vicki big bowls of oatmeal mixed with cream off the top of the fresh milk and honey, the old lady poured some milk in a bowl for Rusty and then Herman gently guided him down once again to the floor where he gratefully began to clean the bowl in record time, then stood, as though waiting a refill.

After they had eaten, the old lady brought a basin of warm water, a clean wash cloth and a towel to the small table by Vicki's bedside.

"I thought you might want to give yourself a little washup. You know, a sponge bath, isn't that what they call it? Then I want to unwrap your ankle and see how that's looking. I'll be gentle, don't worry."

"Can I see, Grandma?" Herman asked.

"See but don't touch. It's still going to be sore for her. Go on, now Herman. Outside with you. Give her a little privacy for washing up. I'll call you when she's done. And take that dog with you. Enough of that tongue bath of his. Keep him on the rope until you put him back in the barn. He will fight to be free, but we have to make sure his ribs heal."

Turning to Vicki she asked, "How's the head? Still sore, I'll wager."

"Just when I forget and roll over on it or reach up there to itch. I sure would like to wash my hair, though."

"I can help you with that. First the body, then the ankle and then the hair washing."

As she began assisting Vicki with all the ministrations, Vicki began to ask questions. Her curiosity was itching and as she and the old lady began to talk, many more questions came floating through her mind.

"What happened to Herman's mother?" Vicki asked.

"Buster's sister had herself a fella once. No good. I tried to tell her but when my husband was killed in a logging accident, that girl just sort of went wild on me. Buster was older and he tried to reign her in, too. Weren't no good. She just did pretty much what she wanted to. All I could do was stand by and pray. Well, like a lot of girls, she got herself with child. Soon as he found out about it, that fella disappeared. Took off like the scared rabbit he was. Buster wasted a lot of time looking for him, but didn't do no good. No good at all. He was long gone. I don't know what Buster thought he would do if he found him. I suppose he thought he could pull off a shotgun wedding, but that never works out for anyone."

"What's a shotgun wedding?"

The old lady was gently removing the wrapping off Vicki's ankle and when she flinched, she said, "Sorry. You want another aspirin?"

Vicki shook her head and said, "Go on. Go on with the story."

It means when a girl gets pregnant and she isn't married, her daddy catches the guilty boy, and holds a shotgun on him until he marries the girl.

The old lady looked at Vicki, grinned and said, "They don't really mean the threat, honey. It's more of a spoken threat to force a boy to "do right" by the girl."

Vicki nodded her head to indicate her understanding.

"Go on with the story," she said.

"Okay." She looked around and said, "I don't like to talk about this with Herman. He and I talked it all out several years ago when he came up with his own questions as to why he doesn't have a mama living with us or a daddy, either."

"Well, to make a long story short," she continued, "After the baby was born, she stuck around for a while but her heart was never in that child; especially when she realized he was going to be a little slow…" The old lady said, pausing to look at the girl, again as though to verify her understanding.

She finished her fresh dressing and binding on Vicki's ankle, and then she said, "How does a cup of tea sound?"

"A cup of your coffee, even if you dilute it with milk. sounds better."

"Alrighty, then."

After the coffee was ready and the old lady had helped Vicki to sit up further, the old lady pulled a rocker closer and she continued.

"Right from the start that baby was more mine than hers and it was okay with me. He was not any trouble; it was almost like he knew he was living on thin ground. If a baby can sense whether or not he is really wanted or treasured or merely tolerated, there must have been times, even as an infant, when Herman seemed to fear he was living on borrowed time, so to speak. I think that is why he tried too hard to please everyone. As he grew older this got stronger. Even though I protect him from Buster, I worry about what will eventually become of him. I often wonder if Buster were to find a woman who would be strong enough to hold her own with him, could it be possible she would also have sympathy and hopefully, acceptance for Herman?" She sighed and went on, "Anyway, when Herman was only about six months old, she went off to the big city of Cincinnati, Tennessee to visit a distant cousin; and she never came back. I don't even know where she lives or anything about her life. I don't remember the baby ever even asking about her... She was here and then she was gone. Buster and me were his family. He avoids Buster as much as he can and Buster allows me to set the rules for him. It worries me some to think about how sad he will be when you and Rusty leave."

Just then Herman burst through the door. Here's the eggs, Grandma. Milk is on the porch. Can I work on the surprise now?"

The old lady grinned and nodded.

"You didn't tell her, did you?"

"No, I didn't tell her."

The old lady turned to Vicki and said, "Herman has asked me for permission to fix you a surprise and I have given it. So, if you hear noises, try to ignore it."

"You have both been so good for me, please don't go to any more trouble."

"It's not trouble," Herman said, "It is going to be fun!"

Just like that he was gone outside. Vicki and the old lady used this time to wash her hair and surprisingly, she was feeling exhausted again. She closed her eyes, and the old lady pulled the quilt covering up to her chin.

When she next woke, it was to a symphony of hammering and sawing and whistling. Herman was definitely up to something. Her curiosity was aroused. It was much later in the afternoon when the noise ceased and a welcome silence enveloped the cabin. It was somehow very homey and restful with the silence, the smell of something good cooking in a big pot, and the sounds of birds outside. How tranquil it all seemed. It was as though this little corner of the world was on its own time schedule; no one was stressed, there was no time-table to meet, no expectations which wouldn't be met without their interference. Sort of a respite from problems and worry which so dominated the world from which she had come. She wondered how old the grandmother was…She seemed to be in such good health, full of energy, but without the feelings of deadlines or pressure most of the adults she was used to seem to always have. Her only anxiety came when she began to wonder where Buster was and when he would be coming back.

When grandma (as gradually Vicki began to think of, and even refer to her) became aware of her being awake, she came over and said, "Do you want to let me help you go to the outdoor potty? It might be too much too soon, but I know it embarrasses you to have me bring you a bedpan to the bed."

This query didn't embarrass the old lady to ask, however; it did discomfort Vicki.

"I would like to try," she answered.

"Okay, here is what we will do," the old lady said, "Herman has found and whittled one end of a sturdy branch you can use for your hurt ankle, and he and I will get on the other side and help you get there. Then we will wait and when you are finished, we will get you back to the porch."

Vicki was actually happy to have a chance to go outside. There seemed to be a breeze outside, and though the window shutters were hooked open in the cabin it was still too warm and stuffy.

"That would be wonderful," Vicki said, "And maybe I could sit outside on the porch for a while?"

"Yes. That would be good for you."

The plan worked good and except for the slow progress and a couple of painful moments when Vicki forgot and put her injured foot down and the weight caused a quick surge of pain. She fought hard to keep from crying each time.

She was offended by the smell in the outdoor privy, but relieved to be able to make her care easier for grandma and Herman (who was usually the one to empty, rinse and return the bedpan).

When the returned back to the porch, they assisted in getting her seated in a rocker. Herman brought his milking stool, and after placing a folded quilt on it, put her injured foot on it so it was almost equal to her rocker seat and made her much more comfortable.

After they assured themselves, she was comfortable, Herman (who had been so obvious about some kind of secret he was guarding) turned to his grandmother and questioned, "Now, grandmother? Now?"

She laughed and said, "Okay, Herman, now."

Herman turned and pointed at a colorful Indian-designed blanket which appeared to be strung up between two huge trees. Each end of the blanket had been sandwiched between two boards, and looked to be nailed to the three making a homemade, but serviceable hammock.

"Look, Vicki, look. I made you a hammock. I can put you in it and you can be outdoors. Do you like it?"

"I love it, Herman! I love it. I can't wait. How will we get me up there?"

"Grandma and me will help you. We will walk you over there, and take the stool and you will step on the stool with your good foot and I will lift you up. You're skinny and you don't weigh very much. It will be easy."

Although Vicki had great trepidation about how easy this would be, she was more than enthusiastic about being able to swing gently outdoors in the big shady tree instead of returning to the stuffy interior of the cabin.

Actually, the walk over to the hammock was the most difficult part of the project, and once she was in the hammock, and allowed her muscles to relax, she gave a big sigh of comfort and enjoyment. She had been worried her weight would bring the blanket too close to the girl, but Herman has strung it good and tight and she really didn't weigh enough to lower the hammock too low.

"Oh, this is glorious! Thank you, thank you, thank you, Herman."

He actually flushed with pleasure at the gratitude she expressed and said, "Oh, it was easy, Vicki. I thought you would like it."

She was moved by his delight in being able to both please and surprise her. She chose this time to ask the question which had been high on her concerns since her fuzzy mind had more or less began to put all the pieces together about the event which had taken place which had resulted in the injuries, she and Rusty were slowly accepting and healing from.

"Herman," she began, "Where is Buster? Is he at work?"

"Buster? No, Grandma sent me to get cousin Abraham' for a while and..." he stopped here long enough to giggle, then continued, "Grandma said if she didn't send him off for a while to think about his behavior, she was likely going to choke him. She was so mad at him. She said that he was lucky she didn't call the sheriff and have him arrested. So, cousin Abraham took him to his house with him to stay awhile."

Herman looked at her and with a somewhat crooked grin he said, "I knew she wouldn't do that; choke him, I mean. She always says we handle our own problems and don't hang out our dirty laundry for everyone to see. I don't understand what our wash hanging out has to do with anything though, do you, Vicki?"

She very carefully kept from laughing and said nothing about the fact she didn't have to worry about Buster showing up unannounced and furious with rage at her for being sent off to some cousin's house.

Curious, she asked Herman, "How long did Grandma say Buster has to stay gone?"

He paused and acted like he was considering his reply. "Hum, I don't know. I guess until she tells him he can come home. I guess it's up to Grandma and Abraham. I like cousin Abraham. He's a good whittler. He's the one who carved those animals of mine. Did you see them? On the mantle inside?"

She had, indeed, noticed the intricate and delicately carvings. They were carved in great detail and smoothed with an excess of sanding which impressed Vicki with the efforts and time which must have gone into their carving.

"Wow, he's a great carver, isn't he?"

"You bet."

She listened to Herman's chatter, and didn't even notice when her eyelids got heavy and she drifted off in her wonderfully comfortable hammock.

Right before she dozed off, she felt a sense of peace and comfort. The combination of her sponge bath, her freshly shampooed hair, the warm breakfast and gentle sway of her homemade hammock all contributed to her overall sense of well-being.

Over the next few days, Rusty was healing nicely and had used his returning health to roam freely where he wanted. At first, she worried about him when he would venture out of her sight and even off into the woods for brief periods; eventually though, she relaxed and allowed him to explore.

Vicki had to laugh when Herman asked her: "Too bad Rusty isn't a girl, huh, Vicki?"

"Why is that?"

"'cause then he could have puppies and you could give me one of my own."

"Yeah, that would be great, wouldn't it?"

* * *

And so, the days passed. Slowly and peacefully. As she healed, she became more mobile, she graduated to walking on her own, with the help of her carefully carved crutch, and then without the crutch, but slowly. Her headaches disappeared in their entirety and even the pain of putting weight on her sprained ankle began to diminish. Her fondness for Herman was also glowing and she was growing almost used to the childlike mind in the large and awkward body.

Some of the things he said were funny but he didn't seem to take offense when she was given to laughter about something he had said. In fact, he enjoyed making her laugh. One day he came outside where she was on the porch with a glass of cool tea. They had no ice, of course, but a jar of water was kept in the creek with water running constantly over and around it. She was learning that many things she once thought necessary in her life were not really necessary; just what she was used to.

"Hey!" Herman said, sitting down on the porch step below.

"Hey yourself," she grinned.

"How are your feet?" he asked.

Puzzled, she asked him, "My feet?"

"Yeah, your feet. I asked Grandma how long she thought you would be here and she said until your itchy feet came back."

Vicki laughed.

"Well, I don't feel any strong itchy feelings yet," she answered him.

"Good. I hope they never itch again."

But the thing she noticed most was the peace and contentment which she not only noticed, but welcomed into her overall well-being. She even joined Grandma in weeding her small garden, enjoying the morning sun and the sounds of the small critters and the abundance of happy noisy birds which kept her company.

One morning she stopped pulling the endless weeds, and sat back on the ground with her injured ankle stretched out on one side and the other leg bent comfortably at the knee and said, out loud "I'm happy." Then she repeated it once again. "I'm happy." Immediately she felt a swath of guilt, thinking of the family she had left back home before she began this adventure. Already so many things had happened. What lay ahead of her? She decided whatever it was wasn't as important as the lessons she was learning about herself at the present moment.

She even allowed a glimpse of shame at the trivial things she used to feel important; the latest style of her friend's clothing, the parties, and the top music of the day, the cutest boy in class, even school itself. It was summer now, but what was she going to do when it was time to go back to school? Would she return home? Was that even an option? Or would she make a new home somewhere; if not here with Herman and Grandma, then somewhere else?

These were questions she mulled over, but not in an anxious of urgent way, just as something she almost casually, and only occasionally wondered about. Of course, she had longer ranging questions, too; as would other girls her age; would she marry and have a family someday? Would she choose a career?

Would something completely unexpected and final happen to make some of these things no longer questions, but steps forward she had no choice in?

She dug her hands into the black, cool feeling dirt, and saw Herman coming back from the wood pile where he had been chopping firewood.

He wiped his forehead with his bandana, and held out a buck and dipper of cool well water to her.

"You have to chop a lot of wood, don't you? Don't you wish you had someone else to help with that?" she asked him.

He looked surprised at the question. "No. I don't care if I have to. Grandma cooks and I chop wood. I help her with the laundry washing and she cleans the house. Those are our chores."

"When Buster is here what does he do?"

"Oh, Buster? Not much. I don't like it when he is home. He talks back to Grandma."

That's not good, is it?"

"No, but she is not afraid of him. She says he is all bark and no bite."

Vicki grinned. "Do you know what she means when she says that?"

"Why, sure. She doesn't take no guff off him."

"Thanks, Herman," she said, handing the water dipper back to him.

"Hey, let's see if Grandma thinks it's safe to get the tape off Rusty today. What do you think? The tape is practically in shreds anyway, and it's dirty."

Herman shivered and said, "Oh, that's gonna' hurt. It will pull his fur."

"True, but I think he will be glad to see it gone, too. Then you and I could give him a nice bath."

After discussing it with Grandma, that's what they did. They put the round washtub on the porch, and Herman and Vicki held the dog in case he might decide to bolt while Grandma got her scissors, and gently, carefully cut the tape. Surprisingly, Rusty stood placidly and stoically as they worked on his coat. It was almost as if he was happy to get rid of this stuff. Vicki wondered if it was itching him under the tape.

After they got the tape off, they filled the tub, and gently soaped his fur, even took the scissors and cut some of it which was gummed up and stuck together. The soap they used was lye soap they made themselves and while its suds up good, there was no sweet perfume smell like she was used to.

The end result, when they let him out of the tub and he shook empathically was very comical and Herman especially could barely control his laughter. The general result was a very poorly given haircut with big gaps of fur missing here and there.

"It's okay, Sweetie," Vicki told the dog, giving him a hug and getting her shirt wet as she did so. "It will grow back. We still love you. We think we're handsome, don't we Herman?"

When they finished, she rummaged through her backpack and found the small plastic case which enclosed the soap she had brought with her from home.

Herman, who had watched her asked, "What's that, Vicki?"

"Look," she said, "Smell this," and she extended her hand out to him. He took the little box and smelled it.

"Oh, that smells pretty!" he said. "What's it for?"

"It's soap. Just like that soap, but they have added perfume to it."

"What's perfume?"

"Toilet water," Grandma said. "Remember when we went down to do some trading once and Buster bought me some with his money?"

"You said that was lilacs. I remember. It smelled like those lilac bushes out back."

"It comes in different scents," Vicki said, "Some smells like lilacs, some smells like roses, some smells like honeysuckle."

A little reluctantly, he held it out to return it and she pushed it back towards him. "No, you keep it. Use it Saturday when you take your bath."

"Will it make me smell like a girl?"

All three of them laughed.

"Who cares? It will be fun, won't it?" Vicki asked.

"Well, I can't do it when Buster comes back. He will laugh at me and call me a sissy."

Vicki felt sorry for the somber change in his expression. She also understood his knowledge as to Buster's probable reaction.

"What else you got in there?" Herman asked.

"Herman!" Grand said sternly. "None of your business. Those are Vicki's things. It's not polite to be nosy."

"Sorry, Vicki," he said.

* * *

When they said grace over supper that evening, again Vicki thought of some of the things which had changed with her during her stay with this confident, intelligent and caring family of two. She didn't count Buster because she could not attribute any of these same qualities to him as she did to Grandma and Herman.

She watched Grandma as she took a venison roast from the smoke house to prepare it one day. She washed it off with cool water, poked some holes in it and pushed whole cloves of garlic in the holes, rolled it in flour, browned all sides in a big black skilled, and then put it in in a big black pot (which reminded her of a witch's kettle from some Halloween story), covered it with water, added whole carrots and onions from the garden, and hung it on an iron rod over a low hearth fire. It made the entire cabin almost unbearably hot that day, but that evening the meat melted in your mouth. It was totally different from the way her mother used her roaster oven or crockpot to cook a roast, but she relished the taste.

Another good thing she noticed was that no matter how hot it got during the day, this high up into the hills, after sundown it cooled off quickly and she didn't feel the lack of any fan or air conditioner like she had at home. In fact, when she woke each morning, she usually found that sometime in the night she had felt cool enough to bring a quilt up to cover herself.

Even when it came to their meal that evening as she enjoyed a big bowl of rabbit stew and cornbread with sliced tomatoes from the garden, she realized it wasn't so long ago she wouldn't even try her brother's frog legs and now she asked for second helpings of the stew.

She felt no sense of guilt when she and Herman went down to the river bank and fished the morning away or when she volunteered to hang the wash out, and week the garden. She drew the line at going hunting with Herman or watching him go behind the barn and clean and prepare a deer. She felt like being able to eat such was a giant step in her evolution. It would be entirely out of her character to watch it being shot or dismembered. Just seeing the meat in the pot helped her dissociate the meal from its source.

Her clothes smelled and felt soft and clean and she smiled to herself when she remembered the bleach, special sweet-smelling laundry soap and softener her mother thought absolutely crucial to a good laundry. What would her mother have thought about having to boil the whites and scrub them on a washboard?

Time seemed to have stopped somewhere in this little mountain hamlet and she was content to slow herself down with it. She wondered at Grandma's energy and strength and tried to guess at her age. She wanted to ask, but out of a sense courtesy, she refrained. Gradually, as the as the days floated by Grandma shared more stories and Vicki learned how her husband had courted and married her when she was only twelve years old and they had lived together in hard times and easy for over forty years before he lost his life in an accident on his railroad job. When she talked about her age at her marriage, she laughed at Vicki's widened eyes when she said, "I was twelve and he was eighteen. Think that's too young, don't you? Well, girls got married early, especially in those days. We; the girls; didn't get much schooling. It was expected we learn how to read and write a little bit; to sew and cook and clean but that was all we needed. It's a little different now, but not much. I was lucky my mother liked to read so I got read to a lot when I was a child. Of course, people told stories in those days, too. Many the tale my grandpa told me late during the winter while we waited out a storm."

They had always wanted more children and had lost one little girl in an early miscarriage which had devastated them both. Buster was the only living child and though the old lady loved him, she was quite aware of his faults; his quick temper and easily aroused rage at little things, his constant complaining and seeming inability to find anything good in his life or in other people.

She spoke of her wonder as to why Buster was so different from her husband or herself; neither of whom was mean or short-tempered. She supposed it could be somehow related to the fast that he was raised pretty much alone; especially after his sister left and with so many years between Herman and himself. Not having a daddy for long, and no real friends except the few months a year he went to the little school probably didn't help things, either. He liked being about his cousins when they went to their place or they made the rare visit to see them; but even then, he treated them poorly or fought over just about everything. He had to always be first or right, and answering a disagreement with his fists was his nature. When he was young, he prided himself on not crying when she spanked him although she always tried reasoning with him first. It was as though he had to show her, he wasn't afraid of her and she couldn't hurt him any.

She said her husband had adored him and in his eyes the boy could do no wrong. She confided that he had had several girlfriends over the years since he got out of school but never kept them long because he didn't know how to treat them right. She had tried to teach him manners, to no avail.

Vicki felt sorry for the old lady but tried not to show it because she knew Grandma was proud and wouldn't want any pity or sympathy from anyone. The look Grandma got on her face when she spoke of Herman showed the love and caring she felt for this boy. She was honest about worrying what would become of him when she went to her reward someday. She supposed if he were lucky Buster would be gone and on his own by then, and perhaps one of the kinder and most gentle of the aunts or uncles might take him in. Problem is none of them had a lot of anything, most had a houseful of their own young'uns and had trouble feeding and keeping up with them until they were old enough to leave home; most to follow the railroad to the bigger cities that had factory work or the occasional still working mine. Any kind of blue-collar job would fit most of them just fine. Work all week, bar on payday Friday nights, sleep it off on Sundays and begin again.

Late Night Assault

One evening, it must have been close to midnight, Vicki was awakened by loud shouting and an assortment of banging, laughter, and strange voices she certainly did not recognize. She didn't know what to do, but feeling she needed to get to her feet; being attacked in her bed was not an option. Heart beating wildly, and breathing fast, she crept towards one of the windows.

Now there came a loud bunch of "pops". Just as she leaned forward to try and see outside, a hand grabbed her arm. She gave a "yelp! Let go, let go!"

"Vicki, it's me, it's me, Herman. I won't let anybody get you. I promise."

"Oh, Herman!" she said, exasperated and filled with relief. "You scared me half to death. What's going on? What's all that noise?"

"Mostly firecrackers. Grandma said it's Buster and Roger."

"Who's Roger?"

"He's my cousin."

"Another cousin?"

"Yeah! He's Abraham's other son."

"Oh." She was speechless.

"Yeah, Grandma says they are probably drunk. She went to get her shotgun."

"Oh, my God," she said, obviously horrified. "She shouldn't do that, Herman."

She grabbed his arm to emphasize what she was saying. "She can't shoot at her own son and nephew."

"Oh, she is a good shot, Vicki. She won't shoot them; she will just scare them and make them go home."

"How do you know that?"

"Cause it's happened before. Buster and Roger get drunk together a lot and then they try to bully everybody. Grandma is not afraid of them."

"But…but…What if she misses and accidently shoots one of them?"

"She won't," he said confidently.

Just then she heard the screen door open and Grandma's voice call out loudly, "Buster! What the heck do you think you're doing? Is that crazy Roger with you? I didn't raise you to act like a crazy man. Where's your good sense?"

"Grandma, we don't mean no harm. You know I wouldn't do anything to make you mad. Roger just wants to meet the girl. I told him about her and he don't believe anything I say. Just let her come outside on the porch and meet him and we'll go back home."

"You been drinking, haven't you, Buster? And you, Roger. Does your dad know you are over here, raising hell?"

There was silence for a few minutes and then Vicki, holding her breath briefly, heard Grandma say, "Ha! I didn't think so. Well, I can't wait to talk to him now, about how his oldest is acting like a real ass. How'd you like to go home with some buckshot in your butt? Huh?"

"You wouldn't do that."

"There's a good way to find out and that's by hanging around keeping a person from a good night's sleep. You two have done some crazy stunts before but this beats all."

"Just let her come out and meet Roger, Grandma, and we'll leave. I promise," said Buster.

"Ha! You don't know how to keep your word. Never have. No, she ain't some prize you captured somewhere. You can't tell me, or her, what to do. Now, I'm going to give you two until I count to ten and then I am going to let go with this shotgun. Usually I am a crack shot, but my eyes are too good in the dark; who knows where the buckshot will land. One…"

She began hollering out the numbers, ignoring anything else the two boys were yelling.

"Two," she said.

Vicki exhaled the breath she had been holding. She was still griping Herman's arm and he gently pried her hand off saying, "Ow, Vicki. Don't worry. She won't really shoot them."

"Three," Grandma called out, and then, "Four,"

"Grandma, come on now, you know you aren't gonna shoot at us."

"Yeah," said Roger, "I just wanna' meet her. Where's the harm in that?"

"Five…Six…Getting closer, fellas."

Vicki was holding her breath again. She was straining to hear anything from outside, but the two boys had not moved any closer but neither had they began to back off.

"Seven…Eight," said Grandma.

Vicki looked outside and focused on Grandma. She gasped when she saw the old lady pull the shotgun up and fit it into her shoulder comfortably.

"Oh, my God," Vicki said, "She's really going to do it."

"Well, let's just say if I was them boys, I'd turn tail and start running," said Herman.

"Nine…and…ten!"

There was a very loud, ear-splitting roar as the shotgun went off. Vicki screamed and so did the two boys. There was a crash of brush being blown apart, and running steps as the boys disappeared into the brush where they had been standing.

The old lady yelled, "Go on home now and stop playing the fool. And don't come back like that; drunk and playing the bully. Next time I won't miss. You're both big and mean enough to make good targets and I got a feeling Abraham is not going to be happy with you"

She came inside, reloaded the shotgun and put it back in its' rack.

"Hey, you two, how'd you like the way they ran?" She laughed. "Nothing like knocking down a couple of big mouths trying to act like bullies."

"Will they come back?" Vicki asked timidly.

"Heck, no. Couple of idiots playing the fool. I can't wait until Abraham hears about this latest stunt."

Herman laughed. "Ain't nobody gets the best of Grandma."

"Aren't you worried they will try something awful to get even?" Vicki asked.

At this both Herman and the old lady laughed heartily.

"If you knew those boys better, Vicki," Grandma said, "You'd know that unless those two boys were filled with liquor, they would not have been brave enough to pull this type of shenanigans. I'm sorry that you had such a fright and I am embarrassed and ashamed that relatives of mine would act like this to our guest. Are you okay? Will you be able to go back to sleep?"

"You don't need to apologize, Grandma," Vicki said, addressing her with Herman's form of endearment, you didn't do anything wrong." She even giggled and then continued, "I do think you scared them a little."

"Good, I wanted to."

Although Grandma tried to talk Vicki and Herman into returning to their beds, neither was the least bit interested in sleeping. They were wound too tightly within their emotions. Finally, Grandma gave up on anyone going to bed, instead she made a fresh pot of coffee and on this occasion, she allowed Herman and Vicki to join her in a full-strength cup of real coffee.

The three of them took their coffee out to the porch and were there to witness and enjoy a glorious sunrise.

"God's good morning to us. What a beautiful day it's going to be," Vicki said.

"Yes," agreed Grandma. Are you familiar with God's sign to Noah in the bible, Vicki?"

"Yes. I remember he sent Noah a rainbow to reassure him of his continued presence. Wasn't that it?"

"Yes," she said, delighted Vicki knew the story. "I believe strongly in signs. I think sometimes we get too busy to see them and we might miss messages which should be easy to see."

"I agree," Vicki said as she began to relax and even laugh along at Herman's rehash of the evening's happenings. While she listened to Herman, her mind roamed over what the old lady had said about signs and she thought of the world she had left which had led her here. Who would believe the events of the previous night? No doubt the two boys would have been arrested, and maybe even Grandma. Vicki doubted things like registering their home owned gun ever crossed their minds.

In her old world a son and nephew would never have pulled such a prank and gotta away with no real punishment. However; she knew Grandma still loved those boys and would put the night behind her.

She also thought of the way Grandma got up before anyone else; fixed coffee and sat on the porch in the early daylight each day to read her bible and get the strength and comfort she needed for the day ahead. Vicki was pretty sure she never dwelled on her own problems and hardships; but instead, felt gratitude for all the blessings she credited to her savior. She felt envy for Grandma's surety.

Despite Herman's continued concern about her feet, when she thought about moving on, she thought of excuses she had for staying. The truth was she was happy here. She didn't really want to leave so quickly. She didn't want to return back to her old home; but she wasn't sure she wanted to tear herself away from these people who had accepted her with no reservations; and no questions asked. They had truly taken up space in her heart. Rusty seemed happy here as well; even going so far as to hunt some, bringing a rabbit he had killed one morning and brought to lay as a gift at Herman's feet.

Vicki tried hard to give him praise because Herman said she should or he would feel she thought he had done something wrong. Grandma cooked it and served it with vegetables from the garden and gravy over biscuits. Surprisingly, Vicki not only ate it; but thoroughly enjoyed every bite.

Vicki was touched when several days later Herman presented her with a soft, cured, and dried rabbit skin he had tightly mounted between small bark-free sticks.

"Oh, it's beautiful! Herman, what a wonderful gift! Thank you so much."

"It's a wall hanging, Vicki. You can hang it up, like a picture.

"I will always treasure it, Herman."

Often; especially in her dealings with the old lady and with Herman, she felt she had found her way backwards into some kind of time warp, and had landed in the past. Perhaps it was all a long dream and she would awake in her "perfect" pink and white (decorated magazine page designed) bedroom. Her computer would be on the vanity and the small television would be on. Then she would look around at the fireplace and the log cabin exterior of the home she called home; at least for now and realize it was no dream but an altogether different reality; one in which she was comfortable.

*　*　*

When Vicki woke one morning with a snap in the air and a definite lower temperature, she got herself a cup of coffee with Grandma's assistance and watched Grandma and Herman building a fire for the big washtub. She saw in one of the porch rockers with her coffee and felt completely at peace. Evidently it was laundry day. She told herself she would spend a little time enjoying her coffee and the morning and then go help with the washing. As she enjoyed the morning, Rusty came and lay at her feet so she would rub his back.

"You're lazy, too, aren't you, boy?"

A few minutes later Herman made a trip to his chopped wood pile, then after carrying some logs over to his grandmother's easy reach for the laundry fire, he came back and said to Vicki: "Hey, Vicki, guess what?"

"Hey, Herman!" she said, teasingly to him. "What?"

Grandma says if we get done with the laundry, I can take you and show you where the biggest blueberry patch is and if we get enough and bring them back, she will make us a blueberry cobbler… and she makes the best cobbler in the whole world."

"That sounds really great, Herman. I love blueberries." Saying this, she sat her empty cup down, she stood and said, "Okay, I'm ready to help."

They worked for little over two hours, but finally, the last of the wash was hanging and blowing in the gentle warm breezes, the tub water had been emptied, and the fire banked safely down.

They hurriedly ate cold biscuits with bacon from breakfast for their lunch, and Vicki changed her shorts for jeans and her shirt for a long-sleeved one after Herman warned her about the thorns. Herman got them each a tin bucket, and whistling for Rusty to follow, Herman led the way to the so-titled "best blueberry bush in the county".

As was usual with Herman, he kept up a non-stop chatter the entire way to the berry patch. Half the time Vicki nodded or gave a simple "Really?" or "Is that true or are you spoofing me?"

Herman was leading the way, and when he pushed back some brush and pausing, looked back at Vicki and said cheerfully, "There, now! Have you ever seen a blueberry path like this before?"

Vicki stepped forward, holding the other side of the brush back as well.

There were many bushes, absolutely loaded with the weight of many berries, and Vicki was truly impressed with the quantity and the large size.

"Oh, my," she said. "You were right, Herman. I have never seen so many beautiful berries in one place. Do we have to fill the pails first or can we eat some?"

He laughed. "Of-course we can. I always eat bunches. If we don't have blue tongues and lips and hands when we go home, well…then we didn't do our job."

She laughed with him.

They began to pluck the berries, saying, "One of you and one for me," each time he placed a berry in the pail or his mouth. They worked steadily for over an hour, then sat and rested for a little while. Down the bank from the berry patch was the cool running river and they bent over, and washed their faces and hands and drank greedily of its' refreshing coolness.

They laughed and made fun of each other's blue fingers and mouths and argued over who had the most berries in their pails.

Later, Vicki would look back on this experience as the last time for a very long time her adventure was truly happy one. Even though the attack from Buster on Herman, Rusty and herself had been injurious, scary and hard to get over, yet it was nothing compared to what took place on what she later termed *"The berry picking day"*. It also became the longest lasting memory of her lifetime and she was rarely able to speak about it again.

When they grew tired of picking berries and very full of eating them, they decided to head back home.

At first, they didn't hear the noise; they had been laughing and remembering the battle with Grandma chasing Buster and Roger off with her shotgun, then Herman grabbed hold of her arm and said, "Wait, wait a minute, Vicki. Listen. Someone is coming!"

They both stopped and she heard it then. It wasn't hard to hear once they quit moving and laughing. It was loud and coming from someone who didn't seem to care how much noise they were making.

As they stood there, hoping the noise would turn some other direction, or stop completely, ahead of them the bushes parted and at first Vicki could not decipher what she was looking at. By the time she recognized what she was seeing, Herman had started screaming, "Run, Vicki, Run!

Rusty had begun barking loudly and his fur was standing up. He growled and placed himself between what looked to be two round furry balls, heading straight towards her. She realized it was two small furry bear cubs and even then, she was unable to recognize the danger therein; while she later realized Herman had immediately recognized and knew the danger.

The enormous and ear-splitting howl of the huge shape bursting through the brush hot on the tail of the cubs was a mountainous roar and changed as she gave up her four-footed gallop to catch her cubs and instead, paused to stand fully up on her two hind feet. Her rage was plain through her howling challenge, both towards Herman, Rusty, and Vicki and as a warning to her cubs.

Rusty had taken a protective stance, showing his willingness to fight to protect Vicki and Herman, which, or course was fool-hardy when acknowledging the opponent, he was facing; yet he stood in his brave, determined, and staunchly set position, ready to meet the attack.

Herman braced himself, and reaching out with both hands, gave a huge push to Vicki, nearly knocking her off her feet, but she caught herself and turned, and starting running as fast as she could.

She thought Herman was right on her heels, but he foolishly he tried to yell Rusty into action, pausing as he yelled, "Rusty, Rusty, come, come on, come, Rusty." By then the mama bear had reached out and with one quick swipe, knocked Rusty completely off the path and into a huge pile of brush. There was an earth-shattering squeal of pain from the dog; which immediately had the reaction of sending Herman off running to follow the path Vicki had followed.

Vicki did not look back; which later would result in a life-long feeling of heavy guilt and an inability to forgive herself. She could not bring herself to return to find out the final results of the attack, but ran all the way home where she sobbed and managed to make Grandma understand that Herman and Rusty were fighting off a big bear. The old lady grabbed her shotgun, made sure it was loaded and took off with Vicki towards the well-known berry patch.

The horror of what they would find there would never leave the old lady or Vicki. Rusty was not quite dead, but was whining in pain and would be dead within the next few minute. His entire belly had been ripped open and his intestines were lying outside his body. Blood was everywhere. He had managed to come back, injured on his front leg and jaw to rejoin Herman and the fight; but of course, to no avail; except to give witness to his bravery right to the end.

Vicki screamed when she saw Herman's body. The old lady cropped to her knees, forgetting all about the shotgun; but there was no sign of the cubs or the mama bear anyway. Herman was no longer breathing and his face was almost unrecognizable. His left arm was torn from the socket and there were other horrendous bite marks. In fact, it was hard to find any place which was untouched on his torso or limbs. It was a bloodbath on the dirt and nearby bushes. His clothes were ripped and torn. The old lady picked up his upper body and rocked back and forth, sobbing uncontrollably. Vicki turned away, continuing her screaming, but unable to look again at Herman. Adding to the overall devastation of the scene, were the over-turned berry buckets and the smashed purple stains on the ground, bushes, and two victims.

Vicki would never be able to estimate how long she and the old lady were there, on their knees in their loud grief; but finally, the old lady said, "Go home and bring me two quilts to cover them. I can't leave them here alone and like this. The bear might come back, or other animals, or people. I don't want no body to see them like this.

I'll wait here. We'll cover them and wait the quilts down with rocks; then we'll go get Abraham and his boys to help us take them home."

Vicki immediately did this; she hurried and when she returned, they did as the old lady wanted. Both intermittently had tears running down their faces. They had no control. They would (either one or the other or sometimes both) find themselves with tears running down their faces, then dry eyes and stumbling along as if zombies, only a few seconds later to find themselves, wet-cheeked and silently weeping uncontrollably again.

Even years later there were nights Vicki would find herself waking to nightmares of Rusty and Herman lying in blood. She thought it odd she didn't wake screaming with visions of the bear bearing down on them; but always on the horrific scene of the bodies.

As things took shape after that, Vicki found herself looking around, trying to find Herman so she could ask him what was happening. Then she would remember he was no longer there to ask.

The old lady would try now and then; when she seemed to remember who Vicki was, and that she was there, to comfort her and help her understand what was happening. And Vicki needed this; she had never even been to any funeral before or even ever seen a dead animal, much less a human.

Later, when she would discuss this event (which wasn't often, in fact, it was very few times in her life) she would have to explain the differences in modern, usual and normal Christian or Jewish funerals than was this Tennessee Appalachian funeral.

Abraham and all the other males in their families, closest friends and neighbors brought both bodies back to Herman and Grandma's home. Vicki was grateful they had brought Rusty's, too. The dog's body was carefully laid out at the side of the house, and was covered as though he were a human, too. Almost immediately someone was sent to the preacher's house to inform him of the death and right afterwards, the bell on the church was rang; (according to Grandma' explanation); one ring for every year of Herman's life, to let the entire community know of the death.

When the bodies were back, Herman's was laid out on his back on the table. Grandma told Vicki, "He has to lay there for the "sitting up with the dead".

Vicki nodded although she didn't know what that meant. One of the older female cousins saw her puzzlement and explained, "Laying him there overnight keeps the body from curling up; and all night long someone will sit up with the body to show we are all grieving with the dead. Later Vicki would understand although they didn't call it a way to avoid rigor motor setting in the body, it served the same purpose. None of those who sat up with body viewed it as scary or weird, but a genuine way to mourn. It was considered an honor to be a member of the family who helps in building the coffin, lining it with white cloth, washing the body with water and camphor, or dressing the body in his or her best clothes. She was told most adults would be dressed in black to be buried and children in white. Coins were placed on the eye lids to keep them closed; "because," one of the cousins told Vicki, "All of us enter heaven with our eyes closed to show our respect to God."

Vicki was astounded at all the food which began to come into the home. Everyone brought food, everyone could eat whenever they were hungry. When she thought about how impoverished most of these families were, she was in awe at the food which poured in. There were excessive donations but also food given to families or neighbors to take to their homes as well.

"After the funeral, it is another honor to be chosen to be one of the men who are asked to fill in the grave after the funeral service, too," said another cousin.

"When will the actual funeral take place?" Vicki asked.

Hearing her question, Grandma came up and put her arms around Vicki's shoulders and said, "We believe the spirit hovers over the body for three days after death before it moves on. It will be my place to be the last one to view Herman before the coffin is closed.

A big honor, and also the signal that the spirit has moved on and only the body is left."

When the women were rubbing the body with camphor, the odor stung Vicki's nose and she knew that smell would also have a place in her memory which she would forever associate with Rusty and Herman. No matter where she traveled and where her life eventually took her; the smell would trigger this memory.

When one of the females offered to take her up to view Herman's body after his body had been cleaned and dressed in his Sunday best; she told Grandma, "I can't. I just can't look at him in that coffin. Do I have to? Please don't ask me to…"

"No, my dear. You do not have to. Just remember him as he was before. Remember his silly grin and how much he liked a good joke. Remember all the good things." This the old lady said with new tears running down her face.

That evening some of the children laid down on the floor to sleep while their parents "sat with the dead". Vicki heard and learned so many things about funerals and death that evening; although some of it didn't register with her until much later when some sight or voice would trigger it.

She was told by someone that the body would be buried facing east. She wondered why this was? She saw that someone else had draped a covering over the only mirror in the cabin and they had also stopped the clock to indicate the time Herman had died.

She had heard that some of Abraham's sons were digging the grave so it would be ready after the funeral. She also heard *everyone would be wearing black and she had nothing black to wear. Would she be allowed to enter the church and attend the funeral if she didn't wear black?*

One of Abraham's daughters came up to her and said gently, "If you don't have anything black to wear for the funeral, we're about the same size and I can loan you something."

Moved by her unasked-for generosity, she almost started crying again, but managed to nod her appreciation and acceptance of the offer.

The girl said, "My name is Addie. Abraham is my father. If you need anything, please ask. my mother. I really liked Herman. He was such a kind person."

Again, Vicki just nodded.

When the grave-digging men returned there was a whispered conversation between them and Grandma. Then the old lady walked over to Vicki and said, "I need to tell you something, girl."

She paused and Vicki waited.

"The men just told me they dug a place for the dog, too."

Vicki gasped in surprise. "They did?"

"Yes, they said the dog died trying to protect and save Herman and he deserves to be buried next to him. I know it's unusual but I hope you don't mind."

Now Vicki reached over and put her arms around the old lady and they both wept. No one paid any attention to their tears; or if they were aware of it, they gave them the privacy of pretending they were unaware of it.

When the funeral was long over and eventually Vicki had moved on, she made it a point to stop by the graveyard, and place wildflowers on both Herman's and on the simple cross over Rusty's grave that merely said, "Herman's Friend, Rusty".

CHAPTER TEN

Difficult Goodbyes

The next few days were a contradiction; at times the days hurried by as in a whirling tumble-weed fashion and sometimes it seemed as they would never pass. The old lady cried every night; and even when she tried to hide it, you couldn't help but feel her pain.

Vicki had been dreading seeing Buster again; but he paid her no mind or notice; not even briefly. She saw him cry several times and with red puffy eyes at other times and she felt better, telling herself he had loved Herman, too. He wasn't staying at the old lady's home; preferring to stay with his male cousins at Abraham's except for the initial "Sitting the Dead" night; and he sat on the floor behind the coffin during the entire night. Listening to some of the conversations around her; she heard that Buster would be moving home to the old lady's house after the funeral so she would not be alone. The old lady argued that whether he moved back or not, she was perfectly able to take care of herself; she was independent and wouldn't even discuss a suggestion she move to Abraham's or one of the other relatives.

"This is my home. I am not being moved out of it. I raised my son here and buried my husband from here. I came here as a new bride, and they can carry me out in my coffin."

Vicki did her share of crying as well, and at times she just wanted it over. She never went up and looked in the coffin; but she knew that they had clothed Herman in a black suit and tie and realized she had never seen him in anything but overalls and faded shirts. She liked to think he might be up "there", looking down and grinning at all this commotion for him. Especially the suit…

He and Rusty both had given their lives to save her; she would never completely lose her feeling of the unfairness or her questions of why she was spared and they were not.

Vicki learned that the reason one of their neighbors; who was big into her pregnancy, did not go up and view the body was because there was an old wife's tale these people believed in that for a pregnant lady to view a corpse their infant would be marked when born.

She had heard so many other customs and beliefs and didn't know which she should take seriously and which had been passed down from generation to generation had no real basis in science or the medical field. She was told that if a picture fell from the wall during the wake, someone else will die soon.

Addie had told her that be careful not to let a bird fly in the house during this time or again, someone else will die soon.

Vicki did not believe some of these things; however, it was very evident that most of these people *did* believe them implicitly.

As she began to put names to faces and pair up the people, she found some were immediate families, some were extended families and could trace their lineage several generations back. Some had even married cousins or second cousins; which of course, she knew from earlier discussions with her mother when she had voiced her intention to someday marry one of her favorite cousins, this would not be allowed in her own society.

She noticed the respect and deference everyone there seem to pay to one older man. She found out he was in reality an uncle of Abraham's, though younger and that he didn't live in the close surrounding hills; but on over the mountain and lived in a small more *civilized* town called Maryville. He was well to do according to these relatives, owning a café and a sporting goods store. Vicki thought she had been to the town once when she rode on one of her father's business trips with him. It had been either that or suffer through a visit to her house of a great aunt who Vicki found hard to tolerate. The aunt was making one of her rare visits for several days and drove Tony and her crazy with her stories and questions. Anyway, Vickie remembered the small rural community. It was considerably larger than the size of her own home town; having a movie theatre, a library, an elementary and junior high school; even a high school and a community college. There was a decent sized shopping mall with good, brand-name department stores of bigger towns or cities, a bus depot and train station.

She sat next to him during the sitting with the dead evenings and he introduced himself to her genially.

"Hello, there young lady. I'm Walter Green; Abraham's uncle. Are you a member of any of these tribes or clans? Who are you here with? Please forgive me if I can't remember, the older I get the fuzzier my mind gets."

Vicki was surprised he had asked. She had gotten used to the strange fact that as of now no one had even asked her about her home or where she was from; that was one of the reasons she liked it here so well. She chose the easiest answer, "I'm with Grandma and Buster."

He jumped to the conclusion she might be related to Herman's absent mother in some way. She knew this because he said, "Were they able to locate Herman's mother? Or is she still long gone? You're not Herman's sister, are you?" Before she could deny this tie, Herman's grandma come over and said, "Walter, the men are planning the transportation for the funeral tomorrow; and we know you came in your automobile. Can you come over and work with them with planning things?"

"Sure, I can. I'd be honored."

He went across the room with Grandma as Vicki wondered how he had found out about the death; none of this gathering clan of people had a phone as far as she knew; they must have sent a youngster in a wagon or on a horse.

Several members of the assembled friends and families chose to place a small personal token into the coffin with Herman. When Vicki spoke about this with the old lady, and was told it was an accepted tradition of love; she asked if she could place the watch, she had given to Herman inside. Grandma gave her a hug and when Vicki asked her to place it for her; because she still could not bring herself to look at Herman's body in the coffin, the old lady placed it inside *for* her. As the gathering moved forward on its' path to the funeral, Vicki realized it was time for her to leave Herman's Grandmother's home and move forward towards whatever the future held for her. Although she felt a sense of cowardice, she just could not face the atmosphere she was sure would follow when the business of the funeral and burial were over. There would be an overpowering of grief and helplessness with Grandma and Buster; indeed, with the entire clan she didn't feel she could cope with. The other reason was that regardless of the way that Buster had ignored her existence since the death(s), she knew she could not share a roof with him, even with her deep concern and caring for the old lady. This recognition was a good assessment of the circumstances even though she did acknowledge a tinge of fear was a part of it. Correctly she credited Buster with an aggressive, bullying personality which she had no doubt would reveal itself once the funeral and burial were over. She would miss the old lady, but always knew she couldn't prolong her stay with her forever; and now was the perfect time to move forward.

She was impressed with the funeral, in which several family members eulogized Herman's gentle spirit and his concern for others. A few told stories of incidents in which he shared or sacrificed his own wants for someone else's comfort or wishes. They hymn they sang were appropriate, but also those which gave comfort and pointed as death being a natural part of life. Death should not only be acknowledged but celebrated as something that comes to all; when it is their natural time. The hymns: "Old Rugged Cross", "In the Sweet by and by", "What a friend we have in Jesus" rang with the voices of the congregation, from the elderly to the children. Vicki was deeply moved.

It was in the following reception celebrations where again, the abundance of food challenged the space on the table, the card tables put up, the wooden planks set up on saw-horses and kitchen counters. She was sitting on one of the steps with her plate on her knees and was surprised by her hunger; the first she really had noticed since the deaths when the old man, Walter Green, brought his plate and sat down next to her.

"Can I share your step?" he asked her cheerfully.

She nodded and moved over a little to accommodate his added bulk.

"All this food looks so good I know I should limit myself or I will regret it later."

She nodded her agreement and replied, "Me, too."

"Herman's grandmother has shared the little she knows about you and your situation…"

He paused and as he did Vicki mused on the little actual facts Grandma had about her, she had simply accepted whatever she had been willing to share; which was very little really.

Walter said, "With your permission, I would like to make an offer; or suggestion, if you will, for you to consider."

Curiously, she looked at him and said, "Go on, what's on your mind, Mr. Green?"

"Well, first, am I right you may have decided this is the good and right time for you to leave Grandma's home to continue your life's path, whatever that is destined to be…Am I right?"

She was surprised, but hid it and answered simply, "Yes."

"I don't know what is in your mind, or what you know about me, but I own several businesses in Maryville." He paused to get her reaction, if any.

"I heard that," Vicki said.

"Well, if you don't already have some specific plans in mind, I am offering you a job. It won't make you rich; just pays minimum wage. I don't even know if you know what that is because I don't know your background and from what Grandma told me, you never shared your past with Herman and her. That's okay. It's a fair wage outside our little hamlet, and more inside it. It even comes with a small dwelling in back of the café. When we bought the property, the last owner had built the little cottage for our own. Since we purchased the property about six years ago, it's been empty and gathering dust. A little cleaning up, maybe a new coat of paint and we believe you might even like it."

"Who is the *we*?"

"My wife and I-married thirty-two years now."

When Vicki paused to consider his words and then she queried, "No contracts? Not promises of time? I'd be free to reject it? I'd be free to leave at any time I wanted to move on? The cottage would be totally mine? No room-mates, no strings attached?"

His face was serious when he shook his head negatively, he said, "You could check me out with Grandma or Abraham or even my own pastor in Maryville. That's my wife, over there in the black and white dress standing next to Herman's grandmother. She wears the pants in our family and has for thirty-two years since we married. I've already discussed this with her and she is ready to open her heart and home to you. She came to these hills as a stranger when she was a child and people treat her as home-grown now. Talk to her. We'll be here until morning; but if you want to think it over for a few days, you can always come later on, after we've gone home. There's no time limit on the offer. Or you can ride over in the car with us."

She was quiet for a minute or two and then she looked at his earnest expression and said, "I appreciate the offer and I promise I will talk to your wife…" Vicki said and then added, "What's her name?"

"Lizzie. Short for Elizabeth."

"I will think about your generous and kind offer, and I'll let you know before you leave."

He nodded, then taking his plate, he stood and said, "I know I shouldn't; but I hear some of that apple pie calling me."

It wasn't until late the same evening when most of the neighbors, family, and fellow mourners had left for the night that Grandma made two cups of hot tea and handing one to Vicki, sat down beside her.

She smiled gently at Vicki and Vicki tearfully laid her head against the old lady's shoulder.

"I am so sorry," Vicki said softly.

"I know, I know. But our faith will carry us through. We must believe God has a purpose." She took a big breath and continued, "Now, to you, my child. I have talked to Walter and his wife. You know how close I have become to you. But though I would welcome you to stay here as long as you would want to, I recognize the problems that would bring with you. Buster already has made his plans to move back here; and he is my son. I cannot, in good faith, refuse to allow him his home. I fear you would never be able to swing his feelings towards you to any kind of acceptance. Unfortunately, he has an unforgiving nature; he is jealous and envious of anyone he sees as a threat to his place in my life. I want you to talk to Lizzie, Walter's wife. She has always been one of my favorite people; as has Walter. If you accept their offer, you don't have to worry that it would be out of any pity they feel for you. I don't know; and because it has never been important to me, what your history or past is—and they; Walter and Lizzie, would never intrude on your privacy or your right to keep those things to yourself. They are smart, caring and generous people. You can trust them when they offer you protection, and a home; even if temporary; the choice will always be yours. Either decision you make, the rest of us will accept and help you in any way we can."

Vicki was openly crying now; her tears were wetting the old lady's shoulder and dress. The old lady was patting Vicki's shoulder and now said, "There, there. I think you should dry those eyes and if they haven't left yet, and if, just if, you have made your decision, I think you should go find Lizzie and ask any questions your may have or answer any she might have."

The old lady pulled a soft old-fashioned hankie, replete with pink crocheted edges, from her apron pocket; she wiped Vicki's eyes.

"Where is she?" asked Vicki.

"The last time I saw her she was on the porch, sitting on the swing, talking to others."

With a final kiss to the old lady's cheek, Vicki left her and walked to the porch. Walter's wife, Lizzie was, indeed, sitting on the porch and as she looked up at Vicki, she patted the swing next to her, inviting her to come join her.

Vicki sat down and began, "Hello, I think you must be Lizzie- ʻ
She was interrupted by Lizzie, "Yes, and of-course, you're Vicki."
Vicki smiled. "Yes 'mam."
"I can imagine you have a lot of questions so fire away!"
Vicki laughed and said, "Well, yes. First of all, why?"
"Why what?"
"Why would you make this offer?"
"Well, you have a big fan in Grandma. She is so fond of you. And I value her love and support as I have for many years. I don't think you know much about me, but I lost a daughter many, many years ago; and without the old lady's support I don't believe I would be here. Also, even though my husband is rough and gruff, he has a big heart and Grandma played matchmaker years ago. Thanks

to her I found my perfect partner. While I'm on the subject of my husband, I know he can be a little intimidating, but he has a generous spirit. Yes, he's cranky and a bit of a curmudgeon often, but he is also caring and sensitive. You don't ever have to be afraid of him. His bark is so much louder than his bite."

"What kind of strings might be attached to this generous offer you and he have made to me?"

"Strings? Humph," the old lady waved her hand. "None. Absolutely none. If you come to stay with us no matter how short or long the time, it will always be your decision to commit however long a visit it is."

"What about privacy? What about decisions? What about choices?"

"You will most certainly have all those things. We offer only a roof over your head, a job where you can earn your own livelihood, and the freedom to share our home and hearth. Figuratively, of course, because I believe Walter told you that we have a small cottage in back of our little café which will be totally your own home and hearth. It sits there, unused and empty so it is no sacrifice for us to allow you to call it your own for as long as you wish."

"What's in it now?"

"A bathroom, small kitchen and living area and an even smaller bedroom. I don't remember what kind of furniture there is; but we will help you get what you need. Nothing fancy, but serviceable."

"What about the job?"

"You have a choice there; you can work in the café; waiting tables, doing dishes…"

When Lizzie said this last, she looked closely at Vicki, maybe to see if she would show any adverse response to being a dish-washer and when she did not, she continued, "or even sales-clerk in the sports department store, cashier in the movie theatre, there are so many options."

Vicki seemed to brighten up, when noting there were so many options possible.

Lizzie said, "So, you don't have to make decisions on all these things right now. In fact, there is no rush on any of them. Just a 'yes or no' as to whether or not you want to give it a shot."

"I'd like to accept now, if that's okay with you," Vicki said, looking straight at Lizzie. If we can work out all the details later. I'd like to spend a couple of more days with Grandma, to help her; if I can, to ease her grief. That's when Buster is coming home so she won't be all by herself. He's going to take a few days off his railroad job, but will be home for the most part. I will make my own way to Maryville. It will give me some time to myself as I come to think over everything."

Lizzie smiled and reached her arms out to hug Vicki to her and pat her back and she said, "Great! Great! I am so excited! Maybe those extra two days or so I can motivate Walter to inventory what's in the cottage and what is missing."

"Please, don't go to any trouble. I'm a hard worker and I want to earn my way."

"Pshaw," Lizzie said as she waved away any concerns as though it were of no real importance.

CHAPTER ELEVEN

New Spaces

Following her plan, Vicki stayed at the old lady's home for two more days. They were quiet days, peaceful, healing and restoring. The old lady shared more of her life story with Vicki and spent some time expressing how much she would miss Vicki.

Finally, to avoid the tears and further grief, early one morning Vicki gathered her backpack and a lunch she had packed the night before after Grandma had gone to bed. It was still dark when she opened the screen door and carefully stepped out on the porch.

She first walked to the small graveyard in back of the little church and placed a handful of wild flowers on Herman's and Rusty's graves. She fought the tears which threatened, and headed down the road towards Maryville.

As she continued, her steps increased and it became very important to her that no one else become aware of her leave-taking. She felt she had spent what she considered her personal mourning time and was ready to gather up her grief to make room for optimism and hope for the future.

She always had a hard time saying goodbye, and with the weight of this new grief, she just couldn't fact Grandma.

Her mood began to lighten and she began to wonder what lay ahead. She spent no time in thinking of her other home and family; and very determinedly concentrated once again on her own possible future.

Around noon time she stopped next to the babbling stream and ate her lunch. She debated on a little nap, but instead decided to continue. It was doubtful she would reach Maryville by nightfall, but she estimated she would by the following day if she continued. It didn't bother her to be back on the road again, but the painful ache in her calves reminded her she had lost the rhythm she had gotten used to, prior to her time with Grandma and Herman. She especially missed Rusty. She kept listening for sounds of him sniffing out things on the trail and the sight of him romping after some critter or other in the bushes.

She took her boots and socks off at one point and waded in the water where it was relatively shallow. The water felt good on her feet, as before.

She noted the cooler mornings, and knew fall was rapidly making its way, winning the race to catch up on winter. If she were home, she would be shopping with her mother for new school clothes; and preparing for her big adventure: entry into middle school and saying goodbye to elementary school.

Wasn't its Shakespeare who said something about putting away childish things? No, she told herself, that's from the bible. *I remember now, it's from Corinthians, 13;11. Paul's letter to the young Corinthians church he had established.* Paraphrasing to herself now, she found she agreed that there were optimum times for grieving, celebrating, planting, sowing, harvesting and planning.

Well, anyway, I am growing up…and older. When I get home after my adventure, I will be much more mature.

How mad will my parents be at me for this adventure? She remembered reading a story once about a child who ran away from home; not forever, and not for an adventure like herself, but because he was angry at his parents. The child had been very worried at the reception he might get when he went back home; but the parents were so very relieved he was safe and sound and home once again, all they could do is hug him and be grateful he was home once again.

Then, of-course, she reminded herself, there was the bible parable about the return of the run- away son in Luke 15:11-32. That father, too, was happy about his return, but his brother wasn't. In her own case, she believed Tony would welcome her home with open arms as would her parents. Perhaps her parents, (and even Tony) would be like that. She wasn't too worried about school starting. She knew her abilities and was always ahead of others. She would be able to quickly catch up. She was a little sad to think of the empty plate they would probably set at the Thanksgiving table for her…She had not made her mind up as to whether she could stay away over Christmas holidays; her very favorite time of the year, or even over her own birthday. She would see where she was and what was happening at that point of her journey. She did intend to go back…eventually. She just wasn't sure how long she intended to continue her journey.

That evening she stopped to rest and dug out the wrapped package of smushed up apple pie she had packed at the old lady's house. It was really a mess to look at; but as she gobbled it down, she enjoyed every bite, even licking the cloth, her fingers and the palms of her hands.

Never had a better tasting pie, she thought.

Again, she felt a surge of sorrow as she made a little nest for sleeping; thinking of Rusty and how his warm body up close to hers had made her feel warm and safe. She missed him immeasurably.

The next morning, she changed shirts and shorts, washed up at the river, combed and re-braided her hair, and felt the excitement and new exhilaration of knowing she would be in Maryville by noon. Maybe she would even get to have a hot lunch at Walter and Lizzie's café.

She whistled as she hiked along, and enjoyed the brisk fall morning as well as the sunny path and noisy birds.

PART TWO

CHAPTER TWELVE

The Home Front

As soon as Ann got off the phone, she called the sheriff and he arrived about ten minutes later.

It would be an understatement to say he was surprised to hear that he had a missing child case in his small township. The town was so small that the law enforcement department consisted of the sheriff, two deputies, and a receptionist-secretary. They had just won two hard-fought battles with their city council in order to get budget approval for the second automobile they had recently acquired.

When he arrived at the home he was met with an expected nearly hysterical mother and they were soon faced with the arrival of the father and brother.

Sheriff Thomas accepted the offer of a cup of coffee; mainly to give the mother something to do with her hands and perhaps enable her to be able to concentrate on this small chore as he questioned the family.

She handed him the notes she had found on Vicki's bed and after reading them he said, "Well, with these notes it would seem an abduction is not the case. She clearly writes she is running away."

Sheriff Thomas mentally relaxed a little. A run-a-way child was quite a different story than a possible abduction. Years ago, when he was just a rookie in the sheriff's office, one couple up in the nearby hill country had their infant daughter abducted and that case had never been solved. He had a softness for children, and it still bothered him that he was no closer to solving that old abduction as he was the day it happened.

"Have you contacted all her friends?" He asked the family.

"Not all, but we have made a list and we are starting to contact all of them as quickly as possible. So far, everyone seems as surprised as we are."

"Do you have a landline phone number?"

"No, each of us, including Vicki, has a cell phone."

"If she should decide to call home, which one do you think she would use to contact you?"

They looked at each other and then Ann said, "Probably mine."

"Well, try to keep that line open, then and use the others for calling all her friends and any extended family.

"Can you think of any reason she would want to run away?"

The parents looked at each other and shook their heads.

"Was she mad at either of you for anything at all, no matter how small?"

"Truly, she wasn't. She isn't a child to get riled up easily. Even when she is being corrected over some behavior or has been refused something she wanted; she just takes it in stride…"

"Not like me," the boy said. "I get mad, especially when I get grounded. Vicki just goes on with whatever."

What about a boyfriend?"

Frowning and speaking with a strong sense of frustration, the mother replied, "Did you forget she's only going on twelve, Sheriff?"

In Sheriff Thomas' mind that was the age most of kids start to believe they're grown and to resent the rules placed on them by parents and teachers; but he said nothing.

"What did she take with her? Have you been able to pin that down? Have you looked? And what was she wearing?"

"None of us have seen her since bedtime last night. It's Saturday and unless we have made plans for the family, we usually allow the kids to sleep in," Joseph said to the sheriff.

"How about you, son? Are you close to your sister? Do you know of any reason she would want to run away?" He looked straight into the boy's eyes as he asked this.

"No sir" he said vehemently, I would tell you."

"Are there any kids," he asked, "You would consider the wrong kind of kid for her to be hanging around?" Again, the three of them shook their heads negatively.

The sheriff looked at Ann; the mother, again and asked, "Are the two of you close? If she was upset or really worried would she feel comfortable coming to you with it?"

Hesitantly Ann looked perplexed when she answered, "I think so. I've always thought we had a wonderful mother-daughter relationship."

The sheriff said, "We will need the latest photo you have, and we will start canvassing the area; neighborhood first, then the township, and then expand it on out. I want to go see her room right now, and you...", he paused and looked to the boy, "You start making those calls. Let me know the minute you learn anything. Make sure people know they can come help with the search."

The sheriff, Joseph and Ann went upstairs to Vicki's bedroom and found it to be very; almost excessively neat. Nothing seemed out of place.

The sheriff commented "Is it always this neat? My own daughter lives in an everyday room of chaos. I don't know how she finds anything."

Her mother looked through the closet and said, "Her hiking boots are gone and her sneakers as well. Her winter jacket, a couple of pair of jeans, and shorts, socks. Her red flannel long sleeved shirt, and…" she paused and then continued, "Several pair of underwear and camisoles."

"What about money? Did she have any?"

"She does lawns around the neighborhood, but it wouldn't be much. She keeps it in that little pig over there on the vanity. She picked it up and first she shook it and then she pulled the little bottom plug and said, "Empty. But it couldn't be more than twenty or thirty dollars at the most."

"How street-worthy is she?"

"What do you mean, street-worthy?" Joseph asked.

"Well, I know you've probably talked to her about strangers and such, but would she know anything about where the bus stop is, and how to get a ticket and avoid notice? Would she know how to find out fees for the bus, or train, and schedules? Would she consider it okay to hitch hike?"

"I don't think so…but then, I never would have dreamed she would run away, either."

The sheriff said to Joseph: "Make sure your boy checks that the children of the families he calls are home. Maybe it's more than one missing. Maybe there's more than just your daughter missing."

He made a note in his little notebook and then said, "Does she get good grades? Would a bad grade be enough to send her running?"

"Of course not. She's an "A" student normally, but school isn't in session now; have you forgotten? It's summer break. She's very excited about being middle school next year."

"What is she like physically?" Sheriff Thomas asked.

"We're already described her to you, sheriff."

Sheriff Thomas could hear the frustration in Joseph's voice, but he took no offense. He was filled with sympathy for them.

"Not her description. Is she strong? Is she an athlete? Does she give up easily on physical limits or targets? Does she have a good appetite? Does she know much about camping or being outdoors? Does she feel she has to have creature comforts? Is she a picky eater? Would you label her "girly" or at home in the outdoors? All these things could be important."

They went downstairs and talked a little more before the sheriff stood, closed his note pad and said, I'm going to meet with volunteers at my office and lay out a grid, beginning with here, and the town and spreading out. Call me if you learn anything, anything at all."

"Should we make some flyers?"

"It's still a little early for that; and chances are good we can find her. Don't give up hope. If we haven't found her by nightfall, I would say that's the next step."

Eyes wide, shocked, Ann said, "Nightfall? Surely you don't think we won't have found her by nightfall?"

"I'm hoping we will, but you never know…"

Tony was sitting at the dining room table, cellphone in hand, calling people and he said, "Yeah, Hope for the best, but expect the worst, Mom. Haven't you heard that?"

"Tony! That will be enough of that kind of talk." Joseph said.

"Ah, Dad, you know I don't mean it. I just think any minute the brat will walk in the door, like nothing happened. Boy, I'm gonna' owe her for all this trouble."

As darkness began to chase the day away, with still no sign of Vicki, there was an increase of activity. So many volunteers were looking for her, the local stationery shop volunteered the paper and printing cost of flyers for free, and were working on those. Neighbors were bringing food and coffee thermoses for the searchers.

One of the deputies had been sent to the bus depot and another to the small train station.

After showing the photo, no one reported seeing a child like that at either. As time clicked on, Sheriff Thomas' worry and distress began to grow but he tried to keep it hidden. His biggest worry was that she had accepted a ride from someone and was being taken miles away every minute. He felt that the later it got, the less chance for a hopeful conclusion to occur. Just like the infant kidnapping years ago in Maryville which was still unsolved; close to ten years ago now.

At the request of Joseph to the local, family doctor, some tranquilizers were sent over to the home for Ann, which she firmly and continually refused to take.

No one got any sleep that evening; there was someone continually crying, and still no sign of Vicki. The next morning volunteers met again at the sheriff's office and Sheriff Thomas had called several nearby small towns; Pigeon Forge, Oak Ridge, even Mascot and Rockville. He asked for their help and they willingly sent some officers to assist. The Federal Bureau of Investigation, located in Nashville, Tennessee, were contacted and they sent two agents to help out.

Thousands of flyers covered small towns and a few bigger cities and a collection for an award was taken up. Even a billboard was leased with information requests and reward offers.

The FBI was not as convinced there was foul-play involved, especially with the notes left by the child, there were hundreds, perhaps thousands of run-a-way children nationally who were never found. Many were later tracked to larger cities living on the street or waylaid by sinister predators who always were looking for innocent youth running away for whatever reasons. Ann herself had just watched a special documentary about children kidnapped and sold into slavery; then even sent out of the country never to be found again.

Days went by, then weeks, and finally, several months. The disappearance was not forgotten; just set aside as an unfortunate run-away-child case; eventually the FBI went home, the neighboring law officers from nearby towns went home and the residue of grief and loss began to ease, for everyone except the family. Joseph had to work and continue earning a livelihood, bills must be paid. Tony must go on with his life and friends and preparation for a new school year in the fall. Tony must continue to grew older and even he reverently prayed she would be found, alive and well before he went back to school.

Her mother insisted her room remain exactly the same as when she left it and would frequently spend the afternoon sitting in there on the pink rocker, crying and demanding an answer from God which never came.

She was isolating herself and much to Joseph's attempt to help her out of the deep depression she seemed to wallow in, she seemed to stop even trying. She did not attend church anymore, she depended on him going to the store when they ran out of things; something he never used to do. Her personal appearance no longer mattered to her and if he didn't try to gently offer to brush her at night, she might have stopped that. Make-up was a thing of the past. Joseph wasn't even sure she took her vitamins, which used to be such a common morning task. The first time she cooked T.V. dinners, he couldn't believe it. She had always made fun of women who did that. Her complete disgust with women "too lazy" to feed their families real food had been a common criticism, even of women who worked long hours and had a houseful of children to care for. No excuses! She would say. When he went to the table and saw the aluminum pans of the dabs of unrecognizable (to him, at least) food, he didn't comment, and he quickly motioned for Tony to close his open mouth, and say nothing. He did see a flush on her face as she sat down and began eating her own.

Joseph hoped this was not to become a regular practice. Ana was a wonderful cook and he always bragged to others about the kind of chef she was.

He knew she bathed because she would get in the tub and stay for what seemed like hours, letting water out as it cooled and adding more hot water to bring the temperature back up to a comfortable level.

Joseph even found himself running out of clean clothes and when he asked gently for fresh laundry, she would look ashamed and apologize for forgetting to do it.

Trying to be patient, and understanding, he started checking the laundry room himself and routinely putting a load in the washer or the dryer, trying to help out.

CHAPTER THIRTEEN

Traces

All hope would have vanished eventually except that the mysterious *traces* began to appear. Not all at once, but realistic and often enough to convince Ann that Vicki was not gone forever and was still alive and well. She did not know where or when or with whom, she just knew she felt with a mother's gift of intuition that she was alive.

When these *traces* at first began to appear, Ann shared them with her husband and son; but eventually when none of these *traces* proved to be provable or true, her family assumed that she was being hysterical or imagining things which they blamed on her grief. Thereafter she never brought these *traces* up to her family again.

The first of these so-called *traces* was a postcard which arrived approximately two months after her disappearance. There was no postmark on the card, and no stamp, it simply was in the mailbox one day with the other mail.

The handwriting *could have been* Vicki's, Ann thought, but not exactly; just similar enough to *could have been*.

The message on the back read:

Mama,

I hope all is well with the family. I am fine. I am making new friends, learning a lot of wonderful things. I will be home in a few months. Don't worry.

Love, Vicki

When she greeted Joseph and Tony at the door that night, they called Sheriff Thomas and he came right over to see the card.

It has no postmark," he said questioning its' authenticity.

"Well, so what?" asked Ana. "It has no stamp, either."

Hidden in her question, of course, was her prayer that no stamp meant that perhaps Vicki had secretly personally come and put the card in the mailbox without anyone seeing her.

Thinking it might have been someone playing a cruel hoax or even someone wanting to make the family feel better by giving them some new possible hope she could be alive and well, Sheriff Thomas took the card to send it off to a handwriting expert to prove it was or wasn't Vicki's writing.

Vicki restrained herself from calling Sheriff Thomas's office every single day to ask if the comparison results had come back. When he finally called her, the results were not what she wanted; a confirmation of it being Vicki's handwriting; but neither was it a total denial, either. The experts came to the same conclusion they had when they received the card: it *could* be Vicki's but then, again, it might not be. There were similarities, but there were slight differences, too.

Nevertheless, the sheriff did not object in giving the card back to Ann with her request. He didn't try to keep it "for evidence" as he could have, but the pity he felt for the mother forbade him from doing so.

The final result of this incident was to make Ann's belief in Vicki being alive and well solidified. The card gave her some much-needed hope and even some peace. She began to think "when" she came home instead of "if". For the most part, though, she used this incident as a much-needed affirmation if Vicki's well-being.

The next "trace" (as Ann began to call these incidents) occurred a few weeks later and was wo unexpected and unusual as to make her doubt her own sanity. She even wondered if she might be sleep walking; even when it was during a daytime nap. She had kept her accounting position, but allowed her mind to wander much more than she ever had before. She kept a framed photo of Vicki on her desk and her eyes would settle on it frequently.

One afternoon, she was eating a sack lunch she had brought from home. She found it more and more difficult to go out for lunch and have to make polite conversation with others and see what she thought was reflected pity in their eyes when they looked at her.

Anyway, she went to the cold drink machine, put the correct change in and returned to her desk. Sitting down, she glanced at the photo again, and then, picking it up, she looked at it. Where there had been nothing before, across the bottom in what she felt certain about, was the inscription, "To my special Mom, from Vicki".

She was *positive* Vicki had not inscribed the photo. Ann remembered taking it; they had been on vacation and while Joseph and Tony had toured the military museum she and Vicki had gone for a long barefoot walk on the sandy beach. If you looked closely at the photo you could see the wide expanse of ocean behind her and the footprints, she had left behind her.

How is this possible? Ann asked herself. *Have I lost my mind? She knew she would not share this with anyone; most especially Joseph. He was such a pragmatist; such a no-nonsense sort of person…*

She made her mind up to keep this to herself, but she wondered at her ability to so quickly attribute so many things to special messages about or from Vicki.

The next week end Joseph unexpectedly had to work some extra hours, Tony was off somewhere with his friends and she was sitting on the back porch, reading a book she had recently gotten from the library. That was something she had begun doing more often, too;

going to the library. It had been one of Vicki's favorite places and it made Ann feel closer to her. It was a book entitled "The Hourglass", written by an unknown (to her) writer named Jackie Smith. She found it both stirring and interesting because it was one Vicki had checked out and it told a story of a young child with the ability to direct people's behavior merely by her own thoughts. She remembered Vicki's many questions about the possibility of such a thing. She had been disappointed when Ann had dampened her enthusiasm by telling her it was just a work of fiction; paranormal fiction, at that.

While reading, a slight cooling and pleasant breeze, carrying the promise of an early winter came over her and she looked up, distracted from her reading. Casually, she placed her bookmark inside, and the book opened up to show the glued-in pocket where the card would be placed when she returned the book to the library. There were several names there; and quite expectedly; since she knew Vicki had checked the book out that time, there was Vicki's name and the date she had checked it out.

Now both our names will be listed there, she thought, and the thought pleased her somehow.

She sat the book, closed and with the bookmark inside, on the end of the whicker table by the swing and went indoors. She checked on the roast she had cooking in the kitchen crock-pot and then decided to take a shower and maybe even take a nap. She went to the back porch and opening the screen, she called out, "Rusty, Rusty, come on in, boy."

Vicki had always wanted a dog but she had a cat and her dad kept putting off another pet to care for and feed until the old Gus passed on. Gus had passed peacefully in his sleep a week after Vicki disappeared but no one had mentioned a replacement yet. It was a few weeks after Vicki had run away that *this* German Shephard had begun hanging around their house. Even though Joseph said, "Don't feed that stray and eventually he will leave and find greener pastures", she felt sorry for the dog and would feed him out by the back porch. Then she had added a bucket of water under the faucet.

Finally, Tony fell for it and named the dog Rusty. When Tony was queried about his choice of name he said, "Well, look at his coat; it has patches of red running through it; sort of like he was left out in the rain and he began to rust out."

They all laughed but agreed. The dog went fishing and bike riding with Tony but his favorite place was their back yard or inside, as though guarding the family.

Joseph relented and gave permission for Tony to claim it.

Actually, the dog was very quiet and well mannered. *Smart, too,* Ann thought, when she saw the way the dog coddled Joseph for his acceptance and behavior. He would wait for Joseph to sit in his recliner and either read something, or watch television and he would come and lie by his chair. When he thought no one else was looking, Joseph would reach down and pat the dog.

Today, as in many days, if no one else was home, Ann would let the dog in for company. She talked to it and it would cock his head and listen as though he understood every word. He had a propensity and liking for Vicki's room, though (and if Ann forgot to close door) he would go in there and lie on the small braided rug by her bed. Ann did not get upset with him, but would gently take him out and close the door. Sometimes this would result in him lying on the floor right outside the closed door.

Ann found herself saying, "*I know, boy, I miss her too...*" and then she felt foolish, knowing they had not had this dog when Vicki was home.

Anyway, on this fall day, the dog came to her call and she allowed him entrance and a doggie milk bone treat before she headed upstairs for her shower. After her shower she dried and put-on fresh jeans and a t-shirt. She was barefoot and as she walked down the hallway; she was toweling her hair with a big fluffy towel when she saw the open door to Vicki's room.

I know I shut that...Maybe I didn't catch the latch on it. She walked over to it and glancing inside, as she expected, saw Rusty lying on the little braided rug.

"You learned to open doors now?" She asked with a chuckle.

She walked over to take hold of his collar and her heart skipped a beat and she gulped a big gasp of air. She took a big step backwards.

"This can't be!" she said aloud.

There, lying on the middle of the bed, open and spread to the page of the bookmark was the book she had been reading down stairs. *And…*she thought, *it's not that I had carried it up here and laid it down to put Rusty out of the room, because I wouldn't have opened it and laid it that way…I already had placed the bookmark inside. And…I specifically remember leaving it outside on the whicker table.*

The dog was looking at her with those big brown eyes as though to comfort her. She sat down in the rocking chair, holding the retrieved book with both hands.

Dear God, she thought *what is happening to me? Am I totally losing it?*

After a few moments her cell phone rang and grabbing the wet towel and book, she called for Rusty to follow, and went downstairs to answer it.

"Hello?"

"Hi, hon. Hey this didn't take as long as I expected. How about going out for dinner? We haven't done that in a long time. I'm kinda' leaning towards a good steak. One I didn't have to cook. What do you say?"

When she didn't answer at first, he said, with a touch of alarm, "What's the matter, Annie? If steak doesn't appeal to you, how about Chinese? I know that's a favorite of yours. Are you…Are you alright?"

"Yes, yes, I'm fine. I just got out of the shower and had to run to get the phone. I'm a little out of breath. Yes. Yes, steak will be fine as long as there is something else on the menu; you know "Tony hates steak.""

"I was thinking just you and I, hon. Like letting him go over to Michael's house and me paying for the pizza. I already okayed it with his folks. Sort of like a date night. What do you say?"

Ann felt a surge of guilt. She had basically cut herself off from Joseph; in fact, from Tony, too. Ever since Vicki's disappearance. The gap seemed to only be getting wider and wider. She had discouraged his overtures. She couldn't even remember the last time they had made love. He had been loving and patient. He missed their daughter too, but she was resentful sometime when he let days go by and never even spoke Vicki's name. They had both agreed not to let each other play the blame game.

Often, she fought the urge just to close the drapes in their bedroom and refuse to even get up from her bed. Perhaps it was time to put forth that extra effort to put things right with him. But could she do that?

After agreeing to his invitation, she hung up and went back upstairs, looking in Vicki's room. The book was still on the bed. She picked it up and took it with her to Joseph's and her bedroom.

Later that evening while Joseph was in the shower and she had finished dressing for their "date", she started down the hallway upstairs. She intended to go downstairs and maybe pour herself a glass of wine to put herself in a more festive mood. She wanted to make Joseph happier with his plan for this evening out with just the two of them She noted a light coming out from under the door to Vicki's room.

Humm, she thought. *I must have turned it on when Rusty and I were in there with that book this afternoon. Funny I don't remember it; but then, I was so upset with the book and all...*She opened the door and walked over to the night-stand and turned the small pink shaded lamp off. Then she went downstairs to get her glass of wine. It had been a long time since she had had anything alcohol to drink and she reminded her self she hadn't eaten all day; she had better watch what she drank until they ate.

When Joseph came downstairs his eyes lit up as he looked at her. Again, she felt shame for how she had been reacting recently, and pity for the very obvious hope she saw reflected in his eyes.

She made herself a promise, silent but no less determined, *to change things in her acceptance of what was and what she made of their future.*

Where did his strength come from? She asked herself once again. *Please, God, be with me; help me. I cannot do this without your help. He and Tony deserve so much better than this.*

They did have a surprisingly lovely dinner; the steak was perfect, the salad fresh and crisp, and the Cabernet delicious. They shared an order of Bananas Foster. Ann had a small, welcome buzz-on from the wine. She even managed to laugh at several funny jokes Joseph told about one of his co-workers.

As they pulled up into the driveway at home, she looked at Joseph and when he reached over to hold one of her hands briefly, she said, "This was a good idea, Joseph. Thank you."

As he unlocked the front door, he allowed her to walk in first and as they turned towards the stairs, he glanced up.

"Where is that light coming from? Is it from Vicki's room? Were you in there today and forgot to turn it off when you left the room?"

Her voice almost stuttered when she answered, because she certainly, most specifically remembered turning the lights off when she retrieved her reading book.

"I…I don't know. I put some things away and chased Rusty out of there once, but…I guess I just thought I turned it off."

"Go ahead to our room and I'll get it, Hon." Joseph said.

Later, though some of the former passion may have lessened, they made sweet and tender love; she fell asleep on Joseph's shoulder, something she had not done in a long time.

Even though it wasn't perfect, as she drifted off to sleep on his shoulder, Joseph wondered if perhaps he had his own share of blame for Vicki leaving. Perhaps if he had encouraged her desire to join Tony and he in the more male type of activities instead force her into the little pink princess role she resisted so adamantly she might have been happier here at their home and more resistant to leaving. Why had he resisted allowing a "tom-boy" and instead insisted on molding her into a miniature version of her mother?

CHAPTER FOURTEEN

Maryville

As Vicki drew closer to Maryville, her thoughts turned; as they often did, to the home and family she had left in her childhood home. She came to some rather remarkable and new revelations about herself and her reasons (or lack of) for her leaving home.

She had never drawn false conclusions or invented non-existent reasons for her leap into this adventure she now found herself immersed in. She had not been neglected nor abused in any way, shape or form…except that she had been invisible. That was one reason she had left the notes to her parents, that, and her desire to free them from worry she had been kidnapped by some malevolent evil creature; human or otherwise.

What was it, then? What's the truth? She asked herself. *The truth, now…No charade or coverup to make you feel better about your actions…*

Okay, then. What was it? Even at her young age she was familiar with games children play to get more attention from their parents or teachers. Deep down, where the truth lies, she had also believed her father favored Tony over her.

He loved having a son. And none of the many attempts she made to compete with Tony in the more masculine activities; fishing, hunting, archery, risky attempts to beat her brother in many, many ways never seem to matter or make a difference. She realized her father would like nothing better than for her to turn into a flirty, girly-girl of pink cotton candy, learning to sew and cook and beg for fashion aware gifts and activities. He was so disappointed when she brought home her choice sheet for fall entrance to middle school and she had marked Auto-Mechanics as one choice. He and her mother also continued to give her clueless gifts of sewing kits, even giving her a kit to make hot pads for the kitchen one birthday. They continued to ignore her personal choices in colors and she was fatigued with their gifts to her which were always pink.

And how did her mother handle these things? Her chosen battlefront was to tell her father to just be patient, ignore these abnormalities in their "little" girl, she would eventually discover boys; not as adversaries or a group she wanted to join, but as membership in romantic interests. Basically, it was "ignore it and it will disappear, this desire to be what she thought her father would appreciate. Several times she had written down what she would say if she had the courage to talk honestly with her parents about these feelings...

She made a dead stop on the path and said aloud to the squirrel on the branch of the closest tree, chattering a warning to her to stay away, "I am invisible to them. The *real* me...is invisible. I'll bet it took most of the weekend for them to even notice I was gone. And who wants to be invisible; especially to your own family? I want them to see and accept me for who I really am. Is that so difficult to ask?"

She saw the way they treated Tony as though he was the eldest child, just because he was a boy and much, much larger physically, just as she was a dainty "little" girl.

She had gone the route of meeting all their expectations, unlike her brother Tony, who followed his own desires and was not held to account for his deviation from their wishes for him.

She rummaged through her backpack and found two slices of homemade bread, wrapped and stuck together with home churned butter and homemade jelly she had wrapped in a clean cloth at Grandma's.

Um, messy but wonderful, she thought. It required some wash-up after she finished and she dipped her hands into the river and splashed some of the cooler water on her face and hair before she resumed her walk.

It felt strange to be walking into a town after so long living in the little valley of Herman and Grandma's life. The further she got into the town, the more she realized how isolated she had been. She couldn't help window "shopping" as she walked. It was a good twenty-minute walk before she saw the sign reading:

"Lizzie's Layover"
Where good friends and good food get together.

She took a deep breath and opened the door and walked inside. She stood, hesitant, and looked around. There was a good scattering of people and the low murmur of private conversations. There were booths, tables, and a serving counter. There was a sign which stated: "Please seat yourself".

She walked over to the counter and an older woman came over and smiled. "What can I get for you, young lady?"

"Is Lizzie here?"

"Yes, she's out in the kitchen. I'll tell her someone is waiting to see her. Meanwhile, can I get you a drink while you wait? Cola, iced-tea, milk or juice?" She quickly added, "No charge, of course. It's on the house. My name is Joyce, shall I give Lizzie your name?"

"Yes, to a cola. Thank you. You can tell her it's Vicki."

As the woman started to turn Vicki said, "Oh, and nice to meet you, Joyce."

The lady looked at her and smiled as she said, "You, too."

Joyce handed her a class of crushed ice, and a bottled coke before heading through a door Vicki assumed led to the kitchen.

She greedily drank some of the coke and felt almost intoxicated by the taste. She had forgotten how much she used to enjoy these carbonated drinks. A very short time later, Lizzie came through the door, wiping her hands on her apron.

She gave Vicki a large, genuine smile and said, enthusiastically, "Vicki! I'm so glad to see you, come give me a hug."

Vicki grinned at her, then slid off the stool and putting her backpack down, went to meet Lizzie's outstretched arms. Vicki was conscious of the great feeling which washed over her from the warmth of the welcome and the hug.

Then, she released Vicki and Lizzie turned towards the girl behind the counter and she said, "Joyce, cover everything for me, I'm going to go with Vicki on an errand and then we'll be back for lunch."

"Got it!" Joyce said.

"Here," Lizzie said, "Give Joyce your backpack until we get back. She'll watch it for you."

Lizzie tucked Vicki's arm through hers and led her outside the front door and led her to the corner of the building. When they reached the end of the next corner, she saw where Lizzie was taking her. There was a small building. It needed painting. It was white at one time, with pale blue shutters but badly needed a paint job now. Weeds surrounded it, but a few hardy little wild flowers waved in the gentle breeze as though to welcome them as they walked to the little porch and front door. The door matched the color of the shutters and like them, needed a new coat of paint.

Lizzie lifted the corner of the welcome doormat, and retrieved a brass key. She unlocked the door and led the way inside. It was musty and hot, and Lizzie went to a window and as she opened it, she said, "See if you can open some of the other windows and prop the door so we can get some fresh air in here.

After they got the windows open there was almost instant relief and Vicki could look around. The front of the little cottage had a combination living/kitchen area. There was a gas stove, and several cabinets. There was a small table which would seat four people and there were four chairs stacked against the counter dividing the living area from the kitchen. She walked down the small hallway and found a small, but serviceable bathroom with a combination shower/bathtub, vanity sink, toilet and a wall medicine cabinet. The far wall had a window with the kind of window you could not see through, but allowed light inside. It looked frosted.

Further down the hall was a small but adequate bedroom. If you put a twin sized bed, you would have room for a nightstand. Maybe one rocking chair. There was a closet with a door. With her imagination Vicki could see curtains on the window, a wall mounted television like she had at home, and a little nightstand with a beside lamp.

Lizzie was looking at her expectantly and with a question in her eyes.

"What do you think?" she asked Vicki.

"Oh, I love it already."

Lizzie laughed, "Well, it's not the Taj Mahal, but it has possibilities."

Vicki said, "I love it already. All my own. I can't believe it. The first thing I am going to do is paint it, inside and out." ·

Again, Lizzie laughed. "I am sure we can get you some help with that. Do you sew?"

Vicki didn't reply for a minute. Then, thinking of how she had resisted all her mother's efforts to teach her how to sew, she said, "No, not really."

"It doesn't matter, hon. I have a sewing machine, and curtains are so, so easy. Just squares with a hem on the bottom and a placket for curtain rods. We'll go to select some material soon and I will show you how to use the sewing machine. I think it's important for you to do most of the work to make this your home; whether you make it temporary or on a more permanent basis. What do you think?"

"Oh, I agree. I want to have a big hand in everything. I just feel so grateful for this opportunity. I want you and Mr. Green to know that."

"Oh, nonsense. First off, no more Mr. Green. You will hurt his feelings. Call him Walter. Everybody does. No one is using this and one of my waitresses gave her notice today, I'm going to need your help. Don't worry. You will earn your keep."

Vicki laughed. "Good, I want to."

"Here's your first job. We'll go and have some lunch, are you hungry?"

Vicki nodded.

"Good, so am I. Well, we will go eat and then I'll give you a tablet and pen and you come back over here and walk through and list everything you will need. No matter how small or large. We are not in a big hurry except for a bed, mattress and box spring. You have to have somewhere to sleep. We have a place to eat; at least for now, but I know, somehow you would refuse to take advantage of my hospitality and stay with Walter and I…right? We do have an extra guest bedroom."

Vicki felt her face warm with a flush as she replied, "I want to keep my independence, so yes, I would rather stay here. I can sleep on just my sleeping bag if we don't get a mattress and springs right away."

"Okay, we will eat lunch, go purchase a box springs and mattress. Hopefully if we smile and are nice, we can get delivery this afternoon."

They walked back to the café, and Lizzie said, "There's the women's room over there; let's wash our hands and take care of any urges we have, then sit down and get something to eat."

After the trip to the ladies' room the two settled in a booth by the window and Joyce came over to get their order.

Lizzie said, "I'm not used to being on this side of the booth. I have to play like I am a guest."

"What should I order?" Vicki said.

"Why, whatever sounds good to you. I may be biased, but I think all the food is good. It's what they call "comfort food".

Lizzie looked at Joyce, "Give us a few minutes, Joyce. Meanwhile, have you seen Walter lately?"

"Yeah, he's putting up a new shelf in the kitchen that Martha wanted for some reason or other. Do you want me to send him out?"

When Lizzie nodded, Joyce turned and headed to the kitchen.

As Vicki looked at the menu her mouth began to water. There were so many wonderful offerings there. So many things she had not had in such a long time.

Lizzie was watching her and she said, "Anything, anything at all, Vicki. Remember, I own the place, we're eating on the house; both of us."

"Well then, I want a cheeseburger and fries and a fresh coke."

"Well, I think that sounds good. I'm kind of leaning towards a grilled cheese, chips on the side and a big glass of sweet iced tea."

In a few minutes, the kitchen door opened, Walter stood there, looking around until he saw them and he started to their booth.

When he reached them, he said, looking at Vicki, "Wow, I'm glad to see you, girl. This woman has been driving me crazy. Every five minutes, 'it's Walter, when do you think she will come? Or, Walter what if she changed her mind?' Maybe now she will stop with the questions. Good to see you. How's Grandma doing?"

"She's having a hard time, but she's strong. She'll manage. She told me she's having trouble imaging Herman with wings."

Walter chuckled. "Not me, if ever a boy deserved wings he does; all those years putting up with Buster."

"How long before you will be through with whatever you're doing in the kitchen?" Lizzie asked him.

"Nothing that can't wait. Why? What do you need, Liz?"

"We need a single sized bed frame, mattress, and box springs and we need it delivered today…" She paused and he replied, "Heck, that's no problem."

"Even getting it today?"

"For the cottage?"

"Exactly."

"Why can't she stay with us a few days?"

"I told her how bad you snore. No one wants to put up with that except me and I'm used to it by now."

When Walter laughed and said, "Funny, Liz, very funny."

"She wants to spend the night in her own place."

"No, no, it's okay. I don't want to be any trouble," Vicki said.

"Oh, come on, now. Show a little backbone there, girl. Fight for what you want. I like spirit, in my friends and in my dogs." Walter chuckled after he said this.

"He doesn't even have any dogs," Lizzie said, "He just loves to be needed."

Then she added, "And, Walter, we need you to get a copy made of this key," She pulled the little cottage key from her apron pocket and handed it to her husband.

Walter said, "I can go down to John Melcher's furniture store. He owes me more than one favor. He'll deliver it today if he has to do it himself or if I have to take my truck and get it."

Then he looked at Lizzie and said, "I'm ahead of you, as usual, hon."

Lizzie looked at him and said, "That will be the day. In what way?"

"I had the electricity turned on in the cottage today."

"Humph. Well, that's the first time, you old fool."

Vicki looked from one to the other. She had never seen her parents; or any other married couple tease each other like this. She liked it, recognized it as teasing and grinned.

"Okay, then, I have my marching orders, see you two later."

Just as Walter left, Joyce brought their order.

Vicki had to watch her manners; she was hungry, hungry for just this kind of meal.

She giggled and Lizzie said, "What's so funny?"

"This is so good, I was visualizing myself gobbling it down by huge bites and you looking on in horror, wondering what you had taken on…"

Now Lizzie almost coked on her food, laughing.

After they finished eating, Lizzie went in the back and came back with a yellow legal pad and a pen.

"Here you go. Go tackle that cottage; remember, no matter how big or how small. And remember to take your backpack. I think everyone here is honest; but why test them?"

"Did we lock the door?"

"No, I needed to give Walter the Key to make a copy."

"Lizzie, I need to say this. I will never be able to pay you back. But I will try. Hard. And I will never make you regret this opportunity you have given me. I will work for free to pay you back."

"Nonsense! This is hard work; you will earn it. Don't go and get all emotional on me. I don't know how to handle soap operas or any kind of pessimistic thinking on this train. Tomorrow will always be better than today, bet on it. Don't let Walter tease you too much until you learn how to give it back to him, you hear?"

Vicki grabbed her backpack and went hurriedly to the cottage. She was so excited.

This is like playing house, only better, she thought.

Forgive me for being so happy, Jesus, she thought guiltily. *I should not feel so happy when I treated my family so badly.* Shocked at the sudden thought she had, she realized it was the first time she felt she had wronged her family in her actions. *I will deal with this later*, she thought.

She began her list and it grew and grew and grew and she wondered if she should scratch some of the items off. *What was the difference between "want" and "need"?* she asked herself.

Then she thought, *I can make sure Lizzie and Walter know there is no rush on any of this, no time limit, I can work towards the list a little at a time.*

After she had been at the cottage making her list almost two hours, there came a knock at the door. When she went to the door there was a truck in the yard and Walter stood there, grinning.

"I came to save a young maiden from sleeping on the floor. Are you that young maiden?"

She smiled. "I think so."

"Okay, fellows, bring everything inside. Put the frame in the bedroom, and leave the mattress and springs out here until we get the frame together." He handed her a sack and said, "I brought you a surprise. I'll bet you and Lizzie forgot all about this."

When the men took the frame in the bedroom and began putting it together, she accepted the sack questioningly and said simply, "Thank you, Walter. What is it?"

"Open it. It's a surprise. Be sure and tell Lizzie I thought of it all on my own. My idea. I get the credit."

She grinned and opened the sack. It contained sheets and pillow cases and a couple of pillows.

"Oh, thank you, Walter! I could have waited on these."

"Naw, it was nothing."

After the men put the frame together, Walter and the two of them carried the box springs and mattress in the bedroom.

Walter said, "I didn't get you a headboard. I figured you could choose one you liked later."

"Oh, yes. I would like that. Thank you so much."

"And here is your new key. We will keep the other one in the café office in case you lock yourself out someday or whatever. Please don't ever hide it under that mat. Everyone does that and it's the first-place bad guys look for keys when you are not home."

"Oh, I won't."

He reached in his wallet and handed each of the men some currency. "Here you go, guys, good job. Get yourselves a six pack tonight. Tell your boss thanks."

After they all left Vicki went in the bedroom and sat on the bed. Tears filled her eyes as she looked at the linens. *There're not pink, either! They're not pink!* They had what looked like tiny blue bonnets, with a blue border on the ends of the pillow cases and the top of the flat top sheet.

She made the bed up and then stood back and looked at it.

Since it wasn't winter weather as yet, she had plenty of time to think about a blanket or quilt. The sheet would be enough.

There didn't seem to be any signs of rain in any near future so Vicki decided to leave the windows open.

About thirty minutes later Lizzie showed up, knocked, and asked permission to come inside.

"Come on in, Lizzie."

She was carrying a mop bucket, a mop, a broom and dishpan and also a spray bottle of bath and kitchen cleaner and a couple of clean rags.

"Hey, thought you could use these."

"Yes, I can."

"I heard about our self-proclaimed super hero. Can I go see the sheets he got? Are they masculine brown plaid or what?"

"Oh, no," Vicki said, "They are perfect. Something I would have chosen myself, come see."

After Lizzie took a look and gave her approval, Vicki asked, "When do I start work? Tomorrow?"

"Oh, heavens, no. Take tomorrow to clean your little home spic and span. Do you know where that came from?"

"What?"

"Spic and span."

"No, where?"

"Used to be the best cleanser on the market and it just caught on. If you got something really, really clean you would call it spic and span."

"Anyway, work here tomorrow, but don't forget to come up front for three meals."

When Lizzie saw a denial building on Vicki's face she horridly said, "No exceptions. If it makes you feel bad, just remember we haven't discussed your salary yet. It's fifteen an hour plus that includes three meals a day. And it's not special to you. Joyce has the same agreement."

"I've never really had a real job before. I mean, I mowed lawns and raked leaves and did some ironing for people; but not a real job. Do I get a uniform?"

Lizzie laughed. "No, but you do get two aprons, one to wear, one to wash and then repeat. Are you sure you will be okay sleeping out here all by yourself this first night?"

"Of-course I will," Vicki answered. Mentally she thought of the past few nights sleeping soundly, alone in the woods.

"Well, you don't have a television or radio or even a book to read. You'll probably get very bored."

"I'll be fine," Vicki said. I wonder if I have hot water?"

"If Walter had the electricity turned on, I am sure he checked out the water heater, lit the pilot and made sure it's working, too. Try it while I'm here to make sure."

Vicki went to the sink and after letting the run for a very short couple of minutes, when it turned hot, she nodded.

"Want to come eat dinner with Walter and I?"

"Sure," Vicki said.

After they walked up the side of the café, Lizzie said, "Make sure you lock up good when you go to sleep. I think this little town is as crime-free as can be, but caution is always a good habit."

After the three of them sat down and ate full platters of chicken-fried steak, mashed potatoes, gravy and black-eyes peas with biscuits, Vicki returned back to her little cottage, tired and full to take a shower and fall asleep within minutes of sliding between her new bedsheets.

For the first time in a very long time Vicki found an urge to take the time to get back out of bed, drop to her knees at the side of her bed and pray her thankfulness to the Lord for her newly acquired blessings and for her family at home as well. As she drifted off, enjoying the cool breeze which drifted through the windows, she realized she was looking forward to working on her improvements for her little home.

She woke early, even before the café had officially opened for business except for the few regulars Lizzie always unlocked the door for; and met with their first steaming hot cup of coffee. Breakfast smells began to waft through the building.

Lizzie presented her with two new orange and yellow aprons with her own cup of coffee after taking her order for breakfast, then sat down to eat with her.

Vicki thought to herself, *Ah, full strength coffee. I am a real grown up. No more children's coffee; half milk and half coffee.*

By the time more customers began to enter, Vicki had finished eating, cleaned her counter space up, and went to the cottage to begin cleaning. By noon she had swept, mopped, and thoroughly washed the windows inside and out. Right before she walked down front to find something for lunch, Walter and two men showed up with ladders, paint, brushes, paint tape and an eagerness to paint the outside of the small cottage.

"I was going to help do that," Vicki told Walter.

"Well, if we're not through by the time you get back, we'll let you. We've all eaten lunch already so you take your time."

After Vicki had chosen and eaten lunch, Lizzie said, "No use you going back there while they're working; you'd just be in the way. Put on an apron, and I'll let Joyce start training you here."

At first Vicki was timid and worried she would make mistakes; especially totaling up the tickets for the customers; but Joyce showed her how to enter everything on the register and it would do all the work for you, including making change and telling you what you owed the customer in return. It was a modern calculator register and kept a running inventory as well. Lizzie was so proud of it; and told Vicki how they used to have to do everything in "old" days. Gradually Vicki began to get the hang of it and began to enjoy introductions by some of the customers to her and make suggestions when they asked her opinion as to a choice to order.

She gained speed as she learned and practiced, and could see approval in not just Lizzie's eyes, but also in the eyes of the other staff members. The afternoon went by very fast and she was surprised when Walter and the two other painters came in to go wash up and then sit down to eat dinner.

It must have been about midafternoon when an old man; clean though somewhat tattered clothing, came in and took a set at a smaller table right inside the front door. His clothing, aside of being tattered and ragged, consisted of an old pair of overalls, and underneath the bib part showed the top part of what looked like "long-johns" like Herman used to wear. The table would only seat one person comfortably, and as he sat, he took off his felt western hat and hung it on the back rung of his chair. When he took his hat off, she noticed most of his gray hair was gone, except for a small fringe which ran over his ears and around the lower back of his head. He had a very long, gray beard.

He did not wait to have someone seat himself, but went straight to the small table and waited quietly there for someone to notice him. Joyce was helping someone at a booth so Vicki took a menu and fresh glass of water over and placed it in front of the man.

He looked at her and said, "You're new, isn't cha?"

She smiled and replied, "Yessir, I am. Do you know what you would like or would you like a few minutes to go over the menu?"

He chuckled and answered her, "Oh, I have the menu memorized already. But I know I want coffee right now, first and foremost."

Vicki brought him a cup of coffee, silver wrapped in a napkin, and several cream packets and a sugar container.

"Wait until I drink my coffee and then come back and we will discuss food, okay?" he asked her.

"Sure," she said cheerfully. When she went back up to the counter to wipe it down after clearing some dishes off Joyce came over and said, "See that old man by the door?"

Vicki nodded and asked, "Yes?"

"He's late today. He usually comes in at breakfast time. Well, his name is Elmer Hodgins. He's a fixture around this town and this café in particular. Never give him a ticket. Never charge him anything. Always be polite and helpful, but never pushy, even if he sits there most of the day. He may come in for one meal day and it might be breakfast, lunch or dinner or all three; doesn't matter. Now look outside there…See that mangy old mutt out there, laying by the side of the door?"

"Yes," Vicki said, after responding and focusing in on a black and white Shephard.

"When you bring the old man's order to him, take two pieces of bacon, and two pieces of buttered toast out to the dog."

"What?" Vicki asked, as though she had heard wrong.

"Yep. And don't forget."

Vicki wanted to ask the why to these instructions, but Joyce turned away and went back to her work station.

So that's what Vicki did. She didn't ask any more questions of Joyce or even of Lizzie or Walter. She figured if it was something, they wanted to share with her, they would; meanwhile she had secrets of her own, what business was it of hers not to allow others their own?

Her feet were hurting at the end of the day but Vicki reasoned it was because it was the first working day and walking or standing most of the day on the concrete would take some getting used to do. She told herself she was young and healthy and if Lizzie and Walter and Joyce, as well as some of the older kitchen staff could toughen up and do it, she could, too.

She asked Lizzie if it were okay if she chose her dinner "to go" and went home to eat.

Lizzie answered her, "Of-course it is. Then take you a nice, hot, soak bath. You've put it a really full work day today. And did a great job, too. I'm proud of you."

Even though it was almost dusk when Vicki, carrying her Styrofoam container with her dinner walked home, she was thrilled to see the white brightness of her little cottage with its' fresh coat of paint and the royal blue shutters like beacons, welcoming her home.

She sat at the small wooden round table to eat; glad she had remembered some utensils.

While she ate, she pulled out her "want" list and circled the word refrigerator. That was something she wanted soon as she could get one so she could keep milk, eggs, snacks and fruits. She was very, very appreciative Lizzie and Walter furnished her meals, but it would be nice to have her own place for "nibblers".

She began to fall into a regular schedule; her body working almost autonomously without any nudging from her conscious mind. She woke within fifteen minutes of sunrise each morning and without setting an alarm; and went to bed within fifteen minutes of nine o'clock each evening. She slept soundly, with no fear, even when she left her windows open for the cool night breezes. For the first time, really, she felt as though she were where she was supposed to be.

Lizzie allowed; in fact, insisted; that she take at least one full day a week off, and she got to choose. She chose Mondays, purely because she noted that was the slowest day of the week in so far as customers went, and she knew the staff would not be as overloaded as they sometimes were on Friday through Sundays.

The first Monday she was off she got up at her regular time, made her bed, then went down and had a leisurely breakfast with Lizzie and Walter.

"What are your plans for the day" Lizzie asked her.

"I'm going to get me a library card and check me out some books. I'm excited about that. I miss reading. And I need some kind of little beside lamp or something so I can read after dark."

"Do you think you might have time to meet me here for lunch and then we could go to the department store and pick out some curtain material and I could give you your first lesson on the machine?"

"Oh, could we? That would be great. And rods…We could get some curtain rods, too."

"Would you want to let Walter put you up some venetian blinds. They aren't expensive and you would have some more privacy; especially until you get some curtains sewn and up."

"I hate for you to go to that expense and trouble, Lizzie. You guys have done so much already."

Walter smiled and said, "Look at it this way, girl. It's an investment for us. When you get tired of us and move on someday, we can rent the place out. Blinds will add to its' value."

"Oh, I am never leaving, I love it here!" Vicki gushed out hurriedly."

"Suits me just fine," Walter said, grinning. "You're fast becoming one of the best waitresses we've ever had."

"I'm sure trying. My tip jar is filling up."

"What are you going to do with all that dough? I might need a loan someday."

The three of them laughed.

After Lizzie and Vicki agreed on a time to meet back at the café for lunch, Vicki headed off to the library.

The librarian was a silver-gray-haired older lady who wore wire framed round glasses and reminded Vicki of the school librarian from home. She even was dressed similarly: navy skirt, white blouse, and gray cardigan sweater. Vicki thought, *I guess that must be a standard librarian uniform. I wonder how long she's been working here?*

When she inquired at the desk about applying for a card, the clerk asked for her address.

"I'm not sure," she began and the clerk looked questioningly at her, and then asked, "You don't know your address?"

Vicki flushed, embarrassed, and then she said, "I'm staying with Walter and Lizzie down at their café. But I don't know their street address."

"Oh, well, here, we'll just note that on the card here and we'll be able to track you down if you don't return your books."

"Oh, I will. I will be good at that. I'll be one of your best customers. How many can I check out at a time?" she added.

"Three at first, but if you build up a good reputation with me, I'll increase it as far as six. Are you a fast reader?"

"Oh, yes. I'd much rather read than watch television."

"Kindred spirits, then. Okay, sign right here; make a note of late charges and stay on my good side by bringing things back on time."

"Oh, I will," Vicki repeated.

Vicki spent more time than she had intended, but when she left to meet Lizzie again, she had Several books in her arms: "Small Great Things" by Jodi Picoult, "Two by Two" by Nicholas Sparks, an old favorite she wanted to read again, "To Kill a Mockingbird" by Harper Lee and a biography of a favorite writer of hers, Betty Smith who wrote "A Tree Grows in Brooklyn".

She took the books home to the cottage, laid them on her table and then went to find Lizzie.

Later that afternoon the two of them roamed the fabric store. The only problem they had there was in making up their minds. They would find one, and claim it was "perfect!", then before they could go to the register to get a clerk to cut the yardage they wanted and find the right thread and the right size rods, according to Walter's measurements written on a scrap of paper, they would spy another pattern they liked. The two of them had decided to put the same pattern and color on all the windows. The cottage was small and for the number of windows it had, too many different patterns or colors would be distracting and chaotic.

After that they went to a local "Dollar Store" and found an expensive little table lamp and a package of spare bulbs.

Vicki was just as excited about the sewing lesson as she was about the project itself and when Lizzie left Walter in charge of the café, (after teasingly telling Vicki how dangerous that was) they headed to Lizzie's house.

Vicki was very impressed and a little surprised when Lizzie gave her a guided tour; there were three bedrooms, a lovely living room with a rock fireplace and big bay window looking out on a large deck which gave a lakeside view of Four Loudoun lake. The lake linked Maryville and Knoxville and was breathtaking. There was a kitchen with hanging exposed copper-bottomed pans and stainless-steel appliances. Vicki was impressed with the wall rack which was magnetized and held a selection of cutlery, which gave the appearance of knives magically just hanging on the wall.

The house had cherry wood cabinets and two full walls shelved with books. Two bathrooms and three bedrooms; one of which had been turned into a sewing room for Lizzie. It had a wall-mounted thread rack that Walter had made for her, made from polished cherry wood, and another wall rack with special hooks for scissors, yardstick, ruler, thread puller, pinking shears, and other assorted tools of the sewing enthusiast. Walter had even made her a cutting table to cut her patterns out on; he had mounted yardsticks on the sides so she could measure and the top was so wonderfully sanded and smooth when you ran your hand across it. *A real act of love,* thought Vicki.

On the floor was a braided circular rug and the rest of the house had beautiful wood floors with scattered splashes of color from area rugs.

All the beds were topped with beautiful quilts and Vicki was surprised to recognize some of the patterns from those her grandmother had quilted: "The Wedding Ring" patterned quilt, "Red Rover Quilt" and "Falling Leaves". Lizzie seemed surprised when she identified these and Vicki explained, "My grandmother used to quilt and she and her friends would always quilt together."

Vicki didn't bring up the quilting class she and her mother had been enrolled in and used to go to on Thursdays. She felt a lump in her throat and could not speak for a few moments as she remembered the unfinished quilt which was to be a riot of colors embroidered on the top. It was going to be a very unusual quilt; involving the explosion of colorful flowers done all in embroidery then the careful quilting of four layers; top, filling, back and binding. They had even discussed entering it in the state fair if they had finished it on time. Vicki wondered if her mother ever worked on it by herself with her gone now; she believed probably not. Since the size of the quilt had been kind size, she knew that even with two people working on it, it would have been a very challenging project. She wondered if her mother had just packed it away and felt another brief flush of guilt.

"Come over here a minute," Lizzie said, and she walked to a huge chifforobe.

"Is this a chifforobe?" she asked Lizzie.

"How in the world did a youngster like you know that?"

"Again, my grandmother."

Lizzie opened the side door and Vicki saw, stacked neatly inside, several quilts.

"Oh, wow," she said, Look at those colors! They're beautiful."

"Years ago, I had a quilting grandma, too. I imagine Herman's grandma had some quilts like these, didn't she? Now days people buy those fancy comforters with pillow shams and they slide all over the bed. Heck, they're not even warm."

"Yes, Herman's grandma had several of them, *real* quilts I mean."

"Well, look at these and pick out your favorite."

"Really? You're going to give me one?"

"Well, that's what I said, didn't I?" Lizzie was grinning.

They got all four quilts out and after spreading them out, looked carefully at them all.

"Oh, how in the world can I choose? They are all so beautiful… Which one should I take, Lizzie?"

"It's *your* quilt, for *your* bed. You decide."

Vicki finally chose one with rows of different colored quilted stars in rows.

"That one will go great with your curtains," Lizzie told her. "Or even another set of curtains later on. It's one of my favorites. I'm so glad you chose that one."

They spent the afternoon cutting the material into the measurements they had taken of the windows, and after showing her how the machine worked and allowing her to practice on scraps of material until she could, as Lizzie put it, "At least sew a straight seam without running her finger under the material guide or jamming too much material at a time, instead of allowing the machine to feed itself slowly and accurately, she allowed Vicki to sew all the hems and plackets.

"Now we'll go find the old man and see if he can spare us the time to put the rods up."

He could. He did. When they hung the curtains, Vicki was ecstatic; the colors were perfect and drew the bedroom together with the beautiful quilt. Vicki gave both Lizzie and Walter a big hug and couldn't stop going in the house, then out, then in again to get the full effect over and over.

She kept saying, "I love them, I love them, I love them. My beautiful curtains."

"Well, they are coming Wednesday to measure for the blinds so you have to take them down for that."

"How long does it take to get the venetian blinds?" Vicki asked.

"Between two and three weeks," Lizzie said.

"Yeah, yeah, yeah, I know. You women are always in a hurry for things. You can close your curtains at night between now and then."

Vicki laughed along with him. As each day passed Vicki felt more at home and happy.

She often asked herself *the reason for this. Was it because she had so much undivided attention and approval from everyone? Not just Lizzie and Walter, but the staff; Joyce invited her to go to the movies sometime and even the old curmudgeon, Mr. Hodgins, had started requesting her by name to wait on him; except he asked for: "The new girl".*

One thing was for sure, she was not invisible here. She got paid each Friday. It was always in cash and when she asked Walter why the rest of the employees got paid in a check, he explained, "Well I pay you *under the table* because if I charged you and held out the taxes you would hardly have anything left."

"Is it against the law to do that? Can I get into trouble?" Vicki asked him.

"Well…A little, but there's trouble and then there's trouble…"

"Well, I sure don't want to go to jail."

He laughed so hard he had to wipe his eyes which had watered up.

"The very worst thing that could happen would be a fine, but believe me, Vicki, the government has more important things to do besides going around looking for a few dollars of tax money. Just keep it a secret between you and me and we won't have any problems. R there's the option of calling you contract labor."

"What's that?"

"Too complicated to explain right now, but just another option"

Vicki took the spiral notebook she had in her backpack and beginning from the back; to avoid mixing her journalistic account of her adventure thus far with her *wish-list* from her "needs and wants" list Lizzie had had her write when she first arrived. She placed these items in order as to what she would do with her money each Friday. She felt a little giddy almost when she got paid the first time. She wasn't young enough or foolish enough to believe she was rich now; but still, it was more money than she had ever had for herself. She would remember the feel of that first payday as Walter counted it out to her many years later, and gave him credit for teaching her how to budget and manage her meager pay each week. She never felt deprived or cheated by the amount; but only gratitude for her first real job and the ability to earn her own money.

She moved the refrigerator down on the list somewhat; and put bedroom table lamp at the top. Now that she had books to read, she enjoyed reading until she got drowsy; but hated having to then get up, go to the wall switch to turn off the light and then return to her bed. She wanted to be able to reach over and snap a lamp off. She could not sleep with the lights on. The only solution was to get a lamp.

She added "computer" to the list, she missed being able to research questions she sometimes had; and even contemplated being able to tune into some online classes she could perhaps monitor, learning what other students her age were working on.

CHAPTER FIFTEEN

A friend for Prince

One morning when she got to work, Mr. Hodgins's dog was lying on the porch to the side of the entrance door; his usual breakfast place, but curled up right next to him was a small furry bundle. When Vicki got closer, she could hear a purring sound and she realized it was a small kitten, cuddled up with the dog.

The dog watched Vicki closely, as though waiting to see her reaction to the cat. When she stooped down, the dog bent his head and gave the kitten a big lick as though showing Vicki the two animals were friends and warning her to not try and interfere or separate the two.

Vicki carefully opened the screen door and held it as she went inside so that it wouldn't slam or make noise. She went to the counter and found Joyce unloading the big commercial dishwasher.

"Hey, how are you this morning?" Joyce asked.

"Hey, yourself. Say, have you seen Hodgins dog this morning?"

"Yeah," Joyce said, raising her head to look towards the front of the café at the dog lying here. "Why?"

""Well, seems he invited and brought a guest to breakfast with him.

Joyce shut the dishwasher and then she grinned, "I know. Can you believe it?"

"Does Lizzie know?"

Yeah, she's the one I showed when I got here."

"What did she say?"

"Just what you would imagine Lizzie to say," said Joyce, grinning.

"And what was that?" Vicki asked, impatiently.

"Feed it, too. So, I gave it a little bowl of warm milk, which it promptly lapped up."

"Do you think Mr. Hodgins knows it's there?"

"Yep. He thanked me for the milk."

Vicki was quiet for a few minutes and then she said, "I've never seen a big old dog allow a cat to sleep on him like that, have you?"

"No, but doesn't it say somewhere about sheep lying down with wolves; wouldn't that be about the same thing?"

"Well, isn't that when the world down here on earth is like heaven?" asked Vicki.

"You're giving me a headache, kid. Don't go all philosophical on me so early. It's just an old dog and a little kitten after all."

"Do you think they would let me have it?" Vicki asked Joyce.

"I'm not the one to ask. Looks like the dog is in charge; or maybe old Hodgins. You might have to ask him. By the way, he's been waiting for you. He acts like you are his own special waitress now days. Remember to take his water and coffee first. You can ask him about the kitten."

"What if he says 'No'?"

"Then he says 'no' and you forget about it."

Vicki took the coffee, water, napkin wrapped silverware over to the old man. He thanked her and then she hesitated and finally he looked at her and asked, "What?"

"Um, I noticed that kitten next to your dog out there…"

"Yes, what about it?"

"Well, I was wondering if it was yours?"

"No, it's Prince's," he said.

"Prince?"

"Yeah, that's my dog's name, Prince."

"Why do you want to know?" Mr. Hodgins added.

"I was wondering if I could have it?"

"You?"

"Yessir. I would take good care of it. I promise."

"Do you have any pets already?"

"No, but I would like a cat."

"Well, Prince has become very fond of that kitten. When we get through with breakfast, if Prince lets you take it from him, you can have it."

"Oh, thank you!"

Vicki went back to Joyce who asked, "Well, what did he say?"

"He said I could have it."

"Oh, me. Oh, my," said Joyce.

"What? "asked Vicki.

"Well, you've taken on a big responsibility. Do you realize that?"

When Vicki just looked at her, Joyce said, "Cat food, milk, kitty-litter box, shots. Just like getting a kid."

"I don't care," Vicki said. "She will be company for me."

"Okay, don't say I didn't warn you, Missy."

Vicki took Mr. Hodgins his breakfast, refilled his coffee cup and took Prince's toast and bacon out to him. The cat was so quiet that for a minute Vicki though it might not be alive. She placed her hand on its warm fur and it wiggled around as though to find a more comfortable place.

Meanwhile Lizzie and Walter had heard the story of the strange pair on the porch and had arrived to go see for themselves.

"Oh, how sweet," Lizzie said.

"Beats every damn thing I've ever seen," Walter said. "Do you suppose that cat is so dumb she thinks that dog is just a bigger cat?"

"The thing of it is," said Lizzie, looking at Walter, "Is that she hasn't learned yet that not all animals are the same. He's warm, he's quiet, and he allowed her to share his space. She's content. And, you need to watch your language, Mister."

"Ah, Lizzie, everybody here has heard 'Damn' before."

When she continued to look at him, he said, "Sorry, everyone."

"So, Joyce said you're adopting this kitten?" Lizzie asked Vicki.

"Yes, mam."

"Well, Let's look in the kitchen for a couple of old soup or salad bowls for water and food. Go look in the clean rag bag for something to make a bed for her, and get Walter to look up in the attic. I thanked have some old wicker baskets. One might do for a bed. And if it cries at night for its mama until it gets a little bigger, we can put a hot water bag or a heating pad for it to cuddle to."

Everyone gathered to watch when Mr. Hodgkin went outside to get Prince. They wanted to see what the dog would do. He stood up, and stretched, which tumbled the cat off him. Then the dog looked around the circle of people until his eyes came to rest on Vicki.

"Look at that," Lizzie said. "It's like he knows it's Vicki's cat now."

The dog watched until Vicki squatted down and gently picked up the kitten. She began stroking it and it immediately began humming and purring.

Then the old man turned and said, "Come on, boy. Let's go home now." And after one last look at Vicki and the kitten, Prince turned and caught up with the old man, to walk by his side. When the two reached the end of the block, and Prince stopped to look back as though to see that the cat was okay. After visually accepting Vicki had the cat in her arms and it was safe, he turned back and went off with his master.

Lizzie helped Vicki carry the basket, bowls, soft clean rags to the cottage where they arranged everything. Food dishes in the kitchen area, basket and bed rags in the bedroom.

Later that day Lizzie gave some milk to Vicki for the kitten. Then Vicki walked down the two blocks to the large grocery store, and using some of her money she bought three cans of kitty food. On the side of the can it designated the food inside to be for young kittens. She bought herself a can opener and an inexpensive heating pad.

After extensive thought on the subject, Vicki; being determined not to name her new kitten something mundane such as Princess, or Blackie or Tiger (she was a beautiful black and gray stripe, except for her four white booties) she named her Aphrodite, after the famous Greek goddess.

She watched the graceful way she moved: slinky, smooth and deliberate. She remembered reading Aphrodite described as beautiful, and wise. She was also associated with love and kindness.

When Joyce asked what she had named her new kitten she looked puzzled when Vicki answered, "Aphrodite" and said to her "Geez I will never remember that, kiddo. In fact, I don't know if I can even pronounce it correctly."

Vicki grinned at her and said, "She's not going to be your ordinary cat. She's special."

"If you say so," Joyce replied.

Vicki took her responsibility seriously; getting up early enough in the mornings to change her litter-box, give her fresh water and cat food. The cat always ran to her first thing when Vicki opened the door in the afternoon and would sit on her lap on the floor so she could get a share of petting and attention.

Several times when she was first new to her little home, Vicki would wake up in the middle of the night with the kitten crying and trying to get up in the bed with her. Though she had her own bed, Vicki would reach down in the dark, and clasping the kitten around her midsection, lift her up and snuggle her closer to her chest, petting her to the humming rhythm coming from the cat and both would sleep. Vicki was worried at first that she might roll over the cat and smother her, but it never happened.

Vicki got her notebook list out and she wrote above the "table lamp" which already had a line drawn through it, added a new notation: "Rocking Chair." She envisioned herself rocking with Aphrodite in her lap, purring while Vicki read her book.

Vicki began to feel at home. Each week on payday, she tried to purchase one thing to cross off her list; her favorite being the rocking chair. It wasn't new; Lizzie took her to the local Salvation Army Thrift store and they found a perfectly good maple finished rocking chair. Over the next few weeks, she acquired a small bedside table. The blinds were delivered and Walter installed them. It was nice to be able to close the world out at night, but it was also nice to be able to adjust the light allowed in each room. She especially loved the effect of the curtains and the colorful quilt in her bedroom. Sometimes she just sat, rocking and petting Aphrodite and she was filled with such a feeling of well-being and contentment she felt like she would never again be this happy.

Occasionally she felt that *the other shoe would surely drop*. Nothing could be this perfect forever. It was as though she were holding her breath, watching and waiting for whatever was giving her this apprehensive expectation of something coming. It reminded her of an old movie she had watched once which had stayed with her. Just thinking about it even now brought her a real sense of forbidding. The movie, taken from a Ray Bradbury book, (entitled "Something Wicked This Way Comes") was a Disney movie, and the entire story carried a sense of bad things to come.

She felt silly about this sense of something scary coming now. Right when she was so contented with her relationship with Lizzie and Walter; her neat little cottage and her new companion, Aphrodite.

She couldn't even blame this feeling on her choice of reading material currently because she

had checked out a very inspiring novel from the library this week: "An Invisible Thread" by Laura Schroff. This book should certainly raise anyone's optimism level. It was full of a wonderful "happy ending" true story.

Is this what people refer to as intuition? If so, why do people usually attach this ability to see into the future as "women's" intuition? Can't men have the same gift? And, most importantly, how would one know if they had this gift or not? Do we just stand around and wait to see what is going to happen?

She tried to shove such thoughts out of her mind.

Answers came. But certainly not the ones she would have expected; no, they were much, much worse.

It was a Saturday and the café was extremely busy. It was difficult in the kitchen because Lizzie had hired another cook. The older one, John; who had been there since the opening of the café was still working there, but the customer bank had grown so much that the older cook could not handle it all by himself. Though the new cook had claimed to have all kind of experience and qualifications, Vicki, watching him as he struggled to follow John's instructions, saw how clumsy and awkward his actions were.

She was aware of John's efforts to keep patience with the new employee but Vicki could tell he was beginning to lose it.

Lizzie saw the brewing problems in the kitchen and without raising her voice, she put herself in the kitchen, giving John an extra pair of hands. This helped a great deal, but the new employee now got in Lizzie's way and almost negated her efforts to help with the backlog.

Finally, she put the new employee at the prep table, and told him to wash and cut necessary things for salads and sandwiches, like lettuce, tomatoes, peppers, pickles, then put them in containers with tight lids, and finally, in the refrigerator. This kept him out of the way temporarily, but all too soon he was edging his way back by John's side. He seemed determined to be actually cooking.

When he saw the oil level in the deep frier a little low, he retrieved a plastic five-gallon jug of cooking oil from the storage closet. No one except Vicki seemed even remotely aware of his actions; and she wasn't sure what his intentions were. She looked for Lizzie, and she was placing orders on the pass-through window which went from the kitchen to the dining area. She didn't want to try and catch Lizzie's attention, fearing it might startle her into dropping some of the orders she had lined up and down one arm and in the other hand.

As Vicki walked to the door to the kitchen, she heard a huge "whoosh" sound and several screams from kitchen staff.

Evidently, the new employee tried to pour oil into the fryer, the container slipped in his hands and spilled across the grill top. Immediately a huge fire began feeding on the oil. Everyone moved as far as they could get away from the flames. Then, totally against any knowledge of the disaster which would follow, the new employee filled a metal pitcher of water and pitched it on the fire.

Even Vicki knew you *NEVER* put water on a grease fire.

It was utter chaos; customers in the front part of the café left their seats and pushed their way out of the restaurant, the fire rapidly caught the cabinets above the grill on fire, and the counters next to the deep fryer began to burn. The smoke was terrible; everyone was coughing and eyes were watering. Lizzie was trying to urge every staff member from the kitchen out the back door. Walter wasn't at the café this morning, to make things even worse. One of the other staff did get a call off to 911 and fire department from her cell phone.

Another waitress thought she could smother the fire, so she whipped off her apron and try to beat the fire out but it was way too late for that. It was just for fuel for the growing fire. As Vicki gradually tried once again to get through the double doors leading to the kitchen, someone from inside the kitchen tried to come back through the other way, the door smacked Vicki in the head and she immediately was knocked to the floor, unconscious. The staff, trying to come through the door merely screamed again, and stepped right over Vicki's still body. Later she would remember thinking how lucky she was she wasn't trampled while lying there in her unconscious state.

Lizzie had finally gotten everyone from the kitchen out the back door; just in time, as the door frame around the screen door was now on fire.

Most of the customers pushing and shoving their way out the front dining room had made it out. Suddenly a huge splash of cold water washed her face and brought consciousness to her again. Vicki stirred and opened her eyes to a wall of smoke and she began to cough. She tried to move, but found her right ankle shoot through with sharp pain. Then, she felt arms reaching for her and a voice said, "Come on girl, put one arm around my neck, there; that's it. Now, use my body to get to a standing position. I don't think I can carry you, but if you can stand and use me for a crutch, we can get ourselves out of here."

I must have gone crazy, Vicki thought, *there's a dog in here. What's a dog doing in the café? Where's the smoke coming from?*

Someone was dragging her up and towards the front door. Her ankle hurt too much to put weight on it, so she was leaning against her human crutch and hopping on the other foot. On the other side was a large dog, pulling her by her jeans with his mouth.

When they reached the front door, someone outside opened the door and assisted them out. A man assisted her human crutch; who turned out to be Mr. Hudgins, in pulling her all the way out and taking her to sit on the lowered tailgate of a truck.

About the same time, two fire trucks turned in, and in a short time, had everyone move their cars and trucks across the street and down the road out of any way harm's way. Then hoses were hooked up and they began to work on putting the fire out. The people from the back of the building came around the front and across the road. One additional fire truck went down the alley and began applying water there. If the firetruck in the back had not wet down the back of the café, the fire might have jumped from the café to the cottage.

It's strange, thought Vicki, when bad things happen how differently people react. Some immediately take note of what "might" have happened which didn't and they considered how lucky they were; others immediately think how bad their luck must be for anything like this to have happened to them.

Right away Lizzie and Walter reassured everyone that as long as no one was hurt, buildings can be rebuilt or fixed back to their original condition but a life cannot be replaced. Mr. Hodgins said, "Thank the good Lord my dog got out safe."

Joyce said to Vicki, "Oh, how lucky you were that Mr. Hodgins saw you were still in there. How brave he was, he and his dog; to go in there and bring you out."

One of the regular customers showed his *'back to normal streak of humor'* when he said, "Somebody should have brought wieners and marshmallows."

A couple of the kitchen staff were taken to the hospital and treated for smoke inhalation; but later released.

Of-course, the café had to stay just like it was until the insurance people came and did their inspection and filed the claim for Lizzie and Walter over the next few days.

Lizzie kept telling Walter, "Now we can go ahead and do those improvements we've been putting off."

Vicki was sitting on the front steps a couple of days later, holding Aphrodite in her lap, and listening to her purr in appreciation when she asked Lizzie, "Lizzie, do you think animals think about things the way humans do?"

"What do you mean? I do believe they are a lot smarter than we give them credit for, but I don't know if that's just instinct kicking in or learned behavior. I always wanted to go to the university one day. I even played with becoming a vet."

Surprised, Vicki looked up at her and said, "Really? I wouldn't have guessed. I guess I always just thought of you and Walter always wanting to run a restaurant."

Lizzie laughed. "I don't seem like university material to you?"

A little embarrassed that Lizzie might think she thought Lizzie wasn't smart enough to go to a university, Vicki hurriedly said, "No, it just seems like you two are very contented with your lives. If you had gone, what would you have studied?"

"Probably psychology," Lizzie answered. "I would have liked learning what makes people tick."

"For instance?"

"Well, Mr. Hodgins, for instance. What's his story? Where did he come from? Did he have any family?"

"Don't you know anything about him?"

"Not really. He just showed up on the porch one day and asked if we had any chores he could do for breakfast."

"I've never seen him do any chores," Vicki said. He raised her hand to block the sun from her eyes as she looked up at Lizzie.

Lizzie laughed. "Well, he doesn't much anymore and I just let it go. We always have been lucky to have plenty; I feel okay sharing."

They were both quiet and then Vicki asked, "Like this kitten," she said, then continued, "Does it know it had a mother once? Does it remember its mother? Does it remember any siblings? Or does it just think about being hungry or sleepy or needing to use her litter box?"

"Well, I don't know; but I do know animals can form attachments, strong ones, for their owners. I've known animals who have even faced danger to protect them."

All of a sudden Vicki remembered Rusty and the bear attack on Herman and herself.

"I believe that, too."

"And I also believe humans can feel that strongly about their pets. You're seen old ladies sometimes who treat their pets like their children; and would even go without to make sure the animal eats, and is safe from harm or bad weather or the cold."

"I sometimes like some animals better than people," Vicki said.

Again, Lizzie laughed and said, "Ain't that the truth?"

"Do you think people can change?" asked Vicki.

"Girl, you sure have a lot of questions."

"Well, that's because I am curious about other people, especially if they are different from me."

"Well, sometimes people have things they don't want to talk about with others and in that case, it's kind of an intrusion to pester them with questions."

"Do you have secrets?"

"Hon, everybody has their secrets. Sometimes that's how you find your one and only; like me and Walter. Sharing some of a person's secrets."

"What did you and Walter do about the new guy?"

"You mean the one who started the fire?"

"Yeah, that one."

"Gave him two weeks' severance pay and told him we couldn't afford to keep him on."

"No, you didn't, did you?"

"Sure did. Was the truth. I didn't really blame him for anything except for lying about his experience. Only a fool would throw water on a grease fire. If I never lay eyes on him again it will be too soon."

"Hum. Well, it's getting hot out here. I think me and Aphrodite are going home."

"Alright, but remember we're eating at mine and Walter's tonight. I invited Mr. Hodgins, too."

"It sure makes the day go slow with the café being closed down."

"Yes, it does, but it won't take long for them to get it back up and running once they start."

Lizzie was right about that. Once the fire department got their report to the insurance company, they wrote a check for the damages and Walter and Lizzie were busy supervising the reconstruction and remodeling. They were in a hurry. Joyce was drawing unemployment; she said she couldn't afford to not have any money coming in and she refused any loan from Walter and Lizzie. Lizzie and Walter insisted on paying Vicki's regular salary on Fridays, just like always and even though Vicki tried to talk them out of it, she was glad to have it.

CHAPTER SIXTEEN

Plants versus Humans

Walter took her to the closest dollar store one week and she got herself a small table lamp for reading at night and to the Salvation Army Thrift store where she purchased a gently used bedside nightstand to set it on.

One morning Lizzie, Joyce, Walter and Vicki got together and began to plan a grand re-opening, complete with door prizes, specials, and a local Country Western Band.

The Open House turned out to be a bigger success than they could have imagined and Local law enforcement even found it necessary to send out some enforcement to conduct traffic jams and good-natured jibes from drivers towards one another.

Thus, the winter passed. The groundhog came out to the delight of the locals, but failed to see and run from his shadow which predicted a short and mild winter season.

There was a contentment from the slow, colder days and Vicki was full of questions about bears and hibernation and questions about why humans couldn't take advantage of the season to regroup and prepare for the glorious spring which was to come, as animals did.

Vicki spent a lot of time reading and when Walter surprised her with a gift of a computer and printer, she began to faithfully do the classwork provided free for students in her grade level. It was satisfying to find she had no problem keeping up with the assignments and one night, lying awake in bed, she wondered if someday she finished this adventure (as she had long termed it, from the beginning) and returned home, what would her reception be?

One early spring afternoon Lizzie and Vicki went to one of the home do-it-yourself stores and looked at seek packets for a planned garden and new small, flower plants for a new flowerbed at the front of the café.

After they selected, then changed their minds, then rechose other small plants Vicki asked Lizzie, "I know plants are considered living things, Lizzie, but why does it not hurt them when they break a leaf, or someone cuts their stems? When animals and people hurt themselves, they bleed and if they bleed too much, they can die…"

She paused and then continued, "So, does it hurt them when they lose leaves or don't get enough water or sunshine…?"

"Well, it's kind of different for plants, Vicki. In fact, sometimes plants do better if you pluck off brown leaves. I read that it takes more energy for a plant to heal a sick leaf than to cut it off and allow a new leaf to grow in its place. Did you ever notice how each spring some plant nurseries trim back branches on some plants and then they grow back even thicker and more beautiful than ever?"

Vicki nodded in agreement. Then she said, "I guess God had it all planned out, right?"

Lizzie smiled and reached out to give Vicki a hug.

Lizzie tried to remember which of the bible verses talked about the time to sow, a time to plant and to reap and that evening she looked it up so she could direct some of Vicki's questions without feeling stupid.

The next day Lizzie gave her bible to Vicki, with a bookmark placed in the book of Ecclesiastes 3:1-2. "Look, I found the verse which answers your questions from yesterday. Read it and tell me what you think later."

Lizzie shouldn't have been surprised with the words which Vicki prepared for her. The girl was so smart she constantly threw a curved ball into the conversation game.

Vicki asked her, "Lizzie, the verses you gave me kind of show that we, as humans, don't have as much to do with our lives as we think. It almost tells us that there is a time designated by God on when it's right to plant, to reap, to live, to die, and all things. Do I interpret it like you do?"

Lizzie was quiet for a few seconds and then she said, shrugging her shoulders and sighing, the most famous answer ever used by a parent faced with difficult questions, "Humph, why don't you go and ask Walter. That question sounds like it's right down his alley."

"Ah," said Vicki, "You don't know the answers, to you, Lizzie?"

Lizzie said, chuckling, "You got it, girl."

Later when Lizzie repeated the conversion to Walter, he asked her, grinning, "Why didn't you explain all about people needing oxygen and plants needing nitrogen?"

"Because I forgot. I never was that big into science, smart-alec."

Over the days, weeks, months that passed since Vicki had joined their family they had grown in love and depend on her; the love was mixed with a little fear which was shown by Lizzie one evening when she asked "Walter, ever think what we would do if she just decided to continue her journey and leave us? I don't think I could bear it…"

"Quit borrowing trouble, Sweetie. She is happy here."

"But?"

He interrupted her, "No more. I don't want to hear it. God sent her here. I really believe that. We lost our girl once and the good lord has seen fit to send us another one."

There was a period of several weeks in which the café flourished in its' new renovated colors and updates and a sense of peace and containment seemed to reign, but unforeseen, the next ripple in their lives was right around the corner and could never have occurred to them.

It happened on what normally would be one of the slow business days for the café; a Monday.

Later they would be thankful it did not occur during Friday through Sunday; the café's busiest and most crowded days.

Lately, if they weren't very busy, Lizzie was allowing Joyce to teach Vicki about the computer cash register and how to ring up sales, hand out change and keep receipts in balance.

When the three came in the café they did not arouse any anxiety, there was a woman and two men. They chose a booth on the back side of the café, even though several of the front booths were empty. Most people enjoyed having a booth near the windows to watch the outside traffic and people passing by.

When the trio entered, Joyce and Vicki were behind the counter, at the register. Joyce said, "I'll get their water and menus."

"Okay," Vicki said.

When Joyce came back to the register she said, "They want a few minutes to look over the menu."

Later, Vicki and Joyce would compare notes on what had taken place and wonder why they didn't give voice to their concerns that something was "off" about the three.

Vicki took her order pad and went over to check on the three's order and once she wrote it down, she went back to the pass-through window to give the kitchen staff the order.

She sensed movement from the booth and what she observed next sent a red flag up. The two men got up and together went to the men's restroom. Often women will go to the ladies' room together; and this was completely usual and accepted as the way women enjoyed gathering and talking together; even in public places.

"How strange was that?" Vicki asked Joyce.

"Yeah, I agree" she replied to Vicki. "How often to men go to the men's room together? Usually, one will go and when he returns, the other one goes."

"Mum hum…And look," Joyce said, "Now the woman is going to the ladies' room. All three are leaving the table at the same time."

They looked at each other and then Joyce asked, "Where is Walter? Is he here yet this morning?"

"I don't think so, I haven't seen him."

Vicki was still watching the booth and just as she started to say something else, the door to the men's room was flung open so wide that it banged on the wall. The two men rushed out, and without even pausing, ran together to the register. It was so sudden and startling, both Joyce and Vicki stepped back from the two men's approach; trying to distance themselves from them.

Out of the corner of her eye, Vicki saw the women's room door burst open.

Joyce let out a scream when they became conscious that all three were now wearing black ski masks. One of the men held a revolver in one hand and he said in a raspy, barely understandable voice, "This is a hold up. Open the register and give me whatever money is in there."

When she hesitated, he continued, "Don't do it…"

Joyce hesitated once again and Vicki yanked on her sleeve and said, "Joyce, give it to him."

"Yeah, Joyce," said the man, waving the gun around, still pointing it at Joyce. "Hurry up before I lose my patience."

When Joyce pushed the change button, the drawer rang up zeros, and there was a ringing bell on the register which made them all jump. The gun went off and Joyce screamed again; but she realized the bullet did not hit anything except the row of glasses sitting behind her on the counter, waiting to be put inside the dishwasher.

Joyce scooped out the currency and handed it to the man who reached for it with his free hand.

"Hurry up, hurry up," the woman said.

The three turned and ran for the door, and several bills fell from the man's hand as he turned and ran.

The cook's face appeared in the open pass-through window for orders and he said, "What the hell was that?" When he took in the scene with the three ski-masked people running for the front door, he immediately ducked down behind the counter. Vicki thought she saw a cell phone in his hand, and hoped it was and that he was dialing 911.

There was a family sitting in a booth by the front window and now the woman there was screaming and the man with her tried to push her down in the booth while the child sitting across from them was gawking out the window at the three masked people.

The father yelled, "Down, Brittany, get down, hurry, get down."

Later when the police came and the interviews began Vicki was surprised that Joyce and herself could remember so little. Descriptions; the main thing they remembered; which was of little and no real assistance, since all wore the black ski masks. Later Vicki said "Those masks are becoming sort of standard equipment for bad guys, right?"

The police officer looked at her rather askance when she said, "The woman had on orange socks."

"Can you think of anything else?" he asked her.

"Well, one of the men had a beard. Both wore jeans, and so did the woman."

The man who was in one of the front booths with his family did identify a black mercury automobile but no license plates.

It was early in the day so there had only been a start-up amount of cash in the register so the perpetrators did not get much.

The main thing was that Vicki told the policeman who interviewed her, "I don't believe he meant for the gun to go off. I think he was nervous and the noise from the other customers startled him."

"That's interesting," the officer said. "I thought the same thing. Still, consider yourselves lucky. It could have had a very, very different kind of ending. We don't get much trouble from this side of town. They may have been outsiders, needing money and noticed fewer cars in the lot; thought this would be an easy hit."

Of everyone there that morning, the one most upset was Joyce. And understandingly, Vicki realized that it was due to her being a single mother and worrying about what would have become of her children if she had been fatally shot.

Lizzie said, after the officers had left, "Well, what's next?"

What do you mean?" Vicki asked.

"Well, they say things come in threes, and there was the fire and now a robbery. What's next?"

Trying to reassure her, Walter put his arm around her shoulders and said, "Well, they say things come in threes, and there was the fire and now a robbery; that's true but good things come in threes sometimes, too. Maybe it will be something good. Don't jinx us by expecting something bad."

"You're right, of-course," Lizzie said.

Although the incident did leave all of them with a heightened sense of anxiety, especially at night and Walter wouldn't let anyone close up in the evening alone. The new rule was at least two at a time to lock up for the night and no one was to walk out to their cars alone at night. Walter took a new rule a step further by making sure he walked Vicki to her little cottage every evening and that he checked out every closet, and under the bed as well as take a walk around the little cottage, checking the bushes and nearby wooded area. She kept telling him it wasn't necessary but he would have none of it; he insisted. For a long time after that, though, she slept with her little table lamp on all night.

Vicki was going through a growth spurt and because of this, Lizzie started more sewing lessons; this time for clothes. They chose simple patterns for skirts, blouses and even a matching skirt and suited jacket. As she grew in talent, she made other things; a new pair of pajamas and a robe. Still, as most young people her age, she loved her jeans and had several pair. Once in a while she couldn't help but remember how her mother took her little tom-boy self and (especially for holidays) would dress her up in frilly, often pink or floral print "girly" clothes. She remembered one Easter for church she had even purchased white gloves and a little summer straw hat. Vicki remembered how she didn't want to wear it, but was relieved that when she was made to do so, there were quite a few other "Young ladies" there dressed like herself.

Eventually she was adding to her little home. Walter and Vicki found a second-hand refrigerator advertised in the newspaper and it was like brand new. She still took advantage of the food from the café, but it was nice to be able to keep cereal and milk and fruit for later snacks in her home.

Vicki got to meet Joyce's children; taking in an occasional movie or even, once, all of them going to the local roller-skating rink for an afternoon of fun and laughter.

Aphrodite continued to grow and was a constant and welcome companion. Lizzie took Aphrodite to a local vet and got all the necessary immunizations to keep her healthy and the cat even grew used to the tiny bell on her collar that Vicki had bought for her. Vicki continued to make her weekly trip to the library and was becoming good enough friends with the librarian that the woman would set aside new books she though Vicki would enjoy.

Now and then they would hear from the police officers who had taken the reports on the robbery, but thus far, nothing came to light. It made all of them think it would never be solved and maybe that it was true they were outsiders, just passing through.

In the spring Lizzie and Vicki had Walter dig up a flower bed around the front and sides of the café and soon there was a riot of spring flowers which was a joy to look at. Next came a little vegetable garden in back of the café, to the side of the cottage. They grew onions, radishes, iceberg lettuce, cucumbers, tomatoes and carrots. They shared the chores of weeding and watering and they delighted in the fresh produce they used for salads.

Looking back on this period of time later Vicki would always remember her happiness. She did often think of her old family, but not with any real remorse; mostly just a vague sense of what she had lost to find this new happiness. Sometimes these thoughts were laced with strong feelings of guilt and shame when she thought of how hurt they must have been when they found her notes and realized she was gone. *How they must have blamed themselves,* she thought, and she *wished she could reveal their non-complicity and that she certainly had made her own decisions.*

One lazy Monday afternoon when the café was closed; perhaps for President's Day or some other holiday (which was rare) she was at Walter and Lizzie's; the weather was cold and Vicki was lying on the floor in front of the fireplace which was giving off a warm and cozy glow. Lizzie was sitting on the floor with her and Lizzie was sharing one of her photograph albums. Vicki was surprised but enjoyed hearing the stories about Lizzie's childhood. For the first time she listened as Lizzie cheerfully told how she and Walter met; how the loss of their child was so difficult and almost caused them to lose one another as well before they finally found a way to use their strength in God to cope. There were many more questions Vicki wanted to ask but she waited for another time.

That night, lying in her bed in her little cottage sanctuary, she realized how many people she had met on this adventure of hers and what she had learned from each of them. How different they all were and yet; how they shared so many of the same hopes, dreams, and forbearance to take what comes and be able to step forward and keep going. Every time Vicki made her bed and spread the beautiful quilt on it; she thought about the embroidered one she and her mother had been making at the quilt classes. She wondered if her mother had stored that away and forgotten all about it? Or, wouldn't it be funny if she had gotten it out and was working on it in her absence?

The Memorial

After the evening of their first "date night" after Vicki's disappearance things did, indeed, seem to get a little better. Especially between Ann and Joseph. Probably not as much as they all wished; but better. Ann was much more attuned to feelings and emotions brewing under the surface, but even she was conscious of her part in trying to drawing Joseph, Tony and herself closer.

That is, until the subject of the memorial arose. One Sunday they had gone to church; something which had gone from every single Sunday before Vicki was gone, to a once in a while when Joseph could cajole, plead, and convince Ann to attend with he and Tony. None of them liked dealing with the sad looks and the whispers from the others or worse yet; their careless questions about any news of Vicki.

They're just concerned," Joseph would tell her and she would immediately come back with, "I don't care. I wish they would just leave me alone. They don't know how I feel or how they would feel if it were their child."

Even Joseph wasn't able to soothe or comfort her and he was caught between showing sympathy or trying to give reasons why they should not give up hope.

It came to a head one Sunday afternoon after they had gone to church and Ann had turned down Joseph's offer to take them all to dinner.

"I don't want to go out to eat," Ann said bluntly.

"Why not? It would be good for all of us and you wouldn't have to cook or cleanup."

"I would rather cook and clean up than sit in a restaurant and have people stare at us with pity in their eyes or come by and ask if there is any news."

"They mean well," Joseph said gently.

"I don't care," Ann said. "I don't want to go. You and Tony can go if you want. I'm not really even hungry anyway."

"Oh, great!" Joseph said, this time with an edge of anger. "Ann, we can't go on like this. It's tearing us apart. This family is not a family anymore. We don't talk to one another; we don't play with one another. We never smile, we never even touch one another."

For just a moment Ann felt a jolt of remorse and sympathy for him. This was the man she had chosen to love for the rest of her life. This was the love of her life and the person she used to lean on for everything and she realized she was shutting him out of her life. Wearily she said, turning away from him and walking to the kitchen for a glass of water, "I'm sorry," she said, "I really am, Joseph. I'm going to try harder, really I am."

When she got the water, he came up behind her and put his arms around her.

"I know, I know," he said. Pastor Willis came up to me today and asked if he could come by this afternoon and visit for a little while."

"Oh, geez. Just what I need. It's not enough I have to listen to his platitudes from the pulpit; every time he looks at me and tries to think of some scripture, he can toss out there for me. Now he is coming here. Why don't you visit with him and I'll just take a long nap or even go for a walk?"

"Oh, honey, don't be like that. He's just trying to help."

"They all are. I know it but it doesn't help. Joseph," she said, turning in his arms and laying her head on his chest, I can't stand it. Where is she? Is she safe? Will we ever find her or know what happened?"

He rubbed her back. "Yes, we will, honey, I know we will. I mean it."

"Every time I see one of her little friends, I want to accuse them of knowing something or I want to cry and inside think horrible thoughts like 'Why wasn't it you, instead of my baby?' I know it's awful and I am ashamed of myself but I just can't help it."

When Pastor Willis came over, she was sitting out on the back porch in the swing and Joseph escorted him back there and offered him one of the other chairs.

"How about some iced tea or coffee, Pastor?" Joseph said.

"The tea sounds great," he said.

"It was good of you to come by," Ann said.

"I've been meaning to come but somehow things get away from me," he said and then continued, "We miss you, Ann. You used to be so active in everything before…" He stopped, obviously embarrassed and not knowing how to go on.

"Yeah," Ann said, "Since we lost Vicki, I can hardly function. I just can't focus on anything."

He cleared his throat and accepted the glass of tea from Joseph.

"I wish I had the words to comfort you, Ann but they are just words. Truth is, I don't know to help. I wish I did. That's what brought me today."

Curious, she listened as he said, "Some of the congregation want to do something."

"What?" Ann said bluntly. "What can anyone do?"

"Well, some have mentioned a candlelit service outside the church some evening or even here, at your home…"

As she heard his words, Ann looked at him incredulously. "A candle light service? Are you kidding me?"

Joseph came to sit by her, "Honey, they're just trying to offer a way to show their hope and bring a little comfort to us."

"Well, they can just keep their candlelight service. She's not dead. She's going to come back. Next, they will want to have a funeral without a body, a gravestone and an obituary in the paper. Write her off as if she never existed. Well," she paused, stood and said, "It's not going to happen. Don't you think I would know if she wasn't alive? If she were gone from this earth? I am her mother, for God's sake. Well, no thank you. That's what keeps me going; just knowing she is alive out there somewhere and I will have her home someday; hopefully soon."

She wheeled away and slamming the screen door behind her, went in the house and headed up stairs.

Embarrassed and mortified, Joseph stood and said, "I am so sorry, Pastor. Please excuse her. She's been like this since Vicki has been gone and instead of getting any better, she just gets worse. Her imagination runs wild with where she is and how she is and who could have her. Quite frankly," Joseph said, with his tears welling up, "I am at my wits end. I don't know how to help her. I don't know what to do. It's even worse for Tony. He never wants to be here at his own home anymore. He somehow feels it might be his fault that he was mean to Vicki and drove her away. He doesn't know how to help his mother. When he tries to say something or to put his arms around her, she just stands there, stiff and unresponsive, or she says something hurtful to him and he closes up like a clam."

"Don't apologize, Joseph," the pastor said, putting his arms around Joseph's shoulders. "I thought it was worth a try and that it might be of comfort to her to see how many of her friends are with her in her sorrow. I thought such a service and would be a beacon of hope, not a signal of surrender. I'll go now, but please tell her later that it was not my intention to hurt her even more. Try to stay hopeful, and let me know if there is anything, and I mean anything at all, I can do, please call me."

After the pastor left, Joseph went upstairs and found Ann, not in their bedroom, but in Vicki's, lying across the pink spread, head mashed into the pillow, sobbing. He lay down beside her and rubbed her back like he was comforting a child, making small sounds of "There, there. He was just trying to help. Of course, he didn't mean she was gone. We know that. She will be coming home, sweetheart."

Ann found more and more comfort in the things she could not explain (even to herself) or even openly speak of with Joseph or Tony. Against everything she believed all her life, she began to find clues and signs which she attributed to Vicki. For instance, the little bedside table lamp continued (in fact, grew) to shut off or own at varied and weird times. She almost began to take it as a game; it would be on when she walked by, carrying the fresh laundry to put away; she would snap it off and an hour or so later she when came upstairs to shower, it would be on again.

Um-hum, she would think, *just a short somewhere, right.*

Often, she would find some of Vicki's clothes in the dirty clothes hamper although it was been months now since Vicki had been here to wear any or put them in the hamper. She would wash, dry, and fold them before putting them away only to later find others back in there.

She could not keep Rusty out of Vicki's room. He had even learned to put his paws on both sides of the knob and mess with it until the door swung open and she would find him, again and again, lying on the little braided rug at the side of her bed.

When she would find him, he would lay his head on his paws and have the most wistful and sad look she had ever seen on a dog. Ann found herself not only accepting the signs she saw as legitimate signs relating to Vicki; but almost living daily expecting something unusual or examples of the nearness of Vicki.

When her birthday arrived Tony and Joseph explained that they wanted to take her out to eat that evening. Tony was at school and Joseph was at work and Ann decided to go ahead and take an early shower in preparation. No one was in the house except herself and Rusty. She had just finished cleaning up the breakfast dishes and as she rounded the stairs onto the landing, she first noticed two things: Rusty was again inside Vicki's room, lying on the small braided rug and the small lamp was; once again, turned on. She walked in the room and turned the lamp off, called Rusty out and closed the door once again.

She walked to the master bedroom and suddenly stood, immobilized, frozen into space there on the threshold. In shock, she gasped, and put her hand up to her mouth. *It's impossible,* she told *herself. How did this happen?* There, spread neatly on her bed, was the dress Vicki had selected for her birthday gift last year…The matching high-heels she chose to wear with it then were placed side-by-side on the floor directly under the dress.

Her purse was sitting on the bed, next to the dress. Her fancy hair comb was lying next to the dress, waiting to be used.

She walked slowly into the room, and sat down in the armchair by the window. She had *not,* most certainly had *not* taken this dress or shoes from the closet.

I really am going crazy, she told herself. That's it. I have flipped on over. She thought about calling Joseph; but almost immediately discarded it. He would simply do what he always did, try to talk her out of it with a multitude of excuses and reasons to explain this. How she must have been preoccupied as she got the birthday dress out; perhaps just going on remembrances of last year's birthday with Vicki safe and sound, here with them. As it was, both Joseph and Tony walked around her as though on hot coals and the slightest thing might set her off. They watched what they did, what they said, and ran interference between herself and the outside world. She wanted; of course, for things to revert back to normal, but most of all, she wanted her daughter back. She would never be "back to normal" (whatever that could be) until Vicki had returned to her rightful place; here, with them.

Rusty came and stood, looking somewhat wistfully at her. When she reached out to pat him, he barked once and went to stand in the doorway.

"What do you want, silly thing?" she asked the dog.

When Rusty barked again, then ran to the top of the stairs, she got up and went to join him.

"Okay, so you want to show me something?" She was speaking out loud and she grinned at the incongruity of having a conversation with a dog.

When Tony got home from school Why not? She asked herself. *Lights that go on or off at will by themselves. Clothes that lay themselves out, postcards with no postmarks. What next?*

When Rusty got to the front door, he stood expectedly, waiting for her to open the door. When she did, she gasped once again, in surprise.

There was a free-standing large basket floral arrangement with a huge yellow bow and a ribbon with "Happy Birthday" emblazoned across it.

She looked around but there was no sign of a delivery van or anyone else. The street was empty.

Well, she thought, *I might not have heard the doorbell when they rang it. They're beautiful. I bet Joseph paid a pretty penny for this. He knows I think cut fresh flowers are almost a waste. They don't last long and they are so expensive. Now I have to rave and rant about how beautiful, how thoughtful, and remember to pretend to be thrilled.*

She carried the arrangement into the house and placed it on the center of the dining room table where it would be on display when they got home. She started to call Joseph but decided to wait until he got home to thank him.

Satisfied with having done his duty, Rusty turned and headed back upstairs to once again lay in front of Vicki's door.

Ann waited to dress for going out until Joseph and Tony got home.

She was upstairs when Tony got home from school and she heard him hang his backpack on the hooks by the door, and then, as usual, headed towards the kitchen to find something to eat. She heard his exclamation when he saw the floral arrangement, "Oh, my gosh! Geez, what is that for?"

She laughed and went to the landing, and looking down she said, "My birthday surprise from your foolish father."

Tony was so happy to see a smile on her face, he immediately smiled back and he said, "And he said the new video game I want is too expensive? I'll bet these flowers cost three times that much!"

"Well, you're not pretty enough, I guess…"

Delighted with her teasing, Tony said, "You're worth it, Mom."

A short time later she heard Joseph's car in the driveway and then as the front door opened and closed, he called out, "Anybody home here? Anyone with a birthday?"

"Dad?" Ann heard Tony question.

"I'm up here," Ann called out.

Tony said to Joseph, "Don't you think you kind of got carried away a little bit, Dad?"

"What do you mean?" Joseph asked and then, as he walked to the stairs, he saw the floral arrangement on the table and he said, "What is that? Where did that come from?"

"You tell me," Tony said. "Did you double up and forget you had already ordered some?"

"I certainly did not. I always give her red roses…always…"

Ann started down the stairs and hesitated when she got a look at Joseph, standing immobile at the bottom of the stairs, holding a green tissue-wrapped bouquet of red roses.

Looking up at her, Joseph said, "Well, I certainly have to admit I have been out done here…Where did those," he nodded his head towards the floral arrangement, "come from?"

"I…I…" Ann hesitated before continuing, "I thought they were from you. There's no card."

"I never get you flowers like that. I always get you red roses. You know that. Are you sure there's no card?"

"Well, you can look again, but I couldn't find one."

"What delivery truck was it?"

"When I got to the door, there was no van or car, or truck. No one."

"Well, there's at least three florists in town. I guess we could call each one and see who ordered and paid for them."

Tony grinned and said, "Uh-oh, Dad. Some secret admirer has a crush on Mom. Better watch out."

A faint blush came on Joseph's face. "Quit being silly, Tony. It could be Grandma."

"Nope. She sends potted plants."

Ann, feeling a little sorry for Joseph; standing there with his dozen red roses, quickly went down to the bottom stair, took his bouquet smelled the flowers and then tip-toed up to reach his face and give him a kiss.

"I love my roses, Joseph. Thank you for remembering."

"You're welcome," he said simply.

Eventually it became a life-long puzzle and sort of guessing game of *who sent the flowers?* It remained a long-standing question and it was difficult to decide who thought about it the most…Joseph or Ann? Even when they called the florists in their town; there was no record of the order.

No definitive answer was ever forthcoming and the mystery remained just that-a mystery.

Along the same sort of unexplainable happenings, Mother's Day that year brought an unmarked, uncancelled Mother's Day card in the mailbox. No one saw anyone around the mailbox and though Ann suspected Tony, he swore it wasn't him. It wasn't signed.

Ann's behavior led to a strong reluctance to leave her alone for any unnecessary length of time. Joseph didn't know what he dreaded or where his apprehension came from, just that he was afraid to leave her, especially overnight. He no longer volunteered to chaperone any of Tony's scout campouts or summer camp parent's days unless Ann was with him.

Almost every day he called home at least once to talk to her and when she accused him of spying on her, he immediately denied it and tried to turn it around and blame her suspicious nature.

She had "tightened the noose" around Tony as well, and he resented it. His dad tried to explain her fear of losing him like she had Vicki and meanwhile he tried to get Ann to relax a little with Tony. He even told her once in exasperation that if she continued to keep such a tight rein on him, she would drive him into doing something drastic. After such confrontations, she would get a little better but when he was gone somewhere with his friends, a football game or a school party, she would call him several times on his cell phone. He didn't like it, but knew if he didn't answer, she would go into panic mode and send his father looking for him.

Often Ann would get accusatory with Joseph or Tony or even her own mother (via telephone) insinuating they were moving on with their lives and forgetting all about their missing girl. At times Joseph felt torn between the two choices; acting forlorn and sad, and bringing up memories of Vicki all the time; or moving forward and trying not to bring her up in fear of sending Ann into a depressed and despondent state which would last for days.

It wasn't that Ann did not make efforts, she did. But often the hopelessness of their family surviving seemed unavoidable. Even such a simple thing about Joseph calling her by her Christian name of Ann instead of his teasing, loving "Annie" which he used to when in a good place.

Sometimes Joseph dreaded going home; he felt an affinity with Tony, in trying to avoid being there. It was as if a tent of gloom had descended over the house. There was no more laughter. They were going through the motions but all the love seemed to have been vacuumed out, leaving nothing but the bare necessities. "The car is due an oil change" Ann might tell Joseph and he would promise to take it the next day and he would follow through.

Many days Joseph would see that they had run out of milk or bread or something else and the note pad on the refrigerator had everything scribbled down; but no one had gone to the store.

One of the most dramatic signs was Ann slipping back into sleeping in late in the morning; not bothering to even get up for coffee with Joseph in the mornings. Sometimes he would come home and find her asleep on the couch, still in her pajamas with her hair still uncombed. She had lost a lot of weight, and often he would wake I in the middle of the night to find her wandering through the house in the dark in a daze. He would persuade her back to bed.

She slept an inordinate amount and refused to go to the doctor. After repeatedly trying to convince her to go for a check-up, Joseph finally gave up. Most of the household chores were either falling by the wayside or when things got too much Joseph and Tony would spend the week-end getting things back in order. Physically Ann and Joseph barely touched one another; even when in the same bed. She had always before loved holidays; any holiday, and decorated for all of them. Now she ignored Christmas décor, New Year's, Valentine's, birthdays, Saint Patrick's Day, Easter, even Groundhog's day and Halloween.

Joseph worried his entire personality was changing.

Tony had complained about the atmosphere and looked for excuses to be anywhere except home.

One day when Joseph made out a check to the school cafeteria for Tony's month of lunches, he dropped him off at school and was surprised to find a new face at his office. He was introduced to a new member of the sales team; a young woman named Rebecca. As they shook hands, he was taken by the sparkle in her eyes and the enthusiasm she showed for her new position. She was petite; probably no more than five ft. three, and had her blond hair up in a professional French braid. Joseph wondered what it would look like if it were unleashed and down.

Joseph had never been one of those married men who even considered philandering and it didn't enter his mind now; but he was drawn to her cheerful and optimistic outlook. What he saw in her was the possibility of a good friend.

She made him (along with others) see her cup; not just half full, but totally full. She enjoyed the most menial of tasks and added such a bright outlook to even be a part of her team was considered a bonus.

He was impressed at her willingness to take on extra chores; and was always early to work and usually one of the last to leave each day. He could not deny his excitement when she was assigned to pair with him the next time he was assigned on an overnight sales convention in Knoxville. He didn't mention her addition to the office to Ann for worry she would feel his interest or approval of her would be inappropriate.

The new employee's cheerful conversation made the trip seem almost like a vacation; rather than the mundane and routine drive it usually was.

He showed her photos of Ann and Tony and touched lightly on having a daughter who he and his wife had "lost". She expressed sympathy and it was sincere and he could feel her empathy.

He anticipated her success in the sales department, with her obvious enthusiasm and seemingly honest belief with their products.

She did not dress provocatively, but still aroused interest and admiration among the masculine members at his office, including himself.

Her presence made him more aware of how much he missed Ann; the "old" Ann. Often, some little feminine gesture or comment from Rebecca even reminded him of how much he and Ann used to relate to each other. It made him feel lonely and even spurred him into new efforts to try to recapture some of the relationship he and Ann used to share. He would go home, filled with new resolve; usually only to be turned away by Ann's lack of interest or response.

If there was any long-lasting effect Rebecca's addition had on him; it was that it did renew his efforts with Ann. He continued to be driven to try and try again.

Sometimes he smiled as he wondered what Rebecca would think if she knew what he drew from her optimistic and positive attitude to make a difference in his own family.

He had never accepted nor appreciated any of the sexist or off-colored attitudes of some of the men in their business circle and had always had a reputation of integrity and fairness among his co-workers. He would "cut them off at the pass" when such comments or attitudes occurred. When Joseph heard gossip of any wrong-doing among their staff, he had no problem with giving his staunch disapproval.

It was true that this gave him somewhat a reputation of being old-fashioned or strait-laced, he was still very much liked and respected by both genders in his workspace. The women found him polite and well-mannered and the men respected and admired his work ethic and dedication to the job.

It was more likely he would give a woman a compliment on a job well done or her cooperation in a project than on her personal appearance.

Still, it was not easy for him (and others) to respond to this new member of their firm. Her constant positivity was very contagious.

Joseph had noticed many of the responses towards Rebecca from the males in the staff; but to her credit, she seemed oblivious to it; especially when it came from some of the less respectful co-workers. She seemed totally unaware of their inuendoes or casual references to anything not work related. Joseph admired her for that.

When they went on that first sales convention, Joseph couldn't help but admire her professionalism as well as her company. She took copious notes, asked many questions about other companies and their products and spoke knowledgably to other representatives about their own products.

At the end of the first day, Joseph asked her: "Want to meet back here for the dinner meeting?"

"Sure," she replied.

They met at the agreed-on time and she had changed from her smart business suit to a less formal dress. He almost didn't recognize her with her hair down, but was aware of the number of looks she got from others as they entered the dining room and found their place cards.

The meal wasn't anything special; the roast beef was dry, green beans tasteless, and the familiar mashed potatoes.

"The best thing about these meals," Joseph said, "is the coffee and pie."

She grinned. "I am so hungry I could eat anything."

He watched without comment as she cleaned her plate.

Some of the speakers were interesting and some were boring, but Joseph enjoyed his conversation with Rebecca more than any of the speakers.

When dinner was over, they allowed some of the guests to file out before they got up to follow, Joseph said, "Would you like to go to the after dinner open bar for a free drink?" he asked her.

"No, I think I'll go on up and go through some of this literature we got today."

"What? Don't want to make some contacts?"

"It's been my experience that most contacts made at things like this are the first forgotten in the light of day. Besides, frankly, I always get "hit" on at these things and I run out of excuses to get away from the married men who view sales conventions like this as opportunities to forget they're married."

Joseph couldn't keep from laughing. "Ah, you've got them figured out, right?"

"You bet."

"Well, I'll see you to your room then and what meeting down here at the restaurant for breakfast?"

He was impressed with her honesty and her decision to skip the bar. He told her good night at her door and whistled as he went on to his. His respect for her went up several notches.

The rest of the conference went smoothly, and as they were driving home, Rebecca saw a roadside stand and she asked Joseph if they had time to stop.

"Sure, we're in no big hurry, are we?"

They pulled in and parked off the road. Rebecca went down the row of good, picking out a small basket of strawberries and some beautiful tomatoes. Then she headed to the other side with a little gleeful sound.

"Oh, look, Joseph; Marigolds! Aren't they beautiful?"

He nodded, and had to agree that their bright golden colors were by far the most beautiful flowers on display.

Rebecca asked the person behind the counter, "It's a little early for these, isn't it?"

"Yes, yes, it is; but these stay inside my greenhouse during the cooler weather. They're my babies. My favorite flowers. I take good care of them. I even named my eldest daughter Marigold."

Rebecca smiled. "Well, they're beautiful, aren't they Joseph?"

He nodded and remembered when he and Ann had been on their honeymoon, he had purchased a small bouquet of Marigolds from a street vender who was selling the bright bunches tied with lavender ribbons. She had been so disappointed when they began to wilt and fade from their place in the hotel glass of water. He remembered he had taken them out, and gently pressed them in one of her books to try and preserve them as a remembrance of their happy trip.

Briefly, looking at the these he was brought back to the happiness of their former lives and wondered if their marriage was a lost cause now and where they would be this time next year; or for that matter, even next month. It all seemed so hopeless somehow. He wondered if those long-ago Marigolds were still pressed somewhere in one of her books…long forgotten and dried, like their marriage seemed to be now.

He was roused back to the present when Rebecca said softly, "Why don't you pick out some flowers to take home to Ann, Joseph?"

He smiled at her, and then looked around and said, "I don't see any roses, do you?"

"Yes, over there," she said as she pointed.

As he started that way, she took hold of his sleeve and said, "No, Joseph. Why not the Marigolds?"

He hesitated and said, "Well, I always get her red roses."

"Well, even better! The Marigolds will be a special surprise."

He got swept up with Rebecca's enthusiasm and picked out a bunch of the Marigolds. The woman wrapped them with a wet tissue on their stems, then a layer of green tissue paper. When Joseph saw her tie the bunch together with a lavender ribbon, he swallowed and felt a warmth in his hands as he took them from her.

"Thank you, that's perfect," he told her.

Although he and Rebecca kept up an interesting and lively conversation on the drive home, his mind kept returning to the small bunch of Marigolds he had lain in the back floorboard behind his driver's seat. *Would she remember the first Marigolds? Why had he not remembered them before this day? When had he changed the traditional Marigolds to roses? And why? Maybe because as the years passed and he earned more money he felt he should invest in a more expensive flower; after all, weren't Marigolds the next thing to a weed? In fact, didn't he sometimes now even buy a houseplant so she could replant it later in her flower bed? Before they married, he remembered once; when they were engaged, but not yet married, they had talked about what their married lives were going to be like. What they would avoid about their own parents lives together and how they would keep the romance alive and growing, no matter what.*

"I'll never go to bed with curlers," she had said, giggling.

"What if I think you are cute in curlers?" he asked.

"You wouldn't think so if you saw me like that," she said

"I will never forget out anniversary," he had said, seriously.

"I will cook your favorite meal at least once a week" she said.

"And I will say it's delicious, even if it's not…"

"I will never go to bed mad at you. I will always make up before then."

"And I will never buy you a household appliance for a present. We will buy things like that together."

"What will you buy me instead of a vacuum or a mixer?" she asked, pulling back from his shoulder to look up at him better.

"Oh, black lacy underwear, beautiful, soft, satiny gowns, jewelry-when we can afford it—sweet smelling perfume and beautiful flowers."

"Did I hear you say you would buy me black lacy underwear and beautiful gowns?"

He looked down at her and said, "Sure. You're the sexiest girl I ever met."

"Oh. Well, thank you but I was planning on sleeping without anything but your arms."

He had laughed then and pulled her close for a kiss. How well he remembered that time and that conversation. How long ago and difficult it was to remember the joy of those days. Where; and most importantly, why; had it gone?

CHAPTER EIGHTEEN

Marigolds and Quilts

"Hey, you daydreaming over there?" Rebecca's voice brought his mind back to the present.

"Sorry, I was just running over what might be on our desks after missing two days."

"How boring, Joseph. Enjoy the rest of this day. Let tomorrow take care of itself."

If only it could, he thought. *If only it could.*

He dropped Rebecca at the office so she could transfer her bags to her car and then waved as she headed to her own home.

When he arrived home, he got his suitcase from the trunk and picked up the small bouquet of Marigolds and set the suitcase down to unlock the door. Since Vicki's absence they always locked doors and windows and were even more vigilant about setting the security alarms.

When he got inside, he hung his key ring on the small wall plaque which said "keys Please", set his suitcase down and called out, "Hello, anybody home? Tony? Ann?"

He heard Tony calling from the back porch, "Dad, we're out here in the back."

He walked to the back porch and saw Tony playing with Rusty, throwing his ball and praising him when he quickly retrieved it.

Ann looked up from where she was curled on the porch swing. She was wearing her night clothes including her robe and her face reflected the weariness which was often common to her expression now days.

Joseph had been holding the small bouquet behind him.

Tony had noticed and he said, "Whatcha' got there, Dad? Did you bring me something?"

"Not this time."

"I'm not too big for surprises, Dad. You should remember that…" Tony was grinning.

Joseph walked over and bending down a little he gave Ann a gentle kiss on her head and reached out to her with the Marigolds.

She looked at them and she gasped, and reached out for them, standing up.

"Oh, Joseph…Joseph…" she said, laying her head on his chest.

She put her arms around him, and she said, "Marigolds! You brought me Marigolds." She began to cry.

Tony looked from one to the other. Then he asked, "Mom, why are you crying? Dad brought you flowers. Doesn't that make you happy? Why are you crying?"

, "Oh, Tony," she said, still looking up at Joseph. "These are happy tears, Tony. Marigolds are special to Dad and me."

"Well, when I'm happy, I smile or laugh. I don't cry."

Ann smiled at Joseph and he took his handkerchief from his inside pocket and wiped her eyes and face with it gently.

"I love you, Ann." Joseph said.

"And I love you, too," she replied.

Tony looked at his parents and seemed slightly embarrassed as he said, "Oh, no…Here comes the mushy stuff."

Both Joseph and Ann laughed and his father said, "Someday you will look forward to this 'mushy stuff', Tony."

"Maybe so, but I wouldn't bet on it. I'm going down to meet with Chad so you guys can cry or get all mushy or whatever. I will see you later."

He left and Ann said, "I'm going to go put these in a little water." As she was walking towards the kitchen, she hooked her arm into Joseph's and she said, "Are you hungry? Did you eat? Want me to fix you something?"

"I am a little hungry. Maybe something small to hold me off until dinner."

"How about an omelet?"

"That's sounds perfect."

He sat on one of the stools and watched as she busied herself in preparing his food.

When she placed it in front of him and poured him a cup of freshly made coffee she said,

"While you eat, I'm going upstairs and take my shower."

"Okay."

Joseph couldn't help it…A warm feeling swept through him. The Marigolds had been just the thing. She had been very moved. Her response gave him hope. Things would and could get better. It would just take patience and efforts from he and Tony.

When he finished eating, he rinsed the dishes and silver and placed them in the dishwater. He picked up his suitcase and went upstairs to the master bedroom to unpack and separate his clothes for laundry and for putting the rest away.

Ann's robe lay on the bed with a pair of pajamas. He heard the water running in the bathroom and then he heard Ann's voice calling, "Joseph…Joseph…Can you come here a minute?"

He walked over to the door to the bathroom, and opening it just a crack he looked into the steamy room and said, "I'm here, Ann. What do you need? Forget a towel?"

He saw the shower door open just a crack, and Ann's face, water and hair dripping down appeared as she said, "Will you wash my back?"

Joseph was stunned. He stood for a minute, then, as she pulled her head back inside the shower, Joseph quickly took his tie, followed by his shirt, shoes, socks, slacks and boxers. He let them lay and opening the other end of the shower he stepped inside the warm stream inside the shower and shut it behind him.

She had her back turned to him but he didn't know if it was a slight embarrassment at this unusual and almost forgotten activity they used to frequently share or just so he had access to her back to lather it up and begin to wash it.

"That feels so good," Ann said.

"It's been a long time since we did this…"

"Too long," she replied.

They took turns lathering each other up and then rinsing off. Joseph accepted the kiss she offered and he whispered "I'm going to subscribe to a daily delivery of Marigolds," he said into her ear.

She laughed. "Cheaper than diamonds and so much more effective, right?"

Joseph got out first and got a big, fluffy towel to wrap around her, then got one for himself.

As they walked into the bedroom, Ann walked over to the bed, and pulled back the covers. She looked at Joseph and said, grinning, "Tony is gone to Chad's, Rusty is outside…How about we jump inside these covers and warm up a little?"

"I'm up for that."

Joseph walked over and stripped her towel off and picked her up and laid her in the bed. Then he pulled his towel off and climbed in next to her. He couldn't help but notice how much thinner she was than she used to be and he fought to keep from losing his composure and tearing up.

* * *

Things got considerably better after that. Ann even began to speak Vicki's name occasionally, instead of avoiding it at all costs. She still affirmed that she knew Vicki was alive and would eventually be home again, but Joseph thought this was the one thing which kept her from giving up and falling completely apart. As for himself, he believed she had met up with some ruthless and unbalanced crazy somewhere and the case would more than likely never be solved. He grieved for his daughter, but it was with an acceptance of her probable fate which Ann simply could not do.

Perhaps the most difficult days were the holidays, including anniversaries and family birthdays. Vicki's birthday was especially difficult. When good-hearted but thoughtless friends and neighbors would try and speak hopefully to her with optimistic inquiries about any fresh news, her eyes would glaze over and she found herself tuning them out. Ann was not good at these conversations and yet, she realized they meant well. All the while they were being grateful it was her family and not theirs which had been struck down with this horrible twist of fate, bad luck, or whatever a person's faith led them to believe was the cause. She could almost read the sympathy she saw in their eyes, and hear the unspoken "why?"

These two words were the ones she, herself, asked the most often. "Why me? Why us?"

But she never had an answer.

Ann was trying hard to retain some of the warmth which came with the Marigolds from Joseph; and she could recognize the same kind of efforts from him but that it took a definite effort on her part was painful. She knew she loved him still, and that none of this was his fault; but often she found herself again asking "Why? What have we done to deserve this?"

It became almost a routine task to stop by Vicki's room and turn the little lamp off; only to find it lit once again later the same day.

One afternoon she felt encouraged to give some of the house a more intensive cleaning; partially because during her lowest days, she had been doing only what really necessary and letting other chores simply slide. She would tell herself: *We never have company anymore, it will be here tomorrow, none of it really matters, does it? No one would notice such activity except for Joseph; who quietly and efficiently "picked up the slack" when he noticed something needed attention. Often his gentle efforts to do much more than his "share" made her realize how important he was to her and how lucky she was that he was the kind of man he was.*

As she tried to replace some photo albums on the shelves in the hall closet where they kept old board games, forgotten and no longer used or even dusted off, several material items fell to the floor, and on her head.

When she began to untangle the mess, she saw the quilt she and Vicki had begun working on last summer together. As a special project they had joined a quilting class at the local YWCA summer program. She got permission to be off one afternoon a week; and she chose Thursdays. Ann would allow Vicki to sleep in a little later, and she would go to work for half a day and then pick her up for lunch and then go to their 1:30 p.m. quilting class. If they were faithful in their attendance, by the end of the summer the two of them would have a finished quilt. It was a very intricate pattern they chose; not just squares of material sewn together for the top of the quilt, but each square had an appliqué to embroider of a different flower. There was going to be a border comprised of bright green leaves. Every other flower square would be Vicki's, alternating with those done by Ann.

Ann sat down on the floor there in the hallway, she spread some of the quilt top out and looked at the brightly colored flowers. There was a purple iris, red rose, yellow buttercup, pink hyacinth, an orchid, sunflower, daisy, blue-bonnet, tulips and a square with holly leaves and bright red berries.

She began to look at the squares which had been emblazoned with the inked pattern but not started with the embroidery as yet. There was an embroidery ring holding the next square to be embroidered, and a needle already threaded with white thread for the white carnation to come to life.

Setting aside the unfinished quilt top, her small sewing box with other threads and needles, she put all the games back up on the shelves neatly, and closed the door.

She finished the laundry she had started, fixed herself a sandwich and iced tea for lunch.

She turned on the television and after she finished her lunch, she picked up the embroidery hoop and began embroidering the half-finished square. At first, she was awkward and it did not feel natural, but as she continued, she began to achieve a sort of rhythm. She enjoyed seeing the flower take shape and color as she worked. She thought to herself, this will be my goal. I will finish the quilt before Vicki gets back, and she will be so surprised. She will also know I thought of her every time I worked on the quilt. Ann knew it was a very substantial goal, but that it was achievable. She was determined to meet the challenge. She also realized that it wasn't just the flower squares, but joining them to one another, making the top. Then, the fill or batting for the inside of the quilt, then the backing, then the quilting of all the layers and the binding. She knew it was a king size and therefore quite the project but she felt the excitement fill her. She was tempted to count how many squares that were left to be embroidered, but resisted it. She didn't want to be depressed at the number which remained. She decided, instead to begin counting with the one she was working on today and see how many she could get done in a day, a week, a month.

For some unknown reason, this project filled her with optimism. She welcomed the feeling of doing something; as though this were a path straight to Vicki. Perhaps Vicki was somewhere right now, remembering their work together on this quilt. The thought was energizing and exciting. Especially when she had heard so many say, "There's nothing you can do except wait and pray, Ann. There is nothing you can do…"

Well, she told herself as Rusty came up on the back porch and lay down by her feet, *Now I have something I can do.*

When Joseph arrived home that afternoon he called out and Ann called back, "I'm on the back porch, Joseph."

When he came out to the porch, he bent his head and she raised hers for the small kiss he bestowed on her cheek.

He picked up a corner of the quilt top and said, "What's all this?"

"Remember when Vicki and I were going to that quilting class last summer? This is the top of it we were going to make all embroidered flowers. I came across it when I was cleaning today and decided to get it out and work on it. That way, maybe I can even have it finished when she comes home."

Joseph felt his heart jump at her words but then he said, "That would be a great surprise for her."

"I think so, too. And I love picking out the colors for the different flowers."

"Any Marigolds on there?"

She smiled at him. "Of course."

"Well, if you need some to look at while you work, let me know and I will run down to the florist and get some."

She grinned. "What kind of reward would you expect?"

"Um, let me think on it." He was smiling, too.

"I was thinking that when I get to the center of the quilt top, I might save the very center square for a poinsettia, with Vicki's name in the center since Christmas was Vicki's favorite holiday. What do you think?"

Joseph had to swallow again before he replied, but Ann was looking down at the quilt top in her lap and she didn't notice his pause.

"I think that would be perfect," he said softly.

After that it was very rare that Ann did not have the quilt top close at hand. In her lap, hands busily going in and out. Joseph fell into the habit of looking at the thread color to see if she was on the same color as when he last looked. He noticed if the thread color had changed; that way he was able to keep track of her progress.

To him it seemed she was flying through squares; but there were so many left he could not even make a guess at how many she could do in a day or a week.

When she agreed to ride along with Tony and him and go sit on the bank while they fished, he was so happy for her willing company he felt grateful for the project. She insisted on bringing the quilt-top along and she spread out a blanket to sit on while they fished. She had packed a basket lunch and midday the guys stopped long enough to come eat. Ann set aside the quilt-top, and She made gentle fun of Joseph's inability to catch any fish while Tony had caught three already.

It was the best day they had had as a family in a long, long time and Joseph eagerly latched on to it as a sign of better things coming their way. True, there was no mention of Vicki, and Joseph knew she was there, underlying Ann's thoughts at the missing part of the family, yet it was still a big improvement over the past few months.

Felling a trifle silly, he thought, *Thank you, God, for the quilt. Thank you for Rebecca's suggestion about the Marigolds. Thank you for giving Ann some hope.*

Thereafter, the little sewing basket went almost everywhere Ann went. Of-course, she did not take it anywhere she needed her two hands; grocery shopping, driving to the pharmacy, bakery, or other places where she was alone. However, if she chose to accompany Joseph to watch one of Tony's athletic events, other fishing trips, even once on a Sunday when Joseph wanted to go into his office to get caught up on some reports, she took it along and worked on it while he sat at his desk and quietly worked on his paperwork.

Even though there were plenty of opportunities to tease her about it; Joseph and Tony both restrained themselves. The quilt-top had taken on a meaning of its own and had changed their lives for the better.

Joseph was a pragmatic man; not given to much imagination or fanciful daydreaming, and yet this quilt was beginning to become a focus in his life. In a sense *he worried about what would happen if Ann finished it and there was still no sign of Vicki. Would she revert back into that dark hole of depression?* He would then reassure himself that the moment was a long way off. According to his questions to Ann, even after all the squares were embroidered, there was sewing them together, doing the filling; whatever that entailed, the back, the binding…So, he would push his worries aside and enjoy the present, more hopeful and optimistic view of the future. True, the somewhat silly or trivial importance he was attaching to the progress of the quilting would not have made perfect sense to others, it did to the three in their now smaller family. They needed something (which in this case had been transferred to the quilt) to mark their hope on…to hold on to as a real measuring advance towards a goal. Their mantra had become *"When the quilt is done…"*

These words weren't often said aloud, but all three often thought them. None of them added or said "if" the quilt were done, or when the quilt is done…but their thoughts were always *when the quilt was finished…*

CHAPTER NINETEEN

Ball Game

Ever years since Tony had been old enough to play "T-Ball"; Joseph had coached in whatever age league Tony played in. It wasn't just that he considered it his duty to volunteer. So many of the parents did not offer to help, yet eagerly signed their children up. Many would attend the games, cheering for their child, but didn't want the commitment to assist with practices or substitute for the coach when necessary. Still, he felt it as his responsibility; and, truth be known, he enjoyed it.

As he prepared for this year's season, Tony had moved up in age and division and Joseph was especially excited when Ann started attending not just the games, but many of the practices. She began to talk with the other parents did came, and she brought her quilting basket and worked on some of the squares while she talked and watched. It wasn't necessary for her to bring the entire quilt; she wasn't nearly far enough along to need to do that; she could pick out some squares, the colors she would need, her embroider hoop and needle (with a spare, just in case) and be all set to go.

Joseph and Tony were both excited at this progress; both in her seeing him play and watching how fond the players were of Joseph and his coaching; but also, the socialization which seemed to indicate progress on Ann's mental health and coping with her grief.

The other parents welcomed her into their circle and Joseph was very happy with their acceptance of her and of the attempt on her part to fit in.

Once, when had hit a wonderful ball way out into left field and the other team member was hustling to try to retrieve it; Tony rounded third base; Ann was on her feet, cheering him on to home, clutching her squares of quilting patterns in one hand and her embroidery hoop in the other. Suddenly, right after Tony touched third and started for home; everyone was on their feet, yelling for him and to her horror, Ann (and Tony) saw that Tony's shoe had come off. He paused, looked back when he realized one foot was shoeless, hesitated and Ann yelled, "Don't go back, Tony! Keep on going, son! Keep going!"

By that time Joseph was hollering the same thing, and Tony aimed his body towards home base and lowered his head and zeroed his focus. The shoe lay where it had come off, and Tony; to everyone's great delight (even members of the other team) he slid safely into home base, saving the run. There he stood, proudly one shoe off and one shoe on, grinning like a banshee as his team members slapped his shoulders and cheered for him.

To herself, Ann said, *I wish Vicki had been here to see that! She always used to nag him about tying those laces up tight.* That evening, after the winning score, Ann even went along with other parents and team members to the Pizza place to celebrate. With quiet amazement, Joseph watched as Ann even joined the toasts and had a beer with the other adults; something she very rarely did. She loved wine, but for her to have a beer with everyone else that evening marked a definite milestone; at least in Joseph's and Tony's eyes. All the way home the glory was relieved, moment by moment and move by move. Joseph began to experience a small additional measure of hope for their future. He would have been thrilled to know that at this exact moment, his daughter was thinking about him.

CHAPTER TWENTY

Same Game, New Coach

As the weather warmed and the flowers began to blossom, Vicki was surprised to see Walter come into the café wearing a T-Shirt, bright orange and emblazoned with a snarling tiger with the letters on the back identifying the team name of "The Fighting Tigers" and on the front was "COACH".

"What's that all about?" she asked Lizzie.

"Oh, my goodness, get ready for crazy season around here. Walter coaches an all-girl's slow pitch baseball team called the Fighting Fighters."

Immediately Vicki thought about her father and Tony and their annual total submersion in baseball. Of-course, theirs was always boy's; whatever section Tony's age had moved him into since last season. Her father had tried to talk her into playing in a girl's league several times but truth was she had no confidents in her ability to even hit the ball, much less catch it.

Walter immediately began an earnest pitch to enlist her on his new team; he claimed that due to members moving, new ones coming in, having birthdays which shifted them around he was short players, as well as assistants.

"Doesn't Lizzie or Joyce play or help coach?"

"They help coach when I need them; but this is a girls' team, no adults allowed. Come on, Vicki, you can help me out here. I need you. Besides, it will be fun."

"I have never even hit a ball or caught one, either. No experience at all."

"We've got time before the season and practices begin; I can teach you all you need to know."

"I know enough that you need good players on first, and third, for shortstop, and catcher."

"See there: You do know something about the game, after all."

After continued begging, alternating with nagging, Vicki began to consider it.

One Saturday morning Walter came in with a sack from the local sporting goods and wearing a huge grin. He sat down in a booth and motioned Vicki to come over.

"It's a little early for lunch, Walter, isn't it?" Vicki asked him.

"I'm not here for lunch. I'm here for a delivery."

"Delivery? For who? For what?"

"For you. Although it's an investment for me…and I guess a gift for me, as well as you."

"For me?"

H passed the sack over to her. "Go ahead, look inside."

Vicki opened the bag. Instead, she found a baseball mitt, a softball, a Tiger Team T-Shirt.

She laughed but said, "Hey, I never said I would do this!"

"I know…but I was counting on your good heart to help me out. Come on, now, Vicki, it will be fun."

Eventually he wore her down and they set up a practice session; first it would be just Walter and Vicki; he wanted to give her some confidence (and skills) before they started meeting with the rest of the team members. He wanted it to turn out a good experience for her; no one feels comfortable doing something brand new and failing.

He was pleasantly surprised to find she had a natural bend for the game. Yes, it would take some practice, he thought, but there was definitely some talent there. He would start her out in the field, and see where her training and interest would take her.

On Vicki's part, she was surprised at the excitement she began to feel for being a participant. It was true she used to watch Tony play, and had a general knowledge of the rules and how the game was played but being a participant was a totally different thing. She actually admitted (only to herself) she liked it.

She understood (and was quite relieved) to find out that Walter was assigning her to left field. She was becoming more confident in her catching abilities; but often felt like she would never be able to connect the bat with that ball. She was embarrassed every time she swung the bat and realized she had been too slow (or too fast).

She asked for an extra shirt so she would have one to wear and one to wash. *Boy,* she thought, *wouldn't Dad and Tony be surprised to see me now?* She was so nervous when she met the other members of the team; but they were all friendly and welcomed her. It helped that she was not the only "newbie"; but there were also some left over from last year's team; still in this age group and she was slightly intimidated by their prowess. She wondered at some of Walter's choices for assignments; but after observing some of them play, she felt impressed with how much she agreed with him. The girl, named Trina; chosen for pitching and Mary-Beth as her alternative were both very gifted and Vicki couldn't help but feel a little envious. She worked very hard at every practice session and began to see some improvement.

When the first game day came her excitement was at war with her nervousness. The questions rolled round and round: *Would she strike out when she came to bat? Would she fall down or get stuck on a base? Would she miss an easy catch out in the field? Would Walter be ashamed of her performance? Would her team win? Many people; not just parents, would come to the games and she was sure many would recognize her from the café. She didn't want to let anyone down.*

When the actual game began, her nervousness began to settle down, except, of course, for the first time at bat. She felt so lucky when the first ball flew by-she didn't strike at it; which was because she didn't even see the pitcher let it go; but this turned out to be a good thing, because the umpire ruled it a ball.

She struck very high at the next pitch and it was called a strike.

The next pitch was termed a ball and she felt good that she had mentally judged it right.

She struck at the next one and missed.

The very next pitch was another ball called by the umpire and thus; she got to walk to first base.

She began her ball experience hoping to have as little attention drawn to herself as possible so if she made a serious bad play, fewer people would now where to lay the blame; but as her confidence improved, she realized most people did not focus in on specific performance (unless a really, really spectacular move by a player occurred) by individual players, she was able to relax somewhat.

As the ump called another ball, *How lucky!* Vicki thought as she jogged to first base.

She didn't realize just how lucky it had been until the next team member up to bat happened to be the best batter they had; their pitcher, Trina.

Trina hit the bat with a resounding loud "crack" and it flew towards the outfield. By the time she dropped the bat she was on her way to first and of-course, Vicki was pressured to get moving. She touched second base, and didn't look back, but continued through second. Ever conscious of Trina coming up behind her, Vicki kept on running, careful to make sure she touched third base, she felt like she was flying as she made it to home plate.

It seemed Trina was almost on top of her when she reached home.

Everyone was yelling and slapping her and Trina on the shoulders; hugs were given and shouts roared out.

The enthusiasm continued after the game started, but it did not turn out to be a pushover, several times during the gave the score was tied; but they did finally win. Final score was eighteen to seventeen. The game victory was even sweeter because the score was so close.

After the game, Walter took the entire team to the café where they enjoyed hamburgers, fries and soft drinks. Lots of laughter, and reliving the favorite parts of the game.

Walter said, "Hey, Vicki, I saw you out there, looking at all the little wildflowers growing in the field."

"I was not!"

"Well, it looked like it to me."

"Lucky you didn't get hit in the head with the ball." He was laughing and she caught on that he was just teasing.

"Well, it was kind of boring. They weren't exactly tip-top hitters."

"Ho, you say that now but they came close. One more run and you might have had to work a little bit out there."

"Don't worry, coach, I had it all under control."

"When can I except a home run from you?"

She almost choked on the coke she was drinking and then said, "Soon, coach, soon."

"You tell him," Trina said.

As her skills increased, so did her love for the game begin to grow. She loved the excitement and the possibility each time she went to bat. She was even proud of the callouses she begin to develop from all her practice at the batting cage. Walter told her not to overdo it; "she was doing fine," he insisted. She was so thrilled when she began to at least get on base with something other than a ball. She was determined to get a home run before the season was over. Each game seemed to not only bring her higher in skills; but also, a sense of camaraderie which had been missing in her life; even before her undertaking of this great adventure of hers. She found herself enjoying the approval of her team-mates and Walter as her coach.

She wondered about her new enthusiasm for this activity. And, when she thought about it; for sewing as well. Was there something in her personality makeup which made her choose arbitrarily against what she suspected was what others wanted or expected from her? So, she chose the opposite of what she perceived others wanted? Had she been guilty of a sort of passive resistance to whatever her parents had wanted for her; just wanting to make her own choices? She wondered what she may have missed out on merely by being contrary.

She hoped this had not been her guiding force; realizing this might mean some of her most productive and positive choices might have been missed merely because she didn't want others to tell her what to do. She knew she did not want to be one of those who often lived-in regret, saying "I wish I had done that."

Meanwhile her life was busy, ball practice and games, working at the café, household chores and care for Aphrodite.

She began to notice a lessoning of energy in Lizzie's days. She thought at first it was just the extremely busy days she kept and the willingness to do for others when they needed it; she wished she would take some time off. Walter noticed it, too. He tried to convince her to make an appointment for a check-up with their doctor, but she refused, making light of his concerns. She reluctantly began taking a one-a-day vitamin; just to pacify Vicki and Walter, but it didn't seem to have any effect. She had trouble sleeping and often Walter would wake to find her sitting on the porch overlooking the edge of the creek and forest in the back of the house. She would make some excuse or another, but another sure point of worry was when she began to accede to someone else closing up at night. They had always had a hard and fast rule that there always be two together, especially if the schedule called for two women to lock up; and usually it had been Lizzie and or Walter being at least one. Now, without too much argument, she allowed others to do it; and she left about 4:30 or 5:00 p.m. before the evening dinner crush.

She began to lose a little weight and while at first, she claimed it was voluntary on her part; she had always been a little overweight and in the past had tried a multitude of diets and her weight had fluctuated up and down. Now it was very noticeable she was losing weight and not gaining it back.

Gathering up her courage and putting aside her concern that Lizzie would be upset with her for forcing the subject, one afternoon when there were fewer customers, Vicki cornered her in the kitchen and as they were both doing prep for the evening dinner trade, she confronted her.

Walter had mentioned that Lizzie could not go the entire night without getting up to go to the bathroom at least once, and usually it was two or three times.

"Lizzie, why won't you go to the doctor for a check-up? At least to set Walter's mind at ease?" asked Vicki.

When Lizzie hesitated briefly before answering, Vicki continued, "We love you and we're worried about you. Are you afraid?"

Lizzie scoffed at the idea. "What have I got to be afraid of?"

"Well, people, myself included, always follow the old saying, 'pray for the best, but be prepared for the worst' Isn't that kind of what you are doing? Wouldn't it be just as likely that, at your age- "Vicki stumbled over these words but Lizzie laughed. Vicki continued, "Might it not be a simple thing, readily fixed with medicine or diet change or…slowing down a little?"

"Yes, I supposed so."

"Well, I would be willing to go along with you."

Now Lizzie laughed again.

"Well, I thank you, child and I know you mean well, but I will make an appointment and go for a physical. It has been a long while. I always seem to be too busy for pampering myself."

"It's not pampering yourself. It's protecting me and Walter. We don't want to end up doing your job as well as ours,"

These last words were said jokingly and Lizzie took them that way.

"It's probably a kidney or bladder infection"

"What makes you think that?"

"Well, for one thing all I seem to do is pee. And when I need to go, it's sometimes too urgent for me to even get to the bathroom."

"Can't they just give you a urine test to either confirm or deny that's what it is?"

"Yes."

"Well, make your appointment. Please."

"Okay, okay. I will do it."

So, an appointment was made and though no one said anything other about it; everyone in the café, from Vicki and Walter, to all the staff knew the exact day and time the visit was scheduled.

She was gone considerable time; at least that was the consensus of everyone; upwards of two hours or so and you could have heard a pin drop in the kitchen when she walked in the back door. No one said anything until Lizzie said, grinning, "Boy, what a waste of time."

"Why? What did he say?" Walter asked.

"Well, the good news is that it is related to my kidneys. One of them isn't working too well. The doctor wants to try some dialysis treatments to see if we can enlarge the opening. Right now, every time I go to the bathroom, When I finish and get up, I am leaving a residue of urine in the kidney. Then; I get prescriptions for antibiotics, take them, the infection goes away, then a short time later, here Is another infection since my kidney is not emptying completely."

"Nothing really, the vampires took several vials of blood, checked my weight; which I might add, he approved of; and took x-rays of my chest, though he said it sounded good, and set up an appointment over at the hospital for a Cat-scan."

Both Walter and Vicki's eyes widened somewhat at this news and Walter asked, "Why was that necessary?"

"Don't get your feathers in an uproar," Lizzie said. He said it's more of case of ruling things out until we find something, we can rule in. He didn't seem overly concerned. I am glad you made me go. He did give me a prescription for some extra iron because he said I was a little anemic. He also said that might account for my drop in energy. He sent the bloodwork and urine same to the lab and will call me and set another appointment to go over all that when it comes back. What a bill all that nonsense is going to cost."

"It's not a waste if you get to feeling more your old self, mean as that often is," Walter said, trying to put some levity into the conversation. Give me the prescription and I'll go to the pharmacy and get it."

"I stopped on the way home and got it."

"Well, where is it? Take one right now and get started."

"I have to eat something first. The nurse said some people get nauseated if they don't."

"Well, go sit down, and decide what you want. We'll get it for you."

"Walter!" she said in reply, "Stop. You're making me nervous. I'm not crippled or wounded or otherwise incapacitated. Don't expect immediate results from the iron. The doctor said it may take up to six weeks to reach my system and start making me feel like Wonder Woman."

"He looked at her rather sheepishly and said, "That sounds more like my regular Lizzie."

"Oh, and Vicki," Lizzie said, "I may send you to nursing school."

Vicki looked at her questioningly.

"Well, he did mention that a change in hormones as we get older can cause lots of weird symptoms. Maybe it's all because I am getting older."

Vicki smiled with her.

Often, in the next two weeks before the doctor called to say the tests results were back, Vicki observed Lizzie making concentrated efforts to do more than she had been; mostly to convince them all that she was feeling better or that the iron pills were miracle workers. She tried as much as could, without allowing Lizzie to notice to take some of the day's loads from Lizzie, and so did Joyce and some of the rest of the staff. She didn't go home early very often and Vicki knew that sometimes Walter would decide to grill something for the two of them to entice her to come home early and keep him company allowing Joyce and Vicki or the long-time staff members to lock up.

Lizzie did go to the nearest hospital where she could get the cat-scan the doctor requested, and she was told they would send the results directly to the doctor to read and he would call her.

One Sunday afternoon the café had been closed because the next day was a holiday; Vicki thought it an unexpected bonus. There were no ball games scheduled, no practices. Without any great regularity, she would occasionally accompany Lizzie and Walter to the small Congregational church closest to their home but on this particular Sunday, she was spending a lazy Sunday afternoon on the back deck of their home with the two. It seemed relaxed, even with the anxious expectation all three had about what the doctor's tests would reveal. Once, when Walter went downstairs to check the smoker from which wonderful smells were beginning to wax from the turkey he was preparing for later. The conversation bounced around with nothing really specific, as often was the case with the three of them. All three were voracious readers and all conversations would have literature interests somewhere; today Vicki had just finished a rather long, but very interesting biography of Henry the Eighth of England and thus they were sorting out all his various wives and the effect one ruler so long ago had held on changing England's reformation from a Catholic to a protestant country. Often Vicki would go on binges where she would get interested in a special genre of literature and read everything, she could find about it until she was saturated with that particular subject. Remembering the oft repeated story about her mother naming her after Queen Victoria, she had just finished reading about her, now she was reading all about Henry the Eighth. Her mother used to tease her about what her name might have been if he her mother had been reading a different book; perhaps one about Queen Catherine or perhaps even Cleopatra.

"You know," said Lizzie, musingly, I read somewhere that Henry the Eighth was credited with having said something extremely profound…"

"About his wives, his son or daughters or his off and on-again treaties with The Emperor or with France, Spain, and the battles he initiated?" Vicki asked with a little sarcasm, "or the heads he had chopped off so easily?"

"Nothing like that. No, one of his cabinet members asked him once in his later years when his health was bad and he realized he might not have long left to live. I guess most people, as they reach this point, began to look back even more than forward…"

"What was it he said?"

"Well, supposedly he asked one of his cabinet members what was the one thing they would want back…"

"Wait, Lizzie, let me see if I can guess…I know it wasn't anything about his marriages nor his children; although he always wanted more sons as heirs… I know he was very rich so it couldn't have related to more money…Was it regret on all the people he was responsible for killing; both in battle and for crimes he had committed himself, after naming himself total ruler over countries and church as total ruler? No, don't answer that. He was known as a man of pride and very big ego. He felt as just a matter of his birth he should be the total leader of his kingdoms…Was it regret for all the people he had put to death merely on the words of others like Thomas Cromwell, and the Pope?"

"Lots of good guesses there, Vicki, but he said more than lost honor, riches, loved ones he would have *time* back. To have youth, courage, strength and vitality as in his younger days. He would choose some *time* to do over."

"I guess that's true of most of us, Lizzie. To live again and do things differently, don't we all long for that? How many people find themselves near death and suddenly try to make bargains with God for a little more time to change things? Is there anyone who has no regrets? That, and I think most people would choose the way they finally want to go…" She paused and then, she patted the cushion on the couch next to where she was sitting. "Come sit here for a minute. I want to talk to you while Walter isn't here."

Vicki felt her heart take an extra jump as she did as Lizzie asked. When she was seated, they could both see Walter from out the nearby window, monitoring the grill and enjoying a cold beer.

She took hold of Vicki's hand and said, speaking slowly and carefully, "You must keep this is complete confidence, Vicki and it is because I believe you can do that, I am willing to trust you."

Vicki, realizing the seriousness of Lizzie's words, nodded and squeezed Lizzie's hand. She said, Of-course, Lizzie. I appreciate your trust."

Lizzie glanced out the window at Walter. She took a deep breath and then she said, softly; but still loud enough for Vicki to hear and understand, "I got the report yesterday and I am not ready to share it with anyone but you…"

"And?" asked Vicki.

"It's cancer, Vicki. Malignant kidney cancer."

"Can't they operate on that? I've even heard of donating kidneys to family members. A love of people lives successful lives with only one kidney."

"The doctor that would be our last choice. Meanwhile, dialysis and antibiotics, changes in diet, rest, drinking more water…"

"So, when does all this start?"

"The doctor said the dialysis is uncomfortable, but we are starting day after tomorrow. But when I pushed Dr. Williams for complete honesty, he said these things may not cure it, and worst-case scenario would be to get on the list for a donated kidney and get me a new kidney. There are some people who get a replacement and have no further problems the rest of their life. And, speaking honestly, there are others who stay on the list and eventually die before finding an appropriate kidney."

Lizzie put her arms around Vicki and said, "You're tearing up, honey. You can't do that or I will too, and I am not ready to share it with Walter or anyone else. I need a few days to gather myself and absorb that it is what it is…"

Walter came upstairs just then and they lost the threads of conversation. Later Vicki was thinking of it, and she told herself, *we all think we have untold time for everything we want to do and live and see. But really, it goes so fast. And no one can hold still for any of it. Time comes and goes as it pleases; both the good and the bad. I pray Lizzie's thoughts are not turning towards the end. I pray she has more years left. I have grown to love these people so…*

There did seem to be at least a temporary boost in energy and attitude from Lizzie and Vicki wondered at her strength to pull herself together for her loved ones. Lizzie started demonstrating some of the other symptoms the doctor had forecast and predicted. Additional fatigue, feet swelling, even more urgency about getting to the bathroom. Thus far, she refused the nurses suggestions about wearing pads or panties designed for leakage of urine.

Lizzie did discuss the idea of eventually having to go on a list for a donated kidney. He told her some people have been on those lists for years. And after a kidney is located there are special and many tests to make sure the intended patient's body will not reject the new, foreign kidney.

The more she heard, the more worried Vicki became for Lizzie.

Walter had already told the doctor that if it finally came to that point, they could have one of his. He tried to argue with the doctor about his being sure he would be a match. Her doctor finally got him to shelve the idea until they reached that point.

* * *

Finally, the day came, and though they lost this particular game; Vicki got her home run. *Not,* she admitted to herself, *a <u>real</u> home room where she knocked it out of the park herself and went all the way around. But she was on first base when her team member knocked it from the park and since there was already someone on second and third, she did bring in a run which counted.*

Eventually, too, she did hit the ball way out to right field and while the other team scrambled to get control and toss it several times, she ran all the way to home; both to Walter's and her teams cheers and her own excitement.

As with anything done with repetition, the changes in Lizzie's life became almost routine. She took her medicine; she went regularly for her dialysis treatments. She took a daily nap. She complained about the lower back pain which seemed to be a regular symptom and simple Tylenol did not make much difference.

As time passed, Lizzie seemed to go downhill rapidly. Eventually they day they had all dreaded came; she began to have problems with high blood pressure, headaches, blood in her urine, trouble sleeping, nausea. The doctor said she needed a replacement kidney. Walter and Joyce both went in and had tests and neither was considered a good enough match.

When Vicki insisted, she wanted to be tested, Walter and Lizzie both insisted "No".

"They can't take a child's kidney for an adult," Lizzie said only to have the doctor say, "Actually you can, as long as the legal guardian signs for the child and the child signs too. It's not as common as adult to adult but it can be done, and successfully."

After that, it was just a question of Vicki wearing Walter and Lizzie down; arguing, crying, even begging, using the reasoning she considered herself as part of the family and it wasn't fair. Finally, Walter and Lizzie, talking with their selves, said, "We might as well allow her the test. We know she's not going to be a match. That would satisfy her settle the whole thing."

So, one day, Walter escorted Lizzie and Vicki down where she took a test.

Walter was right about one thing; whether it was because she didn't anticipate being a match or what, Vicki seemed to be satisfied with that. She quit nagging them and was at least pretending to be satisfied with having being allowed to take the test.

CHAPTER TWENTY-ONE

The Battle Begins

When Lizzie returned, she was smiling; but Vicki felt it a fake smile. Lizzie told them things were better than she had expected and they would talk about it later. The afternoon seemed to drag on and on; and finally, when the last customer had left and the kitchen in order for the next day, Lizzie asked Walter to bring her a class of wine. The day was especially difficult for Vicki because of the earlier confidence Lizzie had shared with her. She dreaded seeing Walter's face when he heard it was indeed, malignant.

"Nothing takes so long as waiting for an appointment in a doctor's office," Lizzie said, calmly. It was obvious to Vicki that Lizzie had prepared for this day.

Walter brought her wine, himself a beer and a coke for Vicki. They took them out to the back porch where the flowers that had planted were in abundant display, and there were bees in full force as well.

They all sat down and Vicki was aware of the deep breath that Walter took.

"Well, do you want the good news or the bad new first?" Lizzie asked, speaking cheerfully while her expression belied the words themselves.

Walter looked at Vicki and she looked at him, they both turned their heads towards Lizzie.

"The bad," they spoke simultaneously.

"Well, it seems that I have developed Kidney cancer."

"How bad is that kind?" Walter asked.

"In relation to what other kind?" Lizzie asked.

"Yes," he replied.

"I don't know." She said, however, the good news is that Dr. Williams said we have treatment options."

"That's good…I think…" said Walter.

"Yes, it certainly is. So, don't 'count me out'."

"So, what do they do?" asked Vicki. "Is the cancer in both kidneys or just one? Does it matter?'

"Well, surgery is out at this stage. It's too far advanced. But the doctor says he has seen remarkable results with a treatment plan with chemo and radiation. Certainly, these can help continue a quality of life which will allow me to stay home and continue my lifestyle; just coming for treatment at the center, then returning home. He said that the day of the chemo itself will not be comfortable, but after that, treatment to treatment will be manageable."

For a moment there was dead silence; so silent, in fact, the three humans could hear the sweet sound of birds outside, and even the chatter of the squirrels who lived in the nearby oak tree next to the porch.

Walter's shoulders slumped, and he reached behind him for a chair as though the strength to stand alone was gone. Vicki moved forward, close enough to take one of Lizzie's hands.

"What can we do?" she asked Lizzie.

"Bless your heart, sweetie. The answer is not much, but I do have some favors…"

Walter looked up from the floor pattern he seems completely emersed in, and asked, "What? What can we do, Liz?"

"I know it will be difficult; but if your days are numbered—"

She was interrupted by Walter, "Don't say that, Lizzie. Medicine is not always right, and there's lots of documentation on remission, in fact there's God. I, myself, still believe in miracles…"

Lizzie was patient with him, when he quit speaking, she said gently, looking straight at him.

"I agree, Walter. What I was trying to say was can we three agree together to make this the best times of our lives? Can we make life beautiful, with, for the most part new memories that you two can dwell on long after I am gone; if indeed I go before you two? That's another thing, who says something won't change around here? You could, God forbid, get hit by a truck tomorrow or get an incurable disease or any number of other catastrophes? Where's your own optimism, your hope, your happiness in the little things? For myself, I am going to try to enjoy each and every day and night I have. I'm going to learn how to play chess. I always was going to; and never did. I am going to finish that Christmas quilt I started. I'm going to stop worrying about dieting; and quit worrying about being fat. I'm going to ice cream every day. I am going to read some books I always meant to read but never did. And I don't want everyone ask me 'How are you feeling today?' very single day. If it's bad, I will handle it or tell you how you can help; if not, just leave me to myself."

At this Vicki grinned; she couldn't help herself.

Walter stood up and walked over to put his arms around Lizzie.

He said, "Well, this doesn't mean I am going to let you win when we play dominos."

She laughed along with the other two.

Vicki thought their future changed as of that date. It was as though there were a shadow or some sort of ghost which rode around on their shoulders; unspoken but greatly felt.

Little things, such as a quickly spoken, "When we have time, we need to…" broken off in mid-sentence when the three thought again that they did not know how many moments they might have left.

When Lizzie asked Vicki one day when she planned to go back to "real" school and what had she thought about colleges, Vicki didn't know what to say.

At times Vicki thought maybe she should share her past with Walter and Lizzie, but she rationalized there was no reason for that and nothing which would help Lizzie in her own present journey

After talking it over with Vicki, Walter secretly spoke with all the staff of the café, and planned a day trip to Louisville. Then he had an advance warning sign placed on the café door to give notice. The excuse he gave was "Personal Family Emergency. Open again in three days."

Janet, Walter, and Vicki had sworn the staff to secrecy, plus as many of the customers as they could. Finally, the night before they were to go, Walter told Lizzie. She didn't even try to talk them out of the trip when she caught their enthusiasm and all their planning they had done.

They went to Louisville and the first place they visited was the Jim Patterson Louisville Cardinals baseball stadium. There was an evening game scheduled and Walter had procured very good tickets and the cooler air made the evening very comfortable. Lizzie pretended to be bored and disappointed; but in reality, she enjoyed it immensely. Next, they took in the Louisville Zoo. They went out to eat several times and each day went back to the hotel room to allow Lizzie time for an afternoon nap, even if she protested, she didn't need it. The final day they visited the Kentucky Derby Museum.

They took a lot of photos, shared a lot of laughter and though Walter and Vicki were worried about the toll the trip was taking on Lizzie, she was obviously having such a good time, they just added ways to minimize her suffering as well as they could.

"I don't know why we never took vacations before…" mused Lizzie.

"We were always too busy with the business," Walter said. "I wish we could do it over."

Lizzie looked at him and said quietly, "Now, now, none of that. You don't know what we might have missed back home at the same time. We've always managed to have lots of fun."

They spent a little time looking for and purchasing souvenirs for the staff at the café, and Vicki even purchased something for Herman's grandma. Walter promised he would make sure she eventually got it.

As the days went by; all too quickly in Vicki's mind, the Chemo treatments began to show their effect on Lizzie. The first time she took a shower which resulted in a large handful of hair coming out in the floor of the shower, she cried.

Vicki and Janet began shopping for and presenting Lizzie with some beautiful scarves and everyone began to accept her new fashion statement.

There did occur days (mostly the day after a Chemo treatment) when she remained in bed all day and mostly just slept. Either Vicki or Walter would take trays and try to strongly encourage at least a little nourishment. She continued to lose weight although the doctor gave them names of super protein drinks and other things to tease her appetite.

Vicki began to read to her sometimes, some of her list she said she had always wanted to read. She enjoyed it; Vicki was a good reader and would read until she noticed Lizzie had fallen asleep

Or until Lizzie stopped her.

Every now and then she would have an unexpected sudden burst of energy or a really good day and during one such day when Vicki expressed a desire to learn, Lizzie began teaching her how to knit. Vicki enjoyed it and wanted to get good enough to knit herself a sweater. The laughter which occurred when the two of them discovered she had gotten close to finishing the sweater before discovering one arm was several rows longer than the other one made it worthwhile to pull out the wrong rows and begin that sleeve all over.

Walter began to lose weight, too and Vicki felt she had to nag him. She often thought she was nursing two instead.

Walter and Vicki were crushed when Lizzie indicated a request to have a bed placed on the back porch. The warm spring nights and the smell of the honeysuckle growing on the porch posts made it especially inviting. Walter went a step further, and seeing how rapidly she seemed to be sinking, he undertook a surprise project he rushed to finish. He got a couple of friends and they screened in half of the porch which would eliminate pesky mosquitoes and other bugs, yet allow the pleasant breeze in and make the moon seem very close. He put up several humming bird feeders and before long they had regular families living in them.

Vicki's contribution was to move Aphrodite's litter box, her food and water dish and her little soft bed into the porch as well. Lizzie tried to protest, but when Aphrodite herself seemed more than pleased with sleeping on the bed with Lizzie, she welcomed her. Many times, Vicki would walk back there to find Lizzie talking to her little companion.

People brought casseroles, most of which they gave to staff, but Vicki played secretary and after sharing the giver and the gift with Lizzie, wrote and mailed thank-you notes.

Even the café's cook, who had been with the couple for over twenty years spent any extra time he found, to cook specialties to tempt Lizzie's appetite. He cooked fancy desserts, her favorite salmon she had always loved, sweet iced tea and thin sugar cookies.

Janet insisted on taking Lizzie's laundry home and lovingly washing, drying, even ironing the soft flannel pajamas and gowns and returning them without letting Lizzie know it was her doing this.

Once a week Vicki went to the library and got new books to read to Lizzie. The library trip itself had lengthened because every person she passed on the way there and home and at the library itself she had to stop and answer their questions about Lizzie. It was hard to know what to say; she didn't want to let people know how drastic it was getting, and to worry, yet, she didn't (or couldn't) admit Lizzie wasn't better.

There was a general pall which surrounded them no matter how energetically they fought it. *It's hard to see the light at the end of the tunnel,* Vicki thought, *when you realistically can't find the end of the tunnel itself.*

Walter found and purchased a "chair" which sat on small legs which was designed for gardeners and on their fortieth anniversary he wrapped it with new floral gardeners' gloves, a new little spade and rake. On days when she felt like it, she could sit out in the midst of the flower bed in the back yard, and weed, or replant or mulch up the black, rich soil. It seemed to renew her spirit and Vicki noticed that on the days she did this she was able to eat a little lunch and take a good nap.

One thing Vicki admired the most about Lizzie was her ability to spur Walter and Vicki into a more hopeful attitude. She deliberately insisted on only "Pollyanna" conversations and refused to look at the black side.

One day she said to Vicki, "Want to hear a secret, Vicki?"

Intrigued by her tone, Vicki said, "Sure, I love secrets."

"I always wanted to write."

"Write what?"

"A book. A novel, if you will…"

If Vicki was surprised, it showed in her expression and she said, "Really? I never would have guessed. What would you write about?"

"Well, all famous writers say to write about what you know and it will be more believable; but I don't know if I agree…"

"Well, look at Louisa Alcott and "Little Women". It was based on a true story of the author and her family; most especially her three sisters."

"Yes, but what about Rudy Kipling's "The Jungle Book? A great book, much loved by many and it was all about talking animals and a human boy raised by wolves. It was successful, and yet, the subject of the book is completely fictional, and readers totally accept the story."

"Are you sure about that?"

"What do you mean?"

"Well, Kipling was abandoned (along with his sister) at the age of six by both his parents to allow them to sail the world. No explanation was ever given the two children as to a reason for this abandonment and they were left with a set of foster parents who mistreated them; particularly Rudyard. His mother finally came back to get him when he was twelve years old; and this experience shows itself in several ways in his writing. His poem, *"Baa Baa, Black Sheep, Baa Baa, Black Sheep"* has reportedly been credited to this dark time in his childhood."

Lizzie was quietly looking out the window and she got a smile on her face when she asked Vicki, "Want to hear what favorite quotation is credited to Kipling?"

"Sure, please!"

"A woman's guess is much more accurate than a man's certainty…"

Vicki laughed out loud. "We need to frame that and hang it in the café."

"You really think Walter would allow that?" Lizzie laughed. "Kipling was such a great writer, and yet had such personal tragedy in his life. His dreadful childhood, his only son missing in action and never found in World War II, and a little daughter lost to pneumonia. Only one of his children outlived him."

Suddenly Vicki couldn't hold it in any longer and she ran over and put her arms around Lizzie. Crying, she said into her shoulder, "Oh, Lizzie, I'm so going to miss these conversations with you. What will I do?"

Lizzie reached for a tissue from the box besides her and pulled Vicki back enough to wipe her tears, then hand it to her.

"I will always be with you, child. Talk to me, any time, all the time. I wish I could be like Houdini; in his belief those loved ones who go before must surely have a way to contact the living.

However, unlike him, I wish I could be successful in learning how to do it."

As the days and weeks, and even hours began to pass, Vicki resented the passage of relentless time. She wanted to slow things down. She refused to think about Lizzie's passing; even going online and investigating stories of alternate methods of cancer treatments, which Lizzie refused to even listen to. When Vicki tried to offer these ideas to Walter, he, too, refused to listen. His only comment was, "Whatever is meant to be will be, Vicki. Who are we to dictate to God? If Lizzie can face it, we need to."

Sometimes Vicki would want to wail and wring her hands in frustration. Sometimes she wanted to stay in bed and cover her head with blankets all day long. And often she wanted to make a list of questions for Lizzie while she was still here. What advice would she want to give Vicki? What was her most treasured memory?

Once, in an almost casual conversation, Lizzie asked Vicki, "Know one of the things I am most thankful for, Vicki?"

"What's that?" Lizzie.

"That when it was time for me, I got a relatively easy way to go. Ever see that old movie or read the book by Nicholas Sparks where his and his wife are terribly, terribly in love, and then as they grow older, he stays much the same, but she gets one of those diseases…I think it's Dementia and she can't ever remember who he is. It's called "The Notebook". Anyway, he reads their story over and over to her. It is so touching. I can almost recite all the words. Each time they see each other in the nursing home and she loves the story, not even realizing it is their personal story. I cry every time I see it. When I watch it, I always hope she will finally recognize who he is."

When Vicki says, "I would like to watch it sometime," Lizzie continues on, "Anyway I am glad both my mind and Walter's are both clear as a bell and we can remember all our pasts."

Abut this time Lizzie unconsciously begins to pepper her conversations to Vicki with lots of conversations beginning with, "Remember to…"

It was always advice and often she would suggest she write it down so she didn't forget it.

Sentences like, "Remember to never just settle. Promise me, Vicki."

Not understanding her meaning, Vicki queried, "Never settle?"

"For second best for something because you couldn't achieve what was first in your heart. If you someday meet someone in love with you who wants you to marry him and nags you unmercifully about it—don't do it because you don't recognize an alternative. If he kisses you and makes your heart race and your body tremble, you'll know he's right. I don't care if he's poor, or doesn't like what you do, like reading, or has a mean and grouchy family or is richer than a king. Same for a job or a promotion or other choices you must make, weigh them carefully; choose the one that makes you take a risk or you feel you cannot live another moment without. Better hamburger meatloaf with someone you love than sirloin steak and caviar with someone who wants to buy you diamonds."

Vicki grinned and asked, "Is it possible I could find someone with all those things together?"

"Possible, but not probable. Did I ever tell you my momma and poppa didn't want me to marry Walter?"

Vicki stopped changing the sheets on the bed and looked at Lizzie. "Why in the world not? He is so sweet-natured and kind to everyone; and he has a wonderful sense of humor. Any woman would be glad to have him. He's also very good looking. And…" she paused here and continued, "He adores you. I think you are very, very lucky."

"Well, they didn't agree. There was another young gentleman who courted me, too. Is that a word they still use sometimes, courted? Probably not. Anyway, his name was Sydney and his family owned; in fact, still do, own the only sawmill on the other side of town. Very well to do, that family."

"What was there about him you didn't like?"

"It wasn't that I didn't like him…I just didn't love him and I knew it. I tried to talked myself into it for a long time, but for one thing he bored me to tears. He rarely laughed, and was so busy trying to impress everyone else, no one even liked being around him. Finally, one evening, when sitting on the back-porch swing and my parents had gone inside, Walter and I were *'making out'; is that an expression you young folks still use?"*

Vicki grinned, "Yes."

"Want to know something else?"

"Walter told me he couldn't stand it any longer and he said, 'Let's go get married, Lizzie. We can cross over the state line, find us a Judge or Justice of the Peace and be back before your parents even know we're gone."

"But what about the wedding? I always wanted a church wedding, and my momma did, too. She'll be heart- broken."

"She will get over it, I will be so good to her, she will be eating out of my hand in no time. And your daddy loves me already. He can't stand that sissy Sydney. He told me so."

"But people might think we *had* to get married."

"What do you mean, had to get married?"

"You know…that I'm pregnant…"

"Lizzie, no one that knows you more than five minutes would every think about you like that and if they did, pardon my language, but I'd beat the shit out of them. Waiting around for a fancy wedding with all that worry and stress and wasted money is just plain old silly. I love you and always will."

Lizzie paused and looked outside. "So finally, I just said yes and we did."

"You did?"

"Sure did."

That's just about the most romantic thing I ever heard," Vicki said, smiling.

"So, how did it turn out? Were your parents just furious?"

"Momma was, but she pretended she wasn't and Walter was right; she was eating out of his hand in no time."

"What ever happened to old Sydney?"

"Oh, he married a girl visiting his family from North Carolina and had a bunch of kids. They come back every now and then but unlike Walter, he doesn't still have his hair, he is bald as a billiard ball and has a belly to match. I'll tell you something else, too. Walter can still cause my heart to jump around. I'm worried about how he will do when I'm gone. Do you believe I'll be able to see him from way up there? Just sort of keep him in line?"

"I most certainly do."

"Something else," she added to Vicki, "Make sure Walter makes Buster bring Grandma over here for the funeral and if you can, give him some flowers to put on Herman and Rusty's grave."

"I promise," Vicki said.

Walter did manage to teach Lizzie how to play chess and although it was obvious, she would probably never reach the Master Player class, she learned enough to enjoy the challenge of a game with him.

An illustration of where Walter's thoughts were constantly one only had to look at his activities to give quality days to this woman, he had loved for so many years. One afternoon he came out on the porch with a big box which had a lovely pink ribbon holding the lid on.

"What's that?" Lizzie asked him.

"A surprise. Something long overdue. Something you have always wanted."

Rather ruefully, Lizzie smiled skeptically and said, "Oh, yeah?"

He gently set the box on her bed and helped her sit up a little closer to allow her to take the lid off.

Before she could even get the lid completely off, out tumbled a small gray ball which looked like a dustmop without the handle.

Lizzie immediately let out a squeal, "Oh, Oh, Oh, it's a Shih Tzu!"

"A what?" asked Vicki.

"A puppy. A wonderful puppy. Small, but supposed to be gentle and a follower, good with kids and old ladies like me! I have always, always wanted one."

Just then, with all the excitement, Aphrodite; who was lying on Lizzie's bed chose this time to wake, yawn very big, and stretch before coming up to nose Vicki into acknowledging her presence.

Vicki grabbed her, frightened the puppy would go after her; after all, aren't dogs and cats' natural enemies?

Lizzie reached out her hand and stopped her, "No, Vicki. Leave them alone and let's see what they think of each other."

"Yeah," Walter said, "The lady I bought her from said she has cats and this little lady doesn't seem to care about them."

The two animals seemed to size each other up, at first, circling and sniffing each other. The little puppy's tail was wagging like a little automated machine and Aphrodite's ears were laid back on her head. Then, as easy as that; all apprehension was gone. The puppy licked Aphrodite, causing her to back up and sneeze. All the three humans laughed.

With tears in her eye, Lizzie looked at Walter and said, "I can't believe you remembered after all these years."

"I should have got you one a long time ago."

Walter reached out and patted the dog who had decided to sit down on Lizzie's lap as though finding her own special place.

"I am not going to say it," Lizzie said.

"Say what?"

"Anything about this being too late for a new puppy or that you shouldn't have done this or any such thing."

Walter flushed pink. "I wasn't going to say that."

"Yes, you were, but there is no argument from me. What if I go into a really long remission and this little puppy is responsible?"

He bent over and kissed her cheek which brought a big lick from the puppy to Walter.

"Yuck!" he said, withdrawing his face and wiping his cheek.

He handed the sack he had brought up with the gift to Vicki and said, "You have got your work cut out for you," he told her. "Start taking her out several times a day; trying to catch her before she pees if you can, not after, but there's some puppy training pads in here, a new collar, a new water and food bowl as well as food and dog biscuits."

Lizzie said, "No more surprises, Walter. I don't like goldfish, lizards are scary, and birds are too messy, way too messy."

Thus, began long and sometimes heated (from Walter) on a name for the new puppy. Vicki suspected it was all a bluff on Walter's part, a fun game to keep Lizzie happy and involved. He kept threatening to grab the dog and give her a haircut; at least giving her some bangs to keep her fur out of her eyes. So far Lizzie had refused to let him do this.

Vicki no longer helped out in the café. Her life had changed without it being verbally established. Her job was to take care of Lizzie (and of course, the new puppy and Aphrodite, as well). There was a serenity around Lizzie now; an acceptance and an appreciation for all the little things done for her without her asking. There wasn't anything any of them would not do; they sometimes felt helpless in their desire for more to do for her. She never asked for anything unless it was something for the dog or cat.

CHAPTER TWENTY-TWO

Angel

One morning when Vicki came early in the morning to make sure she got the puppy out before she peed on the floor, she walked in Lizzie's bedroom and Lizzie was cuddling the dog.

"Hey," she asked Vicki, "I looked Shih Tzu dogs up on my laptop and guess what?"

As Vicki brought the leash over and snapped it on the puppy's collar and picked her up, she asked, "What?"

Her breed is Chinese and the name of the breed means "Lion".

Vicki laughed. "Are you sure you were looking on the right page, Lizzie? This tiny, gentle, furball of a dog is named after a lion?"

Lizzie was laughing too.

"But that's not going to be her name. I have a name picked out. The internet said they prefer two syllable names and can learn them faster…so, I named her Angel."

Vicki stopped and said it while she patted the puppy in her arms. She repeated it several times, "Angel…Angel…Angel. I like it,

Lizzie." The puppy was by now wriggling and squiggling, knowing the leash meant an outside trip.

"Now," said Lizzie, "We have to use it all the time so she knows that's her name."

"Right!"

"When she took Angel outside, she took the leash off and allowed her to explore the back yard and the edge of the wooded forest. Vicki could see Lizzie at the window, holding Aphrodite and watching them.

Actually, the puppy was proving to be very smart. She seemed to recognize her name within a few days. You could call her and she would pause in her activity and cock her head to look at whoever was calling and soon she was coming to the call.

That afternoon Vicki asked, "Lizzie can I ask you a personal question? You don't have to answer and it's really not my business but I have wondered about it a lot."

"Honey you can ask me anything. I am probably the least exciting or adventurous person you know. Go ahead!"

"You, and maybe even Walter mentioned once that you had a daughter once but not what ever happened to her."

Lizzie was quiet for a few seconds. "I can talk about it now, but for years I could not. I thought it would break me and Walter apart, but it eventually brought us closer."

When she paused again Vicki asked, "Was she sick?"

"No, just the opposite. Healthy, robust, beautiful."

"How old was she?"

"Just an infant. Three months."

Vicki gasped as she said, "Just a baby! How did it happen? Was it an accident?"

"No. No accident. She was abducted."

"Abducted? Stolen? How? Where? When? How does someone abduct an infant?"

"Turned out to be pretty easy. At that period of our lives Walter and I were a very young couple, we lived in the little house in back of the café where you live now. We were barely making it financially. It was a necessity both of us work. We interviewed several applicants to serve as a nanny and after lots of investigation we hired a young Spanish American girl in her late twenties. Her name was Juanita. At first, she was perfect. Every time we watched them together, she was loving and caring. The baby was kept clean and was gaining weight and thriving. The baby was a little over three months old when we got word that my only sister was in the hospital with serious surgery. She and her husband had been in a terrible accident with an eighteen-wheeler truck. She lives over in Nashville and she had waited too long to finally agree to the surgery. The doctors didn't think she would survive. Joyce offered to open and close the café and Walter and I asked Juanita if she could just stay here in the little house and take care of the baby for a day or two until we could see if my sister was going to recover.

We were there two days and we called Joyce several times to check on Juanita and the baby. Finally, my sister began to pull through; and her husband was released from the hospital. We came home that next morning and the first thing I did was go back to the cottage to see the baby. When I opened the door, I knew something was wrong. It was quiet, too quiet. The laundry basket where we kept clean baby clothing was gone; as were all the baby's clothes. Her carrier was missing, there were no cans of formula or bottles on the drain board on the sink. You would never know the space had ever held a baby."

"Oh, my God," said Vicki.

"Well, we went through all the normal things you would expect; police, FBI, even tracked down Juanita's family and they had packed up and moved suddenly. They supposedly had crossed the border; but the FBI could not locate proof of this. Searches were held everywhere, flyers, volunteers from all over, on horseback, on foot. I nearly went crazy. Walter and I blamed each other for a while, Joyce even blamed herself. We went through the private detective route, the police and FBI tried their best, though at the time I doubted it. There was a theory by the FBI that Juanita had sold the baby on the black market; but it was just a theory. Thousands of clues came in and were diligently checked out. Days went by, then weeks, then months and finally the year anniversary, then the second and on and on and on. All I could do is pray they wanted a baby so badly they would love her and treat her well. I saw a therapist for a long while and I still dream about her."

"Did they ever find Juanita?"

"No."

"And they never found the baby, either?"

Lizzie shook her head 'no'.

After a brief pause, Vicki asked, "What was her name, Lizzie?"

"The baby's?"

"Yes," Vicki nodded as she answered.

Lizzie looked directly at her and very somberly said, "It was Victoria."

Startled, Vicki said, "Victoria? My name?"

Lizzie nodded affirmatively and softly said, "Yes."

"Kind of makes you think about life being stranger than fiction, right?"

"You never mentioned that before," Vicki said.

"No, I didn't."

"It's going to take me a while to absorb that," said Vicki.

"I know. Imagine how Walter and I felt when we met you over at Herman's funeral…"

"Now I have a question for you," Lizzie said, turning to Vicki.

"What?"

"Why are you away from your own home? Where are your parents and family?"

Vicki was quiet for a moment and then she said, with a tentative smile, "Well, Lizzie, I am not running from the law. I am not in trouble."

"Well, do your parents know where you are and how long have you been gone?"

"I left them a note explaining my absence and telling them I still loved them all. I plan to return someday."

"But why did you leave and where are you going?"

"To find myself. I don't know where I will stop and return home yet, but I will know when I reach the end of my journey. Does that make any sense?"

"But aren't they worrying about you?"

"Probably some. But it's not as if they have no one. I have a brother and he is really theirs."

"What does that mean? Really theirs?"

"I have a brother but not a blood brother. I was adopted."

"Is this a search for your real parents?"

"No, definitely not. My parents; or rather, my adoptive parents were very good to me. Loving, caring, understanding and good to me."

"I don't really understand this, then."

"It's kind of a fairytale story…My adoptive parents tried for several years and couldn't get pregnant. Then, one night a little baby was left on the steps of the nearest Catholic home for unwed mothers, or abandoned children. Because, at that time, there were several consequences for anyone who abandoned a baby, sometimes people would leave them at orphanages; and…I even heard of some people selling babies on the black market; babies they had stolen. My parents were contacted about possibly adopting me, or at least being my foster parents. I was already on their list for wanting a baby. My adoptive mother told me later they were completely taken by surprise; when they went to sign the papers and pick up the b aby and a few diapers and cans of formula provided by the orphanage, they brought me home in a laundry basked lined with a flannel robe from my dad."

Lizzie's cell phone rang just then and Vicki reached over and handed it to her.

Listening to Lizzie's side of the conversation Vicki heard, "Yes, this is Lizzie."

Lizzie was quiet, listening and then she said, "Why? What for?"

She listened again and then she said, "And you want us both to come?"

Again, silence from Lizzie as she listened then she said, "Fine. I will let him know and we will see you then."

Vicki was dying to know who and what that conversation was all about and with difficulty she refrained from asking. Obviously, it was not her business. If it had been, Lizzie would have included her after she hang the phone up and sat thoughtfully, looking out the window.

She turned and asked Vicki, "Would you mind going to find Walter, Vicki, and asking him to come here a minute?"

"Of course not. I'll go right now."

Frequently in the next few days; though always silently, Vicki thought over the circumstances of how Walter and Lizzie had suffered through the loss of their only child. It had not cost them the loss of their relationship, but had seemed to make it stronger. Right from the beginning of her own relationship with the couple, she had been impressed with the love they shared.

The subject of her own past did not come up again, although Vicki expected it. She would be able to discuss it more thoroughly then, and did not deliberately try to put it off.

Often in life, one meets others who seem to have a gift for accepting hardships and instead of folding with each test on their strength of character, kept strong and steady on their path. The joy of being given the opportunity to meet some of these latter humans who find the strength to hold steady in the face of hardship is not to be minimized. Vicki wanted to be in this latter group. She wanted to be able to hold her head up and be proud of the kind of person she was becoming. Vicki thought of the classroom discussions about the old nurture versus nature definitions of what determines the kind of human an individual becomes. This caused her, for the first time, to begin having doubts about this adventure she was currently on. What kind of pain had she been responsible for in by her behavior?

She remembered reading the dedication in some book she read which was a quotation by the famous psychologist, Carl Jung; which stated "It is not where you began your life's journey which is most important, but where you end up…"

After Vicki assured Walter, there was no emergency, but Lizzie wanted to see him, she allowed him to go upstairs without her accompaniment, in case it was privacy they wanted for their conversation. If it was something which concerned, her they would tell her at the right time.

* * *

When Walter came in and closed the door behind him Lizzie said, "Walter, the doctor called…"

"What did he want?"

"He wants the two of us to make an appointment and come see him. Together."

"Sounds a little ominous, doesn't it? What else did he say? What was his voice like?"

"I didn't think he sounded like it was any emergency or anything. Anyway, the sooner we go to see him the sooner we will know what he wants to discuss."

"Well, let's not sit around and spend our time getting all stressed out when it might even be something good. I'll call and see when is the earliest he can see us."

"Yes, do."

Lizzie saw him start to turn and head towards the door; then he hesitated and turned back. Lizzie realized (rightly so) that he had intended to go out of her room to make the call, but realizing she would want to hear the conversation, he reentered the room and dialed the number to the doctor's office.

"I talked to the receptionist," Walter said. "She said for us to come in this afternoon around 5::30. He will be through with patients by then. I told him we'd be there."

Later in the afternoon Walter cleaned up and Lizzie changed her clothes and after turning the café over to Joyce, they made their way to the doctor's office.

Vicki watched them leave, wanting to be invited along, but Lizzie smiled at her and said, "We won't be gone long, sweetie. You and Joyce are in charge."

At the doctor's office, the doctor invited them inside his inner office, offered them coffee or water, and locked the outer door.

Lizzie and Walter both felt their apprehension rise as he did so. Then he waited until both were seated, and he walked around his desk and took his own seat. He smiled at them and said, "I must admit this is the first time in my entire life of practicing medicine I have had this happen. There are two sides to this story and it could be viewed as unpredictable, amazing, wonderful, or maybe unbelievable and crazy. Frankly I don't know what to think."

Walter and Lizzie looked from the doctor to one another. Finally, Walter said, "Look, Doc we have all known each other for years now. You know the kind of man I am and I believe I know you pretty well, too. We've been through some tough times with each other. When our baby girl was abducted you were right there with us and helped us make it through something, we thought would kill us both. What I am trying to say is you can level with us. We are strong people, Lizzie and I. Don't try to soften the words with us. Just speak the truth. We can handle it. Did you get more tests for Lizzie? Are they bad?"

He reached out his hand and took hold of Lizzie's and when he got it, he gave it a squeeze.

She said nothing, but she squeezed his hand back.

The doctor looked down at some papers on his desk, then he pushed his glasses back up on his nose.

"Well, all I can do is tell you I immediately called for a second test when I saw these results at came in and those tests only reaffirmed the results of the first ones."

"Which tests were these? Were these tests on Lizzie's kidney?"

"Not exactly. They were on the viability of Vicki's being a donor."

Lizzie and Walter once again looked at each other.

The doctor cleared his throat and he said, looking at the directly, "Not only is Vicki a viable donor; she had the exact same DNA as you two."

There was total silence in the room.

"What does that mean? What are you saying?" asked Walter.

"It means that Vicki is related to you two. It means that she is your family; probably the daughter you lost all those years ago."

"That's…that's impossible!" said Walter.

"Why?" asked the doctor.

Walter sputtered, "Because…because, it just is…"

"Again, I say why? I had the test done twice, each time with a different lab. I am telling you she is your daughter."

"I can't believe this," Walter said.

Lizzie still had not spoken.

"So, the question is, what do we do now? First is the question of the kidney transplant? Do we allow it?"

"Next," the doctor continued, "Do we share the information with Vicki, who is, after all, a minor, in your care. Having proved a blood relationship here, you two have the authority to give permission for the transplant or not. In fact, you two are the only two who have this authority. So, what do we do?"

"How is this possible?"

"I do not know. Truth is, often, life truly is stranger than fiction. Never mind what forces brought her to your home, the facts are she is here; you are in charge of her. What do we do now?"

Walter looked at Lizzie and asked, "What do we do, sweetheart? What do we do?"

Lizzie was openly crying now and she wiped her eyes with a tissue from the doctor's desk before saying, "Dr, are you aware, do you remember our daughter's name?"

He looked puzzled and then he said, "No, Lizzie, I don't. I am almost afraid to ask."

"It was Victoria. It was Victoria. That is on her birth certificate."

"What do you suggest?" Walter asked the doctor.

"It is not for me to say or suggest, Walter; however, I would not make any hasty decisions. I would say you two go home and think this over. Decide whether or not you want to tell Vicki about this development and the options which this opens up; as well as what this means to your personal relationships."

"But what about Lizzie's surgery…her kidney transplant?" asked Walter. "Do we have time to delay it?"

"We don't need to postpone it any longer than necessary if you decide to go that route, but not immediately, like today or tomorrow. In fact, we need not to jump into something harem-sacrum

here. It needs to be into a well thought out and careful decision."

The doctor cleared his throat again and said, "Do you two want me to talk to Vicki for you or with you?"

They immediately shook their heads in unison and Walter said, "No, no. This is our family and our choices to make."

"Well, let me know when you have come to a decision and I will schedule the surgery …or. not."

"We will call you within the next couple of days," Walter said, then stood. He still held Lizzie's hand and he assisted her to stand.

One they got outside the building, the two of them stood looking around themselves. The sun was shining and the sky a glorious blue. There was a gentle breeze and all seemed right with their world.

As they began walking towards home, Walter said, "Hey, I need to sit down for a few minutes. How about you?"

When she nodded agreement, he pointed towards the small ice cream shop location on the next corner.

"Let's go get a Sundae, what do you say?"

She nodded again and while others might have thought this a frivolous decision, completely out of context with what was happening, it seemed perfect to them. This was one of their favorite places and held many wonderful past celebratory visits so seemed very natural.

They sat down in a booth, and when they had decided on what they wanted, placed their order.

Walter reached across the table and once again took hold of Lizzie's hand.

"I still can't take it in. Is it really possible that Vicki is *our* Victoria?" Lizzie asked him.

"I know…I know. How did we end up getting her back? Where was she in all the years in between? And how did she end up over at Grandma and Herman's?"

"I don't know but I have often wondered. Maybe I was afraid of losing her and that's why I didn't ask more questions."

"Why did we not sense it?"

"Well, we grew to love her very fast. Think about that…"

"Well, how did she end up on the road, a mere child?"

"More importantly, what are we going to do now?"

"You mean about telling her?"

"Yes, that, and about her desire to give you a kidney," said Walter.

"She knows she was adopted. I remember her telling me that; in fact, we were in the midst of a conversation about her past right before the doctor called this morning."

"Wait a minute. Do you think *she* knows she is ours? Do you think she was looking for and then successful in finding us?"

"No! Impossible!"

"Not impossible. Perhaps improbable, not impossible. Perhaps her entire reason for being out on the road was to find her real parents and why they didn't want her, but let her be adopted by strangers."

"There are so many questions. If she knew, was she eventually going to share it with us?"

"I don't believe she knows. I just don't. It doesn't feel right."

"I do know one thing. I had a genuine tug when I learned her name over at Grandma's house. Of course, I have known other girls named Victoria in my life, but this was different. I also felt everything she did illustrated what a kind and caring person she was. She just seemed to fit in our family right from the start."

"Right. I agree."

"Okay, what do we do next?"

"I know what she is going to say when we talk to her…" Lizzie said.

"What?"

"She will insist that only God's infinite wisdom brought her here to save my life with one of her kidneys."

"Oh, I'm sure."

"She will insist it is God's will and demand she be allowed to do it."

"Well, we're the adults and she is still a minor. Well, even more than that, *we* are her parents and our permission would be a necessity."

"Wouldn't we have to get in touch with her legal, adopted parents and coordinate all this?"

"She was kidnapped from us. For God's sake, doesn't that give us the real custody? We didn't *give* her up to anyone. Even those adoptive parents."

"Did she ever mention her mother's name? What if it is Juanita?"

"That's just entirely too much of a reach, Walter. I am sure it wasn't Juanita."

CHAPTER TWENTY-THREE

Healing

It was a beautiful day; falsely pretending to be spring, although it was too early. Ann sat on the back porch with her quilt, pleased with her progress on the embroidery and with the day. She felt blessed with those feelings one sometimes gets which, without anything to back it up, simply fills one with a strong sense of well-being. Just as occasionally individuals will feel a forbidding sense of impending disaster, they may also sense an increasing feeling of happiness. That is what Ann was feeling this morning. She could not put her finger on why or from where this feeling was emerging, but neither could she deny the strength of the feeling. She mentally told herself, *just relax, Ann, and go with it. It's been a long time since you have enjoyed such a glorious feeling. Grab it, hold it close.*

She was a little startled when the doorbell rang. These days no one except Joseph, Tony and herself ever came to the house. She hurriedly put down her quilting supplies and the quilt squares she was working on and walked to the front door.

When she opened the front door, she was surprised to see Susanne Jenkins, Vicki's former home room teacher standing there. She was a tiny little woman; the perfect replica of an old-fashioned schoolmarm. She wore horn-ribbed brown and black plastic eyeglasses, and her hair was back in a neat bun low on her neck.

In a timid, soft-spoken voice she asked, "Hello, Ann. I hope I am not disturbing you." She paused and when Ann shook her head negatively, she continued, "I don't know if you knew I am leaving the school next semester…but I recently married and my husband's job is moving him to Arkansas. Well, I have been going through all my supplies and ten years of teaching here and I came across some old folders from the children. If the children are still attending this school, I am trying to give them back any special work they had done for me. I came across Vicki's Creative Writing folder. She was so gifted in her writing, and several times she even shared she might be a writer someday. I read through her folder once again and was still impressed with the quality of her writing. I could not bear to throw it away and I thought you might want to have it." As she finished saying this, she extended her hand out towards Ann.

In it was a brightly colored and designed pronged-folder with Vicki's name on the front.

Ann's hand was trembling as she reached out to accept the folder. "How very kind of you," she said to the teacher. Thank you so much. Would you like to come in for something to drink or to visit a bit?"

"No, no, I will be on my way, Ann."

"I didn't even realize you had recently gotten married," Ann said. "You were always one of Vicki's very favorite teachers. She loved your class. Are you sure you won't come in and have some coffee or a cold drink?"

"No, really. Thank you, but my husband is waiting in the car. We have so much to get done."

"Well, again, thank you for your thoughtfulness. And good luck in your new school."

After she closed the door, Ann went to the back porch to sit in the swing and she slowly opened the folder read Vicki's writings. There was a poem she had written about winter being so slow to leave each year while spring and summer galloped through in no time at all. She had written a short story about a young girl who had always wanted a dog. It made her sad when she remembered how much Vicki had always wanted a dog and Joseph and herself had always postponed it with many excuses. Ann felt a chill go down her spine when the story described the dog, who had an eerie resemblance to Rusty, the dog they had now; and which spent so much time on the small round rug in Vicki's room. The girl in the story was named Veronica and she had named her new dog Rusty.

Ann inhaled a big breath and tried to steady herself. The story was entitled "Finding Myself".

When Ann read the description of the heroine in the story she had to smile because except for the girl's hair she was an exact copy of Vicki herself. In reality, Vicki's hair was a beautiful chestnut brown, shiny and silky and very thick; however, she had always bemoaned this fact and expressed disappointment she didn't have blond hair. She even suggested to her mother once that when she was grown and her "own person" she was going to dye it. But otherwise, the girl in the story was Vicki.

The girl in the story did not have a brother; which made sense to Ann because Vicki considered him a nuance and probably felt good about writing him out of the story.

In the story Vicki had made the mother beautiful but sort of clueless. Vicki had dismissed her almost as someone content to be a mere housewife with no real goals or achievements. But the father… ah, Vicki had given him great foresight and uncommon intelligence and loads of understanding of himself and the world he lived in. It made Ann quite jealous. She wanted to be the father.

The major illuminating part of the story, though was the deep insight Vicki had shown in understanding what motivation drove others to certain behavior. Her understanding of the love shared between the dog and the girl as well as her deep longing to please the father came through the story, woven like golden threads holding the entire tale together.

In the story, Vicki carefully examines the differences in the love the father and mother have for each other and the love they feel for their daughter. She explains carefully the feeling of jealously the mother feels for the daughter when she spends all her time trying to show her love for her father and ignores the mother's neediness for her love too. In the story, she explains too, the "caught in the middle" feeling the father often feels when both the daughter and his wife vie for his attention and love. Close to the end of the story the mother gets ill and dies and it isn't until after that the girl realizes how much the mother meant to her and the importance she had played in the life of the family. In the story the girl realizes she had endowed the father with everything she viewed as good and kind and brave and the mother as almost a nonentity. She also realizes she, too, (like Ann) wanted to be the father in the story. The girl in the story feels a sense of guilt at not having shown more love for the mother and struggles to overcome it. The very final paragraph of the story the girl vows to leave home to "find herself"; the real person inside which she thus far had shown to no one else.

Ann sat on the porch swing and cried a little. She felt the story showed a depth and a maturity she had never credited her daughter with having. An acceptance of who people really were, and not just as she wanted them to be.

Was this why she had run away? Ann asked herself. And what about the dog? How had she predicted in the past they would have in reality a dog that looked like and acted like the dog in Vicki's story? Ann studied the dog who lay now at her feet, watching her as she studied him.

Where did you come from, boy? How did you find us? Did Vicki send you here? She viewed this, as she had so many of the other "traces" lately as something akin to the old television series "The Twilight Zone". She knew she shared a very active imagination with her daughter; sometimes proven by the literature they both chose to read, sometimes by the way they described things, but it was uncanny how some of these things were happening since Vicki had been gone. It also reinforced her feeling that Vicki wasn't gone forever, but would-be returning home. She didn't know when or how, but she was sure of it.

Ann thought about the story, and the other writings in the folder and made a decision not to share it with Joseph; at least not at this time.

Lizzie and Walter agreed not to rush into such a weighty decision and decided to think on it for a week or so before they talked everything over with Vicki.

Vicki lay in bed that night all but oblivious to what turmoil was happening with Walter and Lizzie and suddenly she sat up and came to her own decision.

What, she questioned herself, if her mother or father, or even Tony got very sick or had a horrible accident and she wouldn't even know about it and they didn't know where she was or how to reach her? She decided she needed to go back home. She needed to tell them all about her journey and what she had learned and all about Lizzie and Walter. She needed to trust them to help her make the best decision about Lizzie's surgery. She would go, hurry home and confide in them, bring them back to meet these people she loved as she did them. She was afraid they would try to talk her out of it, so she would write notes.

She immediately sat down and wrote them both a note telling them she had something very, very important she absolutely had to do so she would be gone a few days. No more than three or four, and she would definitely be back. Would they take care of Aphrodite for her and of each other?

She folded the note inside an envelope and as quietly as she could, she dressed and packed her backpack with a few necessities, including snacks from the refrigerator. She took the note and taped it to the inside door of her little cottage, facing out where they couldn't miss it, and then she went around to the side of the café and hurried down the road.

She made extremely good time the first day and did not even stop when it began to grow dusk. She wasn't afraid, in fact, she welcomed the feeling of somehow being in the right place now at the right time. She prayed for Lizzie and for Walters as she walked and though she considered stopping at Grandma's house when she reached that far, she resisted the impulse. She felt an overwhelming pull of emergency, and picked up her pace. She ate snacks while on the move, and continued. Each scene she passed she remembered something about it; Grandma's house, the church graveyard where she paused only long enough to say a simple hurried prayer over Herman's and Rusty's graves. She would not look towards the blackberry bushes where she and Herman had met the bear, and she ignored the fishing hole. She stopped at about noon on the fourth day, crawled under some thick bushes and took a two-hour nap. Then washed her face and hands in the creek and refreshed, picked up a fast pace.

When she reached the outskirts of town, she searched her jean pockets and found some coins.

When she chided herself for remembering their town no longer had pay phones, she stopped in a small grocery story and asked the clerk if she could pay to us the phone.

"Heck, no charge for that. It's right over there. Do you need a phone book?"

"No, I know the number."

Vicki dialed her mother's work number and when the other girl in the office answered "Hello, Accounting unlimited. This is Shirley. How may I help you?"

Vicki froze at first and then said, "May I please speak with Ann?"

"She's not here right now. You can probably reach her at her home."

"Okay, thank you," Vicki replied. Then she hung up and dialed her mother's cell phone.

It rang a couple of times and then Vicki heard her mother's voice, "Hello?"

Vicki couldn't speak for a minute and then she said, tremendously, almost breaking into tears, "Mama? It's Vicki. Can you come get me?"

* * *

As soon as Vicki explained where she was, Ann called Joseph and Tony and the three of them went to pick her up. They were practically hysterics, with tears, and hugs so strong they prevented letting go of each other long enough to prepare to return home. The amazement Vicki had to find was Rusty there, lying on the small round rug in her old bedroom. She had to question Tony and her parents as to where this particular dog had come into their lives; then explain about the other "Rusty" which lay buried in the small graveyard up in the hills.

No one was hungry but everyone talked at once, only to have to start over and begin again. The three of them were up until well after midnight while Vicki told her story (more than once). Tony sat on the edge of his chair, keeping his hand on Vicki's shoulder the entire time, her mother held her hand and her father sat on the floor at her feet. Many times, they stopped her with questions then the story would resume once again. Tony especially wanted to hear the story about Herman and the bear over and over again with the rather grotesque details. It was repeated several times and then, once she tearfully retold the status of Lizzie and her kidney and her need for their help. Vicki waited until the final part before she confided the part about the identical DNA between herself and Lizzie and Walter. Her parents wanted to hear all about how she survived in the woods all by herself and her lack of fear and where she learned all the things she demonstrated.

For her part, Vicki wanted to hear the story of Rusty and where they got this dog which reminded her so completely of her own "Rusty".

At first there was some disbelief on Joseph, Ann and Tony's part about the DNA but she explained there had been two identical tests from two different very reputable labs and the respectable status of their doctor and the length of time the three had known each other.

Tears were running down Vicki and Ann's faces and Ann said, between sobs, "How is that possible? That these are your real parents? That you should end up with your real parents after ten years with us? People you don't know and whom you have never met?"

"Yeah," said Joseph, "and after being kidnapped and the FBI and all kinds of people searching and searching."

"Yes, and you being drawn to go off on your so titled "adventure", Tony said to Vicki.

With another grin, Tony said, "Yeah, and I want my utility knife back, too."

All three laughed.

Joseph said to Ann and Tony, there is no real road going up there, unless we go round the longer way which would add a couple more days so better dress accordingly, hiking boots, jeans, water bottles and sack lunches. Let's get an early start."

Vicki said, "Yes, I know that Lizzie and Walter are really worried about me, too."

"Just as we have been about you," Ann said, sadly.

"I know. I'm so sorry, Mom. Please forgive me."

"Sure, honey. I am just so glad to have you home again. You're not the only one who has been having strange adventures. There's been enough stress and excitement; but one day you and I will have a long, long talk. I have some hard-to-understand events myself that I want to share with you. Sort of like all those para-normal stories you used to love to read."

As Ann said this, she was thinking of the unexplainable "traces" (as she had called them); including the floral delivers, the unstamped mail, the shortage in the lamp, doors opening and closing magically, the arrival of Rusty…Even her birthday outfit being laid out for her to wear, and her book being moved around.

There were more tears and more telling and then, finally, all agreed to order a pizza, have something to drink, and go to get some much-needed rest. Their immediate agreement on plans were to get a good night's sleep, notify their jobs that they would be taking some time off and leave in the morning.

Tony took hold of her arm and he said softly, "Hey, Vicki, do I have to sleep on the floor right outside your room to make sure you don't disappear again?" Though he had sort of a crooked grin, she sensed he needed assurance she wasn't going to be gone in the morning.

When Joseph and Ann finally slipped between the covers on their bed, Ann said, "We didn't discuss what we are going to do about that lady's kidney…"

"I know. That's going to be difficult."

"Oh, Joseph, you aren't even suggesting that we allow it, are you?"

"Are you forgetting something, Ann?"

"What?"

"We are not her real parents…they are."

"But that would be something for the courts to decide, wouldn't it?"

"I don't know. Let's put it aside until tomorrow."

Suddenly Ann sat up in the bed.

Joseph felt his heart jump. "What? What is it?"

"I forgot to tell Vicki about the quilt."

Joseph let his breath again and pulled Ann down in his arms again.

"We will have plenty of time for that, Sweetheart. Our girl is home."

"What if she doesn't want to stay here? What if she wants to stay at her new home?"

"Shhhh, Annie. Stop worrying. We're who she came to when she had a real problem. We've been her parents for ten years now. That just doesn't go away suddenly."

Vicki lay in her old bed, and took several deep breaths as if to check where she was. The dog her brother had named (or rather, re-named) Rusty lay on the small round rug at the side of her bed, close enough for her to reach her hand down and rub his head.

"Who are you, boy?" she asked. "Where did you come by? Are you reincarnated? Did you come here to comfort them and to wait for me to come back?"

Down the hall Tony lay on his back and thought about tonight and about Vicki's adventure. He thought to himself that he had judged his sister wrong. She was not the namby-pamby sissy girl who always tried to horn in on his friends and himself; he wasn't sure he could have taken off like that; alone, in the dark facing all sorts of scary things. He had made fun of her when she showed distaste for putting her worm on her fishing hooks; yet she and her friend had faced down a mother bear and she had been forced to help clean up his broken and torn body. She had lost a dog she was very fond of and had to bury him, too. Even been involved in a robbery. He wished he had been there to share some of those events with her. And then she had come all the way back to get help for her friends.

In the dark as he lay there, he thought she managed to feed herself, find and make new friends, (here he grinned in the dark) *learned to play baseball.* All the years she had begged to play while her mother encouraged her to sew and plant flowers and wear dresses. Idly he wondered what position she had played and if she had been any good at it? If she had had any home runs? Or even brought a run in?

Though it had become commonplace since she had been gone, he again closed his eyes and he whispered, "Thank you Lord Jesus, for bringing Vicki home safe and sound. Thank you, thank you, thank you."

All three woke early the next morning, probably due to the excitement from the night before and while Ann quickly fixed some breakfast for all three, they assembled what they thought they would need.

Vicki insisted on bringing the new Rusty and Tony cheerfully agreed.

Feeling somewhat fortified and ready, they locked the house up and Vicki was elected leader since this would be her third journey to Maryville. She did plan on stopping long enough to see Grandma and introduce her family to her. She didn't plan a long stop, but felt determined it was the right thing to do.

There was a fresh sense of purpose and of determination as well as togetherness as they began to make their way up the hiking trail up the first trail towards the sloping hills in the distance.

Every now and then one would speak to the others; however, most of their energy was devoted to the uphill trail; breathing became all important and especially Ann began to regret her lack of physical exercise over the past few months. They had to stop and rest more often due to her weakness, but no one complained. The dog would do as the "old" Rusty had with Vicki; moving on up ahead of the humans following him, then circling back to join them again. His energy; of all of them, seemed boundless and he also seemed to know exactly where they were headed.

On one of their rest stop closer to lunch time Vicki showed Tony where she had scooted under the brush and slept several hours. They refreshed themselves with splashes of creek water on their faces and hands and with snacks from their backpacks. Tony noticed and appreciated the variety of birds and number of squirrels and even rabbits they came across.

Vicki couldn't help but revel in her role as leader and explorer; pointing out certain things to the others and the importance in her own former journey.

The others showed their acceptance of her role and there was a growing sense of self-confidence in the way she responded to them. Tony had a growing respect for what she had accomplished and suspected their new relationship would more closely resemble that of equals, rather than big brother-little sister they had shared prior to this event.

Ann's thoughts focused into the possibility of having to deal with a choice on allowing or fighting against Vicki's donation of one of her kidneys to this woman named Lizzie. She was not ready to start referring to her as Vicki's *real* mother, even mentally.

Joseph geared his progress to that of Ann's, realizing her lack of stamina compared to the rest of them, but his thoughts also tumbled around the differences which this experience would make in all of them. Specifically, he knew he and Ann had to face the possibility that Vicki would want to stay with Lizzie and Walter. In fact, knowing they were her biological parents, and they had had certainly not abandoned her, as she originally thought, she might feel even more that she *belonged* to them.

So, though often the climb was silent, as each (probably even Rusty) kept their own personal focus' on their own thoughts, now and then one would bring up a thought or a question, but even in the silences, there was a closeness, a sense of camaraderie which this small family had not embraced for a long time.

Vicki's goal was to try and reach Grandma (and Herman's) home before nightfall and when it seemed that this might not be possible, they cleared a place where the three of them (plus Rusty) could comfortably spread their sleeping bags from their bedrolls and backpacks to spend the night.

When they built a small campfire, they roasted the small already cooked smoked sausages and then marshmallows Ann had packed for them. They did not choose to discuss any of the topics most on their minds, but asked questions about Grandma and Herman from Vicki. She allowed the emotion show when she discussed once again the sweet nature of Herman and how good he had been to her.

She described the hammock project he had made for her and how willing he had cut his grandma's firewood and helped her with her wash day. She tried hard to impart the feeling of being lost in time when traveling through these small villages and settlements where people lived much as their ancestors had generations ago.

Vicki turned to her father where he lay next to her mother in their sleeping bags and she asked, "Dad, remember when I asked you ab out these mountains once and you talked to me about them?"

"Vaguely, but I am sure by this time you know them much better than I did, or do now."

"Well, perhaps, but you ignited me enough that it made me choose this path for my adventure instead of me heading some other direction."

"Uh-oh," he said ruefully, "Now your mother is going to hold me responsible for your curiosity which drove you to set out on this exploration…"

Even Ann laughed at this and she said, "Since when have you ever let someone else guide you in any path but that of your own choosing?"

"Gets that from you," her father said to Ann, laughing.

The next morning, they took time to brew some coffee over the small banked fire, then they carefully put the fire out completely and about noon they got far enough to see the small column of smoke rising from Vicki knew was Grandma and Herman's cabin.

Vicki swallowed from emotion when she saw the multi colored blanket hanging as a hammock between the same two trees. She heard the screen door shut and then she heard the querulous familiar voice of Grandma, "Hello! Who goes out there? Yell out."

"Grandma, it's me…Vicki. Don't shoot us."

"Vicki? Is that you, girl? Really? Come on up here." They began to watch as she propped her shotgun up against the cabin wall, and make her way down off the porch to meet their advance.

Things looked just the same to Vicki, and she went up to hug the old lady before introducing her to her parents and to Tony. They smelled the same, too, she realized. Probably a kettle of cooking venison wafting from the cabin, even to the small water-melon she remembered from the other old lady on the trail.

They gratefully put down their backpacks, and sat on the wicker chairs or the steps as they began to get to know each other. Her parents gratefully acknowledged their appreciation of the kindness' she had shown their daughter; careful not to accuse her of failing to notify them of her presence.

The old lady told how fond she had grown of their daughter and how she missed Vicki after she had moved on. She also reinforced her confidence in sending her own to Maryville with Walter and Lizzie and what good people they were. She even brought up the fact that the couple had lost their daughter as an infant and she felt strongly Vicki would be good for them and vice-Versie Quickly, when Grandma brought this up, Joseph, Ann, and Vicki looked at each other, but none of them said anything about the DNA discovery. For one reason, they didn't feel it their place to share this before they even discussed the entire story with Walter and Lizzie, but with her age and the way she lived with no electricity, television or radio, it was doubtful Grandma would begin to understand any of it.

Vicki did share the sad news about Lizzie's kidney problems, but focused on their being possible solutions without bringing up kidney donations. Grandma promised to add Lizzie to her prayer list.

Grandma insisted on cooking and feeding them a hot lunch. Vicki took Tony with her to rummage through the small garden for any fresh vegetables Grandma might have missed in her own use or her canning. They brought in enough to fix a plate of sliced tomatoes, green onions, radishes and even two cucumbers. When added to what was, indeed, stewed venison and corn-pone with honey, they helped clean up, and feeling full, made their goodbyes and got back on the road. Vicki almost cried again, but took her place at the front of the line. She did take them a little bit off the road into the small graveyard in back of the little white Baptist church and showed them Rusty's and Herman's graves.

They were appropriately impressed, especially with Rusty's. Tony picked some nearby wildflowers and reverently (for him) placed them on the two gravestones.

Vicki told them that if they really "stepped on it" they could reach Maryville, and Lizzie and Walter's place by dusk, but they discussed it, and all decided to stay one more camp out night. They found these days and nights were becoming very important to them; both in comforting them and in showing what they had allowed to escape their family in such a distressing way. They were becoming closer than they had been in a very, very long time. They each wanted to stretch this feeling out and hold on to the emotions they felt stirring inside.

When they were totally worn out, they stopped for the night, allowed Tony to demonstrate his fire building skills, and searched backpacks for something to eat. They had a cloth wrapped package of cornbread reminiscent to Vicki of the package Grandma had sent with her the first time.

Ann pulled out three small cans of canned Sausages as she grinned and said, "No more smoked sausages, but how about these? And I have crackers, too."

"And I have apples," Joseph said.

"And I have my utility knife to cut them with," Tony said, looking at Vicki.

"I'm out of water in my canteen," said Joseph.

"Well, the first trip around, I started drinking from the creek; where the creek water bubbles over the gravel and rocks and I never got sick," Vicki said.

"Well, that's good enough for me," Joseph said, and he got up and went down to the creek.

As they regrouped and started out the next morning, they felt fortified by the hot cups of hot coffee but this was a little offset by the anxiety felt by Joseph and Ann with anxiety about meeting Vicki's "other" parents.

Ann kept tossing questions around silently to herself. Would they like them? What kind of people were these mountain people? They certainly wouldn't be sophisticated, and yet, it was obvious they were educated, and that they had formed a very strong bond with her daughter. Should she be worried about being left behind or with the idea Vicki might feel she had to make a choice between these sets of parents? She was so stressed from this idea she was unusually quietly.

Joseph seemed to understand her feelings and he walked alongside her, frequently giving her a gentle hug or holding her hand for a while.

As they entered the southern side of the little town, Vicki's pace quickened and you could see the excitement in her body language.

"Look, way down there," she said gleefully, "See that colorful sign? See the parking lot? That's it. That's the café. I wonder if Lizzie is upstairs or at her house? If she is feeling pretty good or didn't have chemo yesterday or dialysis, she might be at the café."

Ann felt her mouth go dry and she reached out once again for Joseph's hand.

"Maybe we should rest a few minutes before we go inside," Ann said, "And I need a restroom, too."

"Come on, I'll show you where it is."

Thought entered the café and had to pause a minute coming into the slightly darkened interior after the bright sunshine outside. It was close to the lunch time crowd and at first no one paid any attention to the four of them.

Then, a shout from across the room, and the crash of crockery dropping and breaking on the floor.

"Vicki! Vicki!" yelled Joyce. "Is it really you?" She ignored the broken dishes from the tray she had dropped and rushed over to enclose her in an all-encompassing bear hug.

"It is you! Where have you been, girl? We were so worried."

"I'm glad to see you, too," Vicki managed to squeeze out from Joyce's check where she was still being held captive.

When she managed to withdraw from Joyce's embrace, Vicki said, drawing Ann close to face Joyce.

"Joyce, this is my mother…" Then she pointed at Joseph and said, "And my dad," she paused and said, "And my brother. This is Joyce, everybody," she added.

Joyce ignored Joseph's outstretched hand, and one after another gave each of them a big hug.

Surprisingly, all on his own, Tony went over and began to pick up the broken shards of dishes and put them on the tray. He gave Joyce a grin and said, "Good thing it wasn't full of food."

"Where's Walter and Lizzie?" asked Vicki.

"Walter went with her to the doctor's but they will be home pretty quick now. It wasn't for Chemo; just a dialysis treatment. That's a good thing because those don't make her feel as bad as the chemo. Have you guys had lunch?"

Joseph, Ann, and Tony looked at each other and when they shook their heads no, Joyce insisted they take a booth and sit down with menus and water and silver.

"Well, let's get you fed while you wait. When you decide, call me over. Well, Vicki knows the drill. I'm so excited I can hardly think."

After her parents and Tony were seated, Vicki collected their backpacks and said, "I will show you my place later, but let me take these over there and out of the way first. Decide what you want to eat; it's all wonderful here."

Can I have whatever I want?" asked Tony.

Vicki laughed. "That's exactly the first thing I ever said to Lizzie when I arrived here. Sure, you can."

Joyce came back over and said, "Here, Vicki, let me help you take those to the cottage."

"No, I got this," Vicki said, and doubling up the bags, she left back through the kitchen doors.

She was back in a few minutes, and pulled up another chair to the table.

Joyce was talking to Joseph and Vicki interrupted her, "Well, I had to stop and say hello to everyone in the kitchen. Nothing changed. Everything looks just the same."

Joyce laughed. "If you had come a little earlier old man Hodgkin's and his dog would have still been here."

"I'm sorry I missed him." Vicki turned to her family and said, "He and his dog are the ones who pulled me out of the fire; remember, I told you?"

They nodded.

Joseph said, "I want to thank him when I meet him.

Tony said, "I don't know whether to thank him or yell at him for bringing my brat sister back."

"Tony!" said Ann.

"Just joking, mom."

"Even so, we don't joke like that."

"Well, I guess I have missed her a little."

They were almost finished with their lunch, except of course, Tony's second dessert, when Lizzie and Walter arrived at home.

CHAPTER TWENTY-FOUR

Resolution

Thig s were moving too fast for Vicki to keep up. First, there was her pride in showing her family her own special cottage; then introductions to Aphrodite, and Angel. Arrangements were made for voluntary early closing of the café at the end of the day to allow both families to retire to Lizzie and Walter's beautiful home for the evening.

Walter eagerly volunteered to grill their dinner, and Lizzie (from her wheelchair, to be sure, but otherwise in charge) supervised the side dishes and Vicki was in charge of table setting and beverages. The important but frightening topics yet to be discussed among them was delayed while they all struggled to become more familiar with one another.

Of course, even with the heavy weight of the as yet unspoken topics, there were feelings of well-being and thanksgiving to have assembled what was, in reality, one big and tightly bonded family.

Tony attached himself to Angel and Aphrodite in the back yard and Joseph shared a beer with Walter while manning the grill.

Of course, Vicki, Ann and Lizzie had to examine all of Lizzie's quilts and discussion of the Vicki-Ann Floral quilt left at Ann's home was of course brought up.

Tony was most impressed by the fact that at her young age Vicki was allowed to have her own house; sanctuary, entirely set up to her own choices. At first, he thought it very unjust and he recognized a touch of envy in himself; but as he thought about it, he admitted there had been many things in their family's past history in which he and his father; based totally on gender, had denied membership to Vicki. He wondered just how much of this may have driven her desire to leave home.

When they all sat down to dinner together it seemed only right that they automatically, without instruction; reached out for each other's hands and bowed their heads in thanksgiving. Without being designated as such, Vicki delivered a brief but sincere prayer of gratitude for their being together.

There was also recognized by Vicki, a new sort of deference paid to her. She may have felt invisible before; but now was accorded a newly found acknowledgement of respect from the grownups in her life.

After cleanup, shared by everyone, a cooler breeze, reminiscent of the approaching winter and moved in and Walter lit a fire in the big stone fireplace. Amidst a shared feeling of contentment, they found seats on the comfortable couches and chairs, and even the braided rug.

Joseph approached Ann and whispering so that no one else could hear, asked her if they should speak freely in front of even Tony about the "adult" subjects of Lizzie's health concerns, the DNA which drew them together as one family or should they send him in the other part of the house to play his video games?

Ann quickly said, "No more secrets in this family, Joseph."
He nodded.

As they settled in with beverages and the warmth of the fireplace giving them a feeling of togetherness and joint concerns.

Before anyone else could speak, Vicki stood in her place by the fireplace and she said, "I know I am the youngest person here, but age shouldn't have anything to do with it. I have already made my mind up. I am going to donate one of my kidneys to Lizzie. The doctor has reassured me I will be fine and there is no reason it will curtail my life or health in any way."

This statement brought a gasp from Ann, and the stares of everyone else directed to Vicki.

"Should we postpone this conversation until we can meet together with the doctor?" asked Joseph mildly; maintaining his usual cool head of reason.

Lizzie spoke up then, "I absolutely refuse to allow you to donate one of your kidneys."

"You can't deny me that. It's *my* kidney," said Vicki.

"That may be so, but you must have your parent's permission to donate an organ. You are a minor," said Ann vehemently.

"Let's remember there are two sets of parents here," said Joseph.

"I think it should be up to Vicki," said Tony.

"You are a minor, too. You have no vote." This came from Walter but elicited a strong look from Joseph.

With a touch of sarcasm, Tony said, "There you all go again, totally wiping out the democratic progress. If I'm not allowed an opinion, why not muzzle me or send me from the room?"

"Besides," said Walter, "Joseph is right. There are two sets of parents here. In all honesty, I feel it would be less than civil for us to have to resort to a court battle to decide which set has the absolute right to decide whether Vicki donates or not."

"Also," said Joseph, "We must not lose our sense of family we have begun to establish here, nor our understanding of what is at stake. I think there is some validity to the suggestion that we postpone this conversation until we can have a joint meeting with the doctor; maybe even get more than one medical opinion as to pros or cons on the donation; both on Vicki and on Lizzie.

"I concur," Walter said.

"That's my vote, too; unless you guys are still refusing me a vote," said Tony.

There was a slight cooling in tempers when Vicki suddenly laughed and said, "I feel we should all vote yea or nay now, at least on the motion that we meet with the doctor before forming any decision."

"Yeah," said Tony, "Maybe we should select committee chairmen, judge and jury, too."

"Whatever we eventually decide here," said Walter calmly, "We must keep love in the decision. We all have a stake in this and no one person will decide alone."

Although Vicki certainly didn't agree with this, feeling (perhaps rightly so?) that it should be Lizzie and herself alone who made this decision and since; at least in theory, they were on opposite sides she didn't see how it could be resolved.

Against any other suggestions Tony took the floor again and said, "Okay, then. I vote we all go to bed and I choose to sleep with Angel or Aphrodite. We can call the doctor in the morning."

Everyone else laughed and Lizzie answered him, "I will share one of them, but not both. You pick, Tony."

* * *

The next morning brought smells of bacon and coffee and; as usual, Tony was the first in the kitchen to scrounge for something to eat.

Joyce called to tell Walter and Lizzie to take their time because she had come in to the café early and had everything under control at the café.

After breakfast there was a discussion and Walter was chosen to call the doctor and set up a time for all of them to meet with him and discuss their concerns about any donation of Vicki's kidney to Lizzie.

Tony took his breakfast plate out to the back porch to eat, and was both surprised and amused to see Rusty laying right next to Angel and Aphrodite. Joseph came out, carrying his coffee cup and when he saw the animals he said to Tony, "It's a shame humans can't make friends as easily as most animals. Look at those guys."

"I know, right?"

As Vicki dressed before breakfast, she said to Joseph, "I am so worried. Just think, Joseph, if we were finally driven to get a lawyer and go to court to try and prevent Vicki donating one of her kidneys…"

"Go ahead," Joseph said.

"Well, if my memory is correct, most cases where there is a court test of biological versus custodial "right" to an adopted child, the biological parent wins…"

"Well, not always," Joseph said.

"Well, no, but most of the time."

Joseph put his arms around her and he said, "One day at a time, sweetheart, one day at a time."

"Think of the most famous case of all time on this subject…"

"Which is?"

"In the bible. In verse 2:6 where King Solomon has to decide the mother of a child in which two women claim motherhood and both wanted the child…"

"I remember that verse. It's because of that verse King Solomon earned his reputation for wisdom."

"Yes, and he rightly recognized that the woman who loved the child enough to give him up in order to protect and save him was most certainly the true mother."

"Yes," said Joseph.

"Well, he gave the child to the biological parent."

"Not exactly the same set of circumstances, is it?"

"No, but still…having given birth originally and also the fact that Vicki's real parents did not just give her away, but had her stolen from them is a strong point towards their "right" to decide guardianship."

"There are so many variables to that example, Annie. If we went to court over this, we might; just by the luck of the draw, get a judge who was adopted him or herself or one who would place more value on the ten years she had been ours versus just a few months with her real parents before being abducted. Have you ever wondered why her abductor would go to all the risk and difficulty of kidnapping her, only to leave her at the orphanage? Why not just return her?"

"Well, because she knew she could be arrested and face kidnapping charges herself. Presently she could have had a multitude of choices; leave her at a church, fire-station, police station, all without fear of arrest or questions or punishment. She had obviously realized she wasn't equipped to take care of her on her own."

Still holding her in his strong arms, Joseph said, "Again, honey… One day at a time. Walter and Lizzie are good people. We are good people. There is a fair and just way to a decision here. We just have to work together to find it."

"What if the judge thinks that Lizzie and Walter only want to be named guardians in order to get our girl's kidney for Lizzie?"

"Stop looking t the dark side of it all, honey. One day, one problem, one thing at a time."

Though there was an underlying sense of tension around breakfast, the conversation was a neutral one and did not even touch on what was on all their minds. When it got time to go to their meeting with the doctor, they all loaded up in Lizzie's vehicle and in Walter's truck. Joseph drove Lizzie's car and Walter drove his truck. There were too many for one vehicle and no one argued with Tony's right to be included.

When they arrived at the doctor's office they were shown into a conference and training room which allowed room for all to be seated. Introductions were made and offers of coffee or water were made and rejected.

As was expected and accepted their own family doctor took the head of the table and everyone else filled in on both sides.

Their doctor spoke first, introducing two others who were surgeons which he designated as highly qualified in such surgeries and who practiced in the local hospital. He gave each of them time to talk and to answer questions at the end of his own presentation. Their family doctor allowed the two surgeons to explain the safety of such an operation with donation of a kidney from one individual to another; including the influence of age, gender, condition of the donor and the recipient. They went into success statistics, the possibility of rejection of the organ by the recipient, or ultimate success demonstrated by complete acceptance. They further went into recovery time for both recipient and donor. Then they explained the two families would be choosing the surgeon to perform the surgery; if this was the agreed-on decision. The family doctor announced he had chosen two of the most respected in the field to meet with them today and either would be considered a good choice in his opinion. Both the surgeons he had brought to the meeting today were highly qualified and respected surgeons who made such surgery their specialty. The two often worked together. The surgery would take place here in Maryville's modern and respected hospital where many other such surgeries had successfully been done. Or if it be their choice, it could be done in another hospital of their choice where such surgeries were and had been done.

His audience was quiet and listened intently until the family doctor then announced he would take all questions from them and try to give honest and complete answers. Before he starting taking questions, he asked Lizzie's permission to allow questions about her personal medical condition to be answered in front of the others. She gave her permission easily.

All questions were addressed without consideration of who was asking, giving Vicki and Tony equal time as the adults.

* * *

At the agreed-on finish of the meeting, all questions had been addressed. They all felt they had been given an overload of information with much to go home and digest. There was an agreement that everyone would go home, review all they had learned and then, when a decision had been made whether to move forward to scheduling such surgery, all three doctors would be contacted and the decision shared.

Probably due to the emotional impact of their meeting, Lizzie was exhausted and took the opportunity to retire for a nap. Ann followed her lead and announced she was going out to Vicki's little cottage for her own nap. Walter went to the café to check in with Joyce on any problems which may have occurred in their absence.

Tony asked for and received his father's permission to accompany him on a short review of the local video game store. There was a change of plans when they reached one of the movie theatres and saw a movie they had been wanting to see; a quick decision was made and they went to the movies.

It was agreed on everyone meeting for dinner in the café at a certain time. There was a shared sense of emotional overload. No one welcomed any plan to cook or clean up. All seemed weary and accepting of putting off any decision-making immediately, but to save it until after dinner. Each had promised to just "think things over" before they met again. This was easier said than done and the topic roamed around all their minds silently as they went about their chosen tasks.

They met in the café at the selected time and despite the interruptions from the friendly guests and old friends who came to eat that evening, they pushed two tables together and enjoyed their meal.

Joseph and Ann got to meet Hodgkin's and express their gratitude for his heroic actions during the café fire.

The meal renewed and refreshed them and afterwards they retired to the room above the café for their meeting.

No one seemed to want to be first to speak, when Tony suggested they all do secret ballots with just "yes" or "no" for the surgery. It eased the tension as they all laughed at him and his suggestion.

Vicki said, "What a waste that would be, Tony. We know mom and dad and Lizzie will vote "No"; the meeting with the doctors wouldn't have changed their feeling about this. And I think Walter and you and I will probably vote yes. So, we would have a tie."

"What makes you think I will vote yes?" Tony asked.

"Because you feel it is *my* kidney and I should be able to decide."

Vicki looked around the others and said, "Mom will say no because she is scared something will go wrong and she will lose me. Dad is afraid if he votes yes, mom will be mad at him. Walter feels it isn't his place to voice an opinion so he may decide to not vote at all. Lizzie is very unselfish and thinks it's not right to expect me to go through a surgery like that for her. She will never vote to accept such a sacrifice from me."

"Okay, then, how do we decide?" Tony asked.

Vicki thoughtfully said, "I say we go back to Tony's first suggestion and have written anonymous "yes" or "no" replies on paper; but we have to agree beforehand if we have a majority decision, we will not argue it but agree to accept it as a group and be bound by the decision."

Everyone nodded. Tony passed out paper and pens and there was silence for a few minutes. Then Tony collected the slips of paper. Then Tony unfolded the papers and read out the one-word answers.

When they were tallied it ended with four "yes" and two "no" votes. Most, if asked, would have correctly guessed the two "no" votes were Ann and Lizzie. All the others had made the decision that Vicki should have a heavier vote, with it being her kidney after all; and Ann with her being the mother of the child making the sacrifice. No one went into the "why" and "who" of the vote but most were aware of the correct votes.

Several breathed a visible sign of relief as to at least having reached a decision and it was decided that Walter would call the doctors the next day with their decision. It was also decided that the surgery should be scheduled as soon as possible because there seemed to be no good reason to delay it. It was agreed that Ann and Joseph should be allowed the decision as to hospital and surgeon unless Lizzie had some over-riding reason against the final choices.

Walter's primary duties would be to continue to run the café and depending on the date the surgery was scheduled, Ann, Joseph and Tony would stay at Lizzie and Walter's home and not leave until there was no longer any real assistance they could offer in the recovery of both patients. When an agreed-on date was reached as to his assistance, Joseph would take Tony back to school and home and himself back to work. Ann would remain as head nurse for both patients.

Other smaller, but necessary decisions were made; such as who would accompany the two patients to the hospital for the actual surgery, the care of Angel and Aphrodite, answering phone calls, flowers and gifts from friends and employees. As all this planning and organization was taking place, the two families were growing closer to one another. They begin to feel as though they were all six an actual family and they tried to make it as easy on each other as they could.

The doctor prescribed mild pain medication for Lizzie as well as sleeping aids since she was understandingly nervous about the upcoming surgery.

Vicki cheerfully submitted herself for any tests the doctor and surgeon asked of her and tried to eat and exercise well as though these things would add an additional layer of success on the surgery. She read to Lizzie often and Tony volunteered for Angel and Aphrodite outside duties and feeding and making sure they fresh water. He took these volunteer duties quite seriously and prided himself on never needing any reminders.

Ann took up laundry duty and light housekeeping; not out of necessity, but mostly to keep busy.

They had an excess of volunteers from the employees and from the community at large.

Things moved rather rapidly after the initial decision was presented to the team of doctors and on the night before surgery, they had a final dinner together, early so as to meet Vicki and Lizzie's necessary nothing to eat or drink after ten o'clock, when they checked into the hospital.

The medical team was enthusiastic about predicted results and though both Lizzie and Vicki successfully tried to hide their apprehension, they, too, felt very positive.

It was gratifying to learn that the two patients could be dismissed from the hospital in four days, providing everything went according to plan and there was no reason to anticipate any problems.

After the surgery Vicki joked that she and Lizzie had the easiest assignment; they merely slept through everything while the others paced the floor in the waiting room and hospital hallways.

The hospital room filled with flowers and cards which Lizzie and Vicki immediately directed the hospital staff to give other patients; especially those who had none in their own rooms.

Ann volunteered to write all the thank-you notes and see that they got mailed out.

Everyone breathed a sign of relief when the surgeons came out of the operating room with wide smiles and the good news that the surgery had gone great.

After that, things went very smoothly. After the patients were discharged from the hospital, and a follow-up check -up went smoothly for both patients came and went with successful results, Joseph and Tony left for home, taking Rusty with them.

Ann stayed for another week and then, with insistence from both Vicki and Lizzie, left for home by ambulance escorting Vicki. There she would be checked out thoroughly by the medical staff in their home town, then released in her mother's care for the rest of her recovery period.

The end of the story

Often the end of the story is a surprise or has an unexpected twist. Most people enjoy happy endings and yet many sad stories are satisfactory and enjoyable. The best ending of a story usually is one which makes the reader yearn for more.

The story of Vicki, the young explorer may someday require a sequel but until that decision is made, let it be sufficient to announce Vicki and Lizzie both survived their surgeries with no negative resulting problems.

Vicki's two families agreed on a sharing plan in which Vicki spent much of her summers with Lizzie and Walter and the school year with Joseph, Ann, and Tony.

Tony completed college on a full baseball scholarship, and then went on to become a high school teacher and coach.

Vicki completed college, and then medical school; ending up with a residency at the same hospital where the transplant had taken place. In her spare time, she is writing a young adult book about her explorer adventure as a child.

Inspired by her daughter, Ann went back to school and received her degree in mathematics then became a high-school math teacher. Joseph continued coaching little league baseball and going further up the corporate ladder.

At last visit, Aphrodite was fat and sassy and moving into cat "old-age" lying in the sun on the back porch except during the summers when she accompanied Vicki to the little cottage in back of the café. The "new" Rusty was approaching doggie years of thirteen and still chasing squirrels wherever Vicki hung her hat.

The café is still a popular eating spot with good comfort food and friendly community customers.

Mr. Hodgkins and Prince still have their daily reserved table for breakfast.

* * *

www.ingramcontent.com/pod-product-compliance
Lightning Source LLC
Chambersburg PA
CBHW061609190726
48288CB00007B/2240